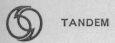

TANDEM

D1419004

## Vornan-19

It is 1999; the century is about to turn.

The civilised world is prosperous, there has been no major war for generations, yet the horror of a final apocalypse hangs over men's heads. Will the new century begin and end on January 1, 2000?

Into a world sliding towards hysterical chaos floats Vornan-19, claiming to be a visitor from the year 2999. Does he hold out a hope for the future of mankind, or a satanic threat to the last remnants of civilisation?

# Vornan-19

Robert Silverberg

TANDEM
14 Gloucester Road, London SW7

Originally published in the United States by Ballantine
Books, Inc., 1968, under the title *The Masks of Time*

First published in Great Britain by Sidgwick and Jackson
Ltd, 1970
Published by Universal-Tandem Publishing Co. Ltd, 1972
Copyright © 1968 by Robert Silverberg

Made and printed in Great Britain by
Hunt Barnard Printing Ltd., Aylesbury, Bucks.

*For A. J. and Eddie*

# * ONE *

A MEMOIR OF this sort should begin with some kind of statement of personal involvement, I suppose: I was the man, I was there, I suffered. And in fact my involvement with the improbable events of the past twelve months was great. I knew the man from the future. I followed him on his nightmare orbit around our world. I was with him at the end.

But not at the beginning. And so, if I am to tell a complete tale of *him,* it must be a more-than-complete tale of *me.* When Vornan-19 arrived in our era, I was so far removed from even the most extraordinary current matters that I did not find out about it for several weeks. Yet eventually I was drawn into the whirlpool he created ... as were you, all of you, as was each of us everywhere.

I am Leo Garfield. My age is fifty-two as of tonight, the fifth of December, 1999. I am unmarried—by choice—and in excellent health. I live in Irvine, California, and hold the Schultz Chair of Physics at the University of California. My work concerns the time-reversal of subatomic particles. I have never taught in the classroom. I have several young graduate students whom I regard, as does the University, as my pupils, but there is no formal instruction in the usual sense in our laboratory. I have devoted most of my adult life to time-reversal physics, and I have succeeded mainly in inducing a few electrons to turn on their tails and flee into the past. I once thought that a considerable achievement.

At the time of Vornan-19's arrival, a little less than one year ago, I had reached an impasse in my work and had gone into the desert to scowl myself past the blockage point. I don't offer that as an excuse for my failure to be in on the news of his coming. I was staying at the home of friends some fifty miles south of Tucson, in a thoroughly modern dwelling equipped with wallscreens, dataphones, and the other expectable communications channels, and I suppose I could have followed the events right from the first bulletins. If I did not, it was because I was not in the habit of following current events very closely, and not because I was in any state of isolation. My long walks in the desert each day were spiritually quite useful, but at nightfall I rejoined the human race.

When I retell the story of how Vornan-19 came among us, then, you must understand that I am doing it at several removes. By the time I became involved in it, the story was as old as the fall of Byzantium or the triumphs of Attila, and I learned of it as I would have learned of any historical event.

He materialized in Rome on the afternoon of December 25, 1998.

Rome? On Christmas Day? Surely he chose it for deliberate effect. A new Messiah, dropping from heaven on that day in that city? How obvious! How cheap!

But in fact he insisted it had been accidental. He smiled in that irresistible way, drew his thumbs across the soft skin just beneath his eyelids, and said softly, "I had one chance in three hundred sixty-five to land on any given day. I let the probabilities fall where they chose. What is the significance of this Christmas Day, again?"

"The birthday of the Savior," I said. "A long time ago."

"The savior of what, please?"

"Of mankind. He who came to redeem us from sin."

Vornan-19 peered into that sphere of emptiness that always seemed to lurk a few feet before his face. I suppose he was meditating on the concepts of salvation and redemption and sin, attempting to stuff some content into the sounds. At length he said, "This redeemer of mankind was born at Rome?"

"Bethlehem."

"A suburb of Rome?"

"Not exactly," I said. "As long as you showed up on Christmas Day, you should have arrived in Bethlehem, though."

"I would have," Vornan replied, "if I had planned it for its effect. But I knew nothing of your holy one, Leo. Neither his birthday nor his birthplace nor his name."

"Is Jesus forgotten in your time, Vornan?"

"I am a very ignorant man, as I must keep reminding you. I have never studied ancient religions. It was chance that brought me to that place at that time." And mischief flickered like playful lightning across his elegant features.

Perhaps he was telling the truth. Bethlehem might have been more effective if he had wanted to manipulate the Messiah effect. At the very least, choosing Rome, he might have come down in the piazza in front of St. Peter's, say at the moment that Pope Sixtus was delivering his blessing to the multitudes. A silvery shimmer, a figure drifting downward, hundreds of thousands of the devout on their knees in awe, the messenger from the future alighting gently, smiling, making the sign of the Cross, sending across the multitude the silent current of good will and repose best befitting this day of celebration. But he did not. He appeared instead at the foot of the Spanish Stairs, by the fountain, in that street usually choked by prosperous shoppers surging toward the boutiques of the Via Condotti. At noon on Christmas Day the Piazza di Spagna was all but empty, the shops of Via Condotti were closed, the Stairs themselves were cleared of their traditional loungers. On the top steps were a few worshippers heading for the church of Trinità dei Monti. It was a cold wintry day, with flecks of snow circling in the gray sky; a sour wind was blowing off the Tiber.

Rome was uneasy that day. The Apocalyptists had rioted only the night before; rampaging mobs with painted faces had gone streaming through the Forum, had danced an out-of-season Walpurgisnacht ballet around the tattered walls of the Colosseum, had scrambled up the hideous bulk of the Victor Emmanuel Monument to desecrate its whiteness with fierce copulations. It was the worst of the outbreaks of unreason that had swept through Rome that year, although it was not as violent as the customary Apocalyptist outburst in London, say, or for that matter in New York. Yet it had been quelled only with great difficulties by *carabinieri* wielding neural whips and wading into the screaming, gesticulating cultists in complete ruthlessness. Toward dawn, they say, the Eternal City still echoed with the saturnalian cries. Then came the morning of the Christ Child, and at noon, while I still slept in Arizona's winter warmth, there appeared out of the iron-hard sky the glowing figure of Vornan-19, the man from the future.

There were ninety-nine witnesses. They agreed in all the fundamental details.

He descended from the sky. Everyone interviewed reported that he appeared on an arc coming in over Trinità dei Monti, soared past the Spanish Stairs, and alighted in the Piazza di Spagna a few yards beyond the boat-shaped fountain. Virtually all of the witnesses said that he left a glowing track through the air as he came down, but none claimed to have seen any sort of vehicle. Unless the laws of falling bodies have been repealed, Vornan-19 was traveling at a velocity of several thousand feet per second at the moment of impact, based on the assumption that he was released from some hovering vehicle just out of sight above the church.

Yet he landed upright, on both feet, with no visible sign of discomfort. He later spoke vaguely of a "gravity neutralizer" that had cushioned his descent, but he gave no details, and now we are not likely to discover any.

12

He was naked. Three of the witnesses asserted that a glittering nimbus or aura enfolded him, exposing the contours of his body but opaque enough in the genital region to shield his nakedness. A loin-halo, so to speak. It happens that these three witnesses were nuns on the steps of the church. The remaining ninety-six witnesses insisted on Vornan-19's total nudity. Most of them were able to describe the anatomy of his external reproductive system in explicit detail. Vornan was an exceptionally masculine man, as we all came to know, but those revelations were still in the future when the eyewitnesses described how well hung he was.

Problem: Did the nuns collectively hallucinate the nimbus that supposedly protected Vornan's modesty? Did the nuns deliberately invent the existence of the nimbus to protect their own modesty? Or did Vornan arrange things so that most of the witnesses saw him entire, while those who might suffer emotional distress from the sight had a different view of him?

I don't know. The cult of the Apocalypse has given us ample evidence that collective hallucinations are possible, so I don't discount the first suggestion. Nor the second, for organized religion has provided us with two thousand years of precedent for the cold statement that its functionaries don't always tell the truth. As for the idea that Vornan would go out of his way to spare the nuns from looking upon his nakedness, I'm skeptical. It was never his style to protect anyone from any kind of jolt, nor did he really seem aware that human beings needed to be shielded from anything so astonishing as the body of a fellow human. Besides, if he hadn't even heard of Christ, how would he have known anything about nuns and their vows? But I refuse to underestimate his deviousness. Nor do I think it would have been technically impossible for Vornan to appear one way to ninety-six onlookers and another way to the other three.

We do know that the nuns fled into the church within

moments after his arrival. Some of the others assumed that Vornan was some kind of Apocalyptist maniac and ceased to pay attention to him. But a good many watched in fascination as the nude stranger, having made his dramatic appearance, wandered about the Piazza di Spagna, inspecting first the fountain, then the shop windows on the far side, and then the row of parked automobiles at the curb. The wintry chill had no apparent effect on him. When he had seen all he wished to see at that side of the piazza, he sauntered across and began to mount the stairs. He was on the fifth step and moving without hurry when a frenzied-looking policeman rushed up and shouted at him to come down and get into the wagon.

Vornan-19 replied, "I will not do as you say."

Those were his first words to us—the opening lines of his Epistle to the Barbarians. He spoke in English. Many of the witnesses heard and understood what he had said. The policeman did not, and continued to harangue him in Italian.

Vornan-19 said, "I am a traveler from a distant era. I am here to inspect your world."

Still in English. The policeman sputtered. He believed that Vornan was an Apocalyptist, and an American Apocalyptist at that, the worst kind. The policeman's duty was to defend the decency of Rome and the sanctity of Christmas Day against this madman's exhibitionist vulgarities. He shouted at the visitor to come down the steps. Ignoring him, Vornan-19 turned and serenely continued upward. The sight of those pale, slender retreating buttocks maddened the officer of the law. He removed his own cloak and rushed up the steps, determined to wrap it around the stranger.

Witnesses declare that Vornan-19 did not look at the policeman or touch him in any way. The officer, holding the cloak in his left hand, reached out with his right to seize Vornan's shoulder. There was a faint gleaming yellowish-blue discharge, and a slight popping sound, and the

14

policeman tumbled backward as though he had been struck by an electric bolt. Crumpling as he fell, he rolled to the bottom of the stairs and lay in a heap, twitching faintly. The onlookers drew back. Vornan-19 proceeded up the steps to the top, halting there to tell one of the witnesses a bit about himself.

The witness was a German Apocalyptist named Horst Klein, nineteen years old, who had taken part in the revelry at the Forum between midnight and dawn and now, too keyed up to go to sleep, was wandering the city in a mood of *post coitum* depression. Young Klein, fluent in English, became a familiar television personality in the days that followed, repeating his story for the benefit of global networks. Then he slipped into oblivion, but his place in history is assured. I don't doubt that somewhere in Mecklenburg or Schleswig today he's repeating the conversation yet.

As Vornan-19 approached him, Klein said, "You shouldn't kill *carabinieri*. They won't forgive you."

"He isn't dead. Merely stunned a bit."

"You don't talk like an American," said Klein.

"I'm not. I come from the Centrality. That's a thousand years from now, you understand."

Klein laughed. "The world ends in three hundred seventy-two days."

"Do you believe that? What year is this, anyway?"

"1998. December twenty-fifth."

"The world has at least a thousand more years. Of that I'm certain. I am Vornan-19, and I am here as a visitor. I am in need of hospitality. I would like to sample your food and your wine. I wish to wear clothing of the period. I am interested in ancient sexual practices. Where may I find a house of intercourse?"

"That gray building there," said Klein, pointing toward the church of Trinità dei Monti. "They'll take care of all your needs inside. Just tell them you come from a thousand years from now. 2998, is it?"

"2999 by your system."

"Good. They'll love you for that. Just prove to them that the world isn't going to end a year from New Year's Day, and they'll give you whatever you want."

"The world will not end quite so soon," said Vornan-19 gravely. "I thank you, my friend."

He began to move toward the church.

Breathless *carabinieri* rushed at him from several directions at once. They did not dare come within five yards of him, but they formed a phalanx barring him from access to the church. They were armed with neural whips. One of them flung his cloak at Vornan's feet.

"Put that on."

"I do not speak your language."

Horst Klein said, "They want you to cover your body. The sight of it offends them."

"My body is undeformed," said Vornan-19. "Why should I cover it?"

"They want you to, and they have neural whips. They can hurt you with them. See? Those gray rods in their hands."

"May I examine your weapon?" the visitor said affably to the nearest officer. He reached for it. The man shrank back. Vornan moved with implausible swiftness and wrenched the whip from the policeman's hand. He took it business end first, and should have received a stunning near-lethal burst, but somehow he did not. The policemen gaped as Vornan studied the whip, casually triggering it and rubbing his hand across the metal prod to feel the effects it produced. They stepped back, crossing themselves fervently.

Horst Klein broke through the crumbling phalanx and flung himself at Vornan's feet. "You really *are* from the future, aren't you?"

"Of course."

"How do you do it—touch the whip?"

16

"These mild forces can be absorbed and transformed," said Vornan. "Don't you have the energy rituals yet?"

The German boy, trembling, shook his head. He scooped up the policeman's cloak and offered it to the naked man. "Put this over yourself," he whispered. "Please. Make things easier for us. You can't walk around naked."

Surprisingly, Vornan consented. After some fumbling he managed to don the cloak.

Klein said, "The world doesn't end in a year?"

"No. Certainly not."

"I've been a fool!"

"Perhaps."

Tears ran down the broad, unlined Teutonic cheeks. The frayed laughter of exhaustion ripped through Horst Klein's lips. He groveled on the cold stone slab, slapping his palms against the ground in an improvised salaam before Vornan-19. Shivering, sobbing, gasping, Horst Klein recanted his faith in the Apocalyptist movement.

The man from the future had gained his first disciple.

* TWO *

IN ARIZONA I knew nothing of this. If I had known, I would have dismissed it as folly. But I was at a dead end in my life, sterile and stale from overwork and underachievement, and I paid no attention to anything that took place beyond the confines of my own skull. My mood was ascetic, and among the things I denied myself that month was an awareness of world events.

My hosts were kind. They had seen me through these crises before, and they knew how to handle me. What I needed was a delicate combination of attention and solitude, and only persons of a certain sensibility could provide the necessary atmosphere. It would not be im-

17

proper to say that Jack and Shirley Bryant had saved my sanity several times.

Jack had worked with me at Irvine for several years, late in the 1980's. He had come to me straight from M.I.T., where he had captured most of the available honors, and like most refugees from that institution he had something pallid and cramped about his soul, the stigmata of too much eastern living, too many harsh winters and airless summers. It was a pleasure to watch him open like a sturdy flower in our sunlight. He was in his very early twenties when I met him: tall but hollow-chested, with thick unkempt curling hair, cheeks perpetually stubbled, sunken eyes, thin restless lips. He had all the stereotyped traits and tics and habits of the young genius. I had read his papers in particle physics, and they were brilliant. You must realize that in physics one works by following sudden lancing insights—inspirations, perhaps—and so it is not necessary to be old and wise before one can be brilliant. Newton reshaped the universe while only a lad. Einstein, Schrödinger, Heisenberg, Pauli, and the rest of that crew of pioneers did their finest work before they were thirty. One may, like Bohr, get shrewder and deeper with age, but Bohr was still young when he peered within the atom's heart. So when I say that Jack Bryant's work was brilliant, I do not mean merely that he was an exceptionally promising young man. I mean that he was brilliant on an absolute scale and that he had achieved greatness while still an undergraduate.

During the first two years he was with me, I thought he was genuinely destined to remake physics. He had that strange power, that gift of the shattering intuition that pierces all doubt; and, too, he had the mathematical ability and persistence to follow up his intuition and wrest firm truth from the unknown. His work was only marginally connected with mine. My time-reversal project had become more experimental than theoretical by this time, since I had moved through the stages of early hypotheses

18

and now was spending most of my time at the giant particle accelerator, trying to build up the forces that I hoped would send fragments of atoms flying pastwards. Jack, on the contrary, was still the pure theoretician. His concern was the binding force of the atom. There was nothing new about that, of course. But Jack had doubled back to reexamine some overlooked implications of Yukawa's 1935 work on mesons, and in the course of reviewing the old literature, had generally reshuffled everything that supposedly was known about the glue that holds the atom together. It seemed to me that Jack was on his way to one of the revolutionary discoveries of mankind: an understanding of the fundamental energy relationships out of which the universe is constructed. Which is, of course, what we all ultimately seek.

Since I was Jack's sponsor, I kept an eye on his studies, looking over the successive drafts of his doctoral thesis while devoting most of my energies to my own work. Only gradually did the larger implications of Jack's research dawn on me. I had been looking at it within the self-enclosed sphere of pure physics, but I now saw that the final outcome of Jack's work had to be highly practical. He was heading toward a means of tapping the binding force of the atom and liberating that energy not through a sudden explosion but in a controlled flow.

Jack himself did not seem to see it. Applications of physical theory were of no interest to him. Working within his airless environment of equations, he paid no more heed to such possibilities than he did to the fluctuations of the stock market. Yet I saw it. Rutherford's work at the beginning of the twentieth century had been pure theory too, yet it led unerringly to the sunburst over Hiroshima. Lesser men could search within the core of Jack's thesis and find there the means for total liberation of atomic energy. Neither fission nor fusion would be necessary. *Any* atom could be opened and drained. A cup of soil would run a million-kilowatt generator. A few drops of water would send a ship to the moon. This was the atomic energy of fantasy. It was all there, implicit in Jack's work.

But Jack's work was incomplete.

In his third year at Irvine he came to me, looking haggard and depleted, and said he was halting work on his thesis. He was at a point, he told me, where he needed to pause and consider. Meanwhile he asked for permission to engage in certain experimental work, simply as a change of air. Naturally, I agreed.

I said nothing whatever to him about the potential practical applications of his work. That was not my place. I confess a sense of relief mingled with the disappointment when he interrupted his research. I had been reflecting on the economic upheaval that would come to society in another ten or fifteen years, when every home might run on its own inexhaustible power source, when transportation and communication would cease to depend on the traditional energy inputs, when the entire network of labor relationships on which our society is based would utterly collapse. Strictly as an amateur sociologist, I was disturbed by the conclusions I drew. If I had been an executive of any of the major corporations, I would have had Jack Bryant assassinated at once. As it was, I merely worried. It was not very distinguished of me, I admit. The true man of science forges ahead heedless of the economic consequences. He seeks truth even if the truth should bring society tumbling down. Those are tenets of virtue.

I kept my own counsel. If Jack had wished at any time to return to his work, I would not have attempted to prevent it. I would not even have asked him to consider the long-range possibilities. He did not realize that any moral dilemma existed, and I was not going to be the one to tell him about it.

By my silence, of course, I was making myself an accomplice in the destruction of the human economy. I might have pointed out to Jack that his work, extended to the extreme, would give each human being an unlimited access to an infinite energy source, demolishing the foundation of every human society and creating an instant decentralization of mankind. Through my interference I might have caused Jack to hesitate. But I said nothing. Give me no medals of honor, though; my anguish remained in suspension so long as Jack remained idle. He was making no further progress on his research, so I had no need to fret over the chances of its successful outcome. Once he got back to it, the moral problem would face me again: whether to support the free play of scientific inquiry, or to intervene for the sake of maintaining the economic status quo.

It was a villainous choice. But I was spared making it.

During his third year with me Jack pottered around the campus doing trivial things. He spent most of his time at the accelerator, as though he had just discovered the experimental side of physics and did not tire of toying with it. Our accelerator was new and awesome, a proton-loop model with a neutron injector. It operated in the trillion-electron-volt range then; of course, the current alpha-spiral machines far exceed that, but in its day it was a colossus. The twin pylons of the high-voltage lines carrying current from the fusion plant at the edge of the Pacific seemed like titanic messengers of power, and the great dome of the accelerator building itself gleamed in mighty self-satisfaction. Jack haunted the building. He sat by the screens while undergraduates performed elementary experiments in neutrino detection and in antiparticle annihilation. Occasionally he tinkered with the control panels just to see how they worked and to find out how it felt to be master of those surging forces. But what he was doing was meaningless. It was busywork. He was deliberately marking time.

Was it really because he needed a rest?

Or had he seen the implications of his own work at last—and been frightened?

I never asked him. In such cases I wait for a troubled younger man to come to me with his troubles. And I could not take the risk of infecting Jack's mind with my own doubts if those doubts had not already occurred to him.

At the end of his second semester of idleness he requested a formal counseling session with me. Here it comes, I thought. He's going to tell me where his work is leading, and he'll ask me if I think it's morally proper for him to continue, and then I'll be on the spot. I came to the session loaded with pills.

He said, "Leo, I'd like to resign from the University."

I was shaken. "You have a better offer?"

"Don't be absurd. I'm leaving physics."

"Leaving—physics—?"

"And getting married. Do you know Shirley Frisch? You've seen me with her. We're getting married a week from Sunday. It'll be a small wedding, but I'd like you to come, Leo."

"And then?"

"We've bought a house in Arizona. In the desert near Tucson. We'll be moving there."

"What will you do, Jack?"

"Meditate. Write, a little. There are some philosophical questions I want to consider."

"Money?" I asked. "Your University salary—"

"I've got a small inheritance that somebody invested wisely a long time ago. Shirley's also got a private income. It's nothing much, but it'll let us get by. We're dropping out of society. I felt I couldn't hide it from you any more."

I spread my hands on my desk and contemplated my knuckles for a long moment. I felt as though webs had begun to sprout between my fingers. Eventually I said, "What about your thesis, Jack?"

"Discontinued."

22

"You were so close to finishing it."

"I'm at a total dead end. I can't go on." His eyes met mine and remained fixed. Was he telling me that he didn't *dare* go on? Was his withdrawal at this point a matter of scientific defeat or of moral doubt? I wanted to ask. I waited for him to tell me. He said nothing. His smile was rigid and unconvincing. Finally he said, "Leo, I don't think I'd ever do anything worthwhile in physics."

"That isn't true. You—"

"I don't think I even *want* to do anything worthwhile in physics."

"Oh."

"Will you forgive me? Will you still be my friend? *Our* friend?"

I came to the wedding. It turned out I was one of four guests. The bride was a girl I knew only vaguely; she was about twenty-two, a pretty blonde, a graduate student in sociology. God knows how Jack had ever met her, with his nose pushed into his notebooks all the time, but they seemed very much in love. She was tall, almost to Jack's shoulder, with a great cascade of golden hair like finespun wire, and honey-tanned skin, and big dark eyes, and a supple, athletic body. Beyond a doubt she was beautiful, and in her short white wedding gown she looked as radiant as any bride has ever looked. The ceremony was brief and nonsectarian. Afterwards we all went to dinner, and toward sundown the bride and groom quietly disappeared. I felt a curious emptiness that night as I went home. I rummaged among old papers for lack of anything else to do, and came upon some early drafts of Jack's thesis; I stood staring at the scrawled notations for a long while, comprehending nothing.

A month later they invited me to be their guest for a week in Arizona.

I thought it was a *pro forma* invitation and politely declined, thinking I was expected to decline. Jack phoned and insisted I come. His face was as earnest as ever, but the little greenish screen clearly showed that the tension and haggardness had been ironed from it. I accepted. Their house, I found, was perfectly isolated, with miles of tawny desert on all sides. It was a fortress of comfort in all that bleakness. Jack and Shirley were both deeply tanned, magnificently happy, and wonderfully attuned to each other. They led me on a long walk into the desert my first day, laughing as jackrabbits or desert rats or long green lizards scuttered past us. They stooped to show me small gnarled plants close to the barren soil, and took me to a towering saguaro cactus whose massive corrugated green arms cast the only shade in view.

Their home became a refuge for me. It was understood that I was free to come at any time on a day's notice, whenever I felt the need to escape. Although they extended invitations from time to time, they insisted that I avail myself of the privilege of inviting myself. I did. Sometimes six or ten months went by without my making the journey to Arizona; sometimes I came for five or six weekends in a row. There was never any regular pattern. My need to visit them depended wholly upon my inner weather. *Their* weather never changed, within or without; their days were forever sunny. I never saw them quarrel or even mildly disagree. Not until the day that Vornan-19 careened into their life was there any gulf visible between them.

Gradually our relationship deepened into something subtle and intimate. I suppose I was essentially an uncle figure to them, since I was in my mid-forties, Jack was not yet thirty, and Shirley hardly into her twenties; yet the tie was deeper than that. One would have to call it love. There was nothing overtly sexual in it, though I would gladly have slept with Shirley if we had met some other way; certainly I found her physically attractive, and the attraction increased as time and the sun burnished from her some of the charming immaturity that made me at first think of her as a girl and not as a woman. But though my relationship to Jack and Shirley was a triangular one, with

24

emotional vectors leading in many paths, it never threatened to break down into a seamy experiment in adultery. I admired Shirley, but I did not—I think—envy Jack his physical possession of her. At night, when I heard the sounds of pleasure sometimes coming from their bedroom, my only reaction was one of delight in their happiness, even while I tossed in my own solitary bed. One time I brought a woman companion of my own to their place, with their approval; but it was a disaster. The chemistry of the weekend was all wrong. It was necessary for me to come alone, and oddly I did not feel condemned to celibacy even though my sharing of Shirley's love with Jack fell short of physical union.

We grew so close that nearly all barriers fell. On the hot days—which meant most of the time—Jack was accustomed to going about in the nude. Why not? There was no one in the neighborhood to object, and he scarcely needed to feel inhibited in the presence of his wife and his closest friend. I envied him his freedom, but I did not imitate it, because it did not seem proper to expose myself in front of Shirley. Instead I wore shorts. It was a delicate matter, and they chose a characteristically delicate way to resolve it. One August day when the temperature was well above one hundred degrees and the sun seemed to take up a quarter of the sky, Jack and I were working outside the house, tending the little garden of desert plants they cherished so warmly. When Shirley emerged to bring us some beers, I saw that she had neglected to don the two strips of fabric that were her usual garments. She was quite casual about it: setting the tray down, offering me a beer, then handing one to Jack, and both of them totally relaxed all the while. The impact of her body on me was sudden but brief. Her ordinary daily costume had been so scant that the contours of her breasts and buttocks were no mysteries to me, and so it was purely a technicality, this crossing of the line between being covered and being revealed. My first impulse was to look away, as if I were an unexpected intruder coming upon her by surprise; but I sensed that this was precisely the inference she wished to destroy, and so I made a determined effort to equal her sangfroid. I suppose it sounds comic and preposterous, but I let my eyes travel deliberately down her bareness, as though some fine statuette had been presented to me for my admiration and I was showing my gratitude by examining it in detail. My eyes lingered on the only parts of her that were new to me: the pinkish mounds of her nipples, the golden triangle at her loins. Her body, ripe and full and lustrous, gleamed as though oiled in the bright midday sun, and she was evenly tanned throughout. When I had completed my solemn, foolish inspection, I downed half my beer, arose, and gravely peeled away my shorts.

After that we ceased to observe any taboo of nudity, which made life very much more convenient in what was, after all, quite a small house. It began to seem wholly natural to me—and, I assume, to them—that modesty was irrelevant in our relationship. Once when a party of tourists took the wrong fork in the road and came down the desert track to the house, we were so unaware of our nakedness that we made no attempt to hide ourselves, and only slowly did we realize why the people in the car seemed so shocked, so eager to swing about and retreat.

One barrier remained forever unbreached. I did not speak to Jack about his work in physics, or about his reasons for abandoning it.

Sometimes he talked shop with me, inquiring after my time-reversal project, asking a hazy question or two, leading me into a discourse on whatever knot currently impeded my progress. But I suspect he did this as a therapeutic act, knowing that I had come to them because I was in an impasse, and hoping that he could bring me past the sticking-point. He did not seem to be aware of current work. Nowhere in the house did I see the familiar green spools of *Physical Review* or *Physical Review Letters*. It was as if he had performed an amputation. I tried to imagine what my life would be if I withdrew wholly from physics, and failed even to picture it. That was what Jack had done, and I did not know why, and I did not dare to ask. If the revelation ever came, it would have to come unsolicited from him.

He and Shirley lived a quiet, self-contained life in their desert paradise. They read a good deal, had an extensive musical library, and had outfitted themselves with equipment for making and playing back sonic sculptures. Shirley was the sculptor. Some of her work was quite fine. Jack wrote poetry which I failed to comprehend, contributed occasional essays on desert life to the national magazines, and claimed to be working on some large philosophical tome, the manuscript of which I never saw. Basically I think they were idle people, though not in any negative sense; they had dropped out of the competition and were sufficient unto themselves, producing little, consuming little, and thoroughly happy. By choice they had no children. They left their desert no more than twice a year, for quick trips to New York or San Francisco or London, pulling back hurriedly into their chosen environment. They had four or five other friends who visited them periodically, but I never met any of them, nor did it seem as though any of the others were as close to them as I. Most of the time Jack and Shirley were alone together, and I gather that they found one another completely rewarding. They baffled me. Outwardly they might seem simple, two children of nature romping nude in the desert warmth, untouched by the harshness of the world they had rejected; but the underlying complexity of their renunciation of the world was more than I could fathom. Though I loved them and felt that they were part of me and I of them, yet it was a delusion: they were alien beings, in the final analysis, detached from the world because they did not belong to it. It would have been better for them if they had managed to sustain their isolation.

27

That Christmas week when Vornan-19 descended upon the world, I had gone to their place in deepest need. My work had become hollow to me. It was the despair of fatigue; for fifteen years I had lived on the brink of success, for brinks border not only abysses but also precipices, and I had been scaling a precipice. As I climbed, the summit receded, until I felt that there was no summit at all, merely the illusion of one, and that in any event what I had been doing was not worth the dedication I had given it. These moments of total doubt come upon me frequently, and I know them to be irrational. I suppose that everyone must give way periodically to the fear that he has wasted his life, except, perhaps, for those who *have* wasted their lives and who mercifully lack the capacity to know it. What of the advertising man who breaks his soul to fill the sky with a glowing, pinwheeling cloud of propaganda? What of the middle-echelon executive who pours his life into the shuttling of tense memoranda? What of the designer of automobile hulls, the stockbroker, the college president? Do they ever have a crisis of values?

My crisis of values was upon me again. I was stymied in my work, and I turned to Jack and Shirley. Shortly before Christmas I closed my office, had mail deliveries suspended, and invited myself to Arizona for an indefinite stay. My work schedule is not keyed to the semesters and holidays of the University; I work when I please, withdraw when I must.

It takes three hours to drive to Tucson from Irvine. I locked my car into the first transportation pod heading over the mountains and let myself be whirled eastward along the glittering track, programmed for a short-run trip. The clicking mind in the Sierra Nevada did the rest, omnisciently detaching me from the Phoenix-bound route at the right time, shunting me onto the Tucson track, decelerating me from my three-hundred-mile-per-hour velocity, and delivering me safely to the depot where the manual controls of my car were reactivated. The December weather on the Coast had been rainy and cool, but here the sun blazed cheerfully and the temperature was well into the eighties. I paused in Tucson to charge my car's batteries, having robbed Southern California Edison of a few dollars of revenue by forgetting to do it before I set out. Then I drove into the desert. I followed the old Interstate 89 for the first stretch, turning off onto a county road after fifteen minutes, and leaving even that modest artery shortly for the mere capillary leading to their pocket of uninhabited desert. Most of this region belongs to the Papago Indians, which is why it has avoided the plague of development enveloping Tucson, and just how Shirley and Jack acquired title to their little tract of land I am not at all sure. But they were alone, incredible as that may seem on the eve of the twenty-first century. There still are such places in the United States where one can withdraw as they had done. The final five-mile stretch I traveled was a pebbled dirt track that could be called a road only by semantic jugglery. Time dropped away; I might have been following the route of one of my own electrons, backward into the world's dawn. This was emptiness, and it had the power to draw forth torment from a cluttered soul like a heat pump soothing the dance of the molecules.

I arrived in late afternoon. Behind me lay rutted gulleys and parched earth. To my left rose purple mountains dipped in cloud. They sloped off toward the Mexican border, leading my eye straight around to the flat, coarsely pebbled desert on which the Bryant house was the only modern intrusion. A dry wash through which water had not flowed in centuries rimmed their property. I parked my car beside it and walked toward the house.

They lived in a twenty-year-old building made of redwood and glass, two stories high in the living quarters, with a sundeck to the rear. Beneath the house was its life-system: a Fermi reactor that powered the air-conditioning, the water circulators, the lighting, and the

29

heating. Once a month the man from Tucson Gas & Electric drove out to service the unit, as required by law wherever a utility has declined to run power lines and has supplied an isolated generating unit instead. The fifty-yard storage unit below the house held a month's supply of food, too, and the water purifier was independent of city lines. Civilization could disappear entirely, and Shirley and Jack might remain unaware of it for weeks.

Shirley was on the sundeck, busy with one of her sonic sculptures, spinning a feathery thing of intricate lines and glowing textures, whose soft birdlike twitter had immense carrying power as it crossed the desert to me. She finished what she was doing before she rose and ran toward me, arms outstretched, breasts jouncing. As I caught her and embraced her, I felt some of my weariness ebb away.

"Where's Jack?" I asked.

"He's writing. He'll come out in a little while. Here, let me get you moved in. You look *terrible*, darling!"

"So they've been telling me."

"We'll fix that."

She snatched my suitcase and hurried into the house. The saucy twitching of her bare rump reassured and refreshed me, and I grinned at the two firm cheeks as they vanished from sight. I was among friends. I had come home. At the moment, I felt that I might stay among them for months.

I went to my room. Shirley had everything ready for me: fresh linens, a few spools beside the reader, a nightglow on the table, a pad and stylus and recorder if I wanted to set down any ideas. Jack appeared. He pressed a flask of beer into my hand and I thumbed it open. We winked in mutual delight.

That evening Shirley conjured a magical dinner, and afterwards, as warmth fled from the desert on this winter evening, we sprawled in their living room to talk. They said nothing whatever of my work, bless them both. Instead we discussed the Apocalyptists, for they had come to be fascinated by the cult of doom that now was infesting so many minds.

"I've been studying them closely," said Jack. "Do you follow it at all?"

"Not really."

"It happens every thousand years, it seems. As the millennium comes to its close, a conviction spreads that the world is about to end. It was very bad toward 999. At first only peasants believed it, but then some very sophisticated churchmen began to catch the fever, and that did it. There were orgies of prayer and also the other sorts of orgies."

"And when A.D. 1000 came?" I asked. "The world survived, and what happened to the cult?"

Shirley laughed. "It was quite disillusioning for them. But people don't learn."

"How do the Apocalyptists think the world is going to perish?"

"By fire," said Jack.

"The scourge of God?"

"They expect a war. They believe that the world leaders have already ordained it and that hellfires will be loosed on the first day of the new century."

"We haven't had a war of any size in fifty-odd years," I said. "The last time an atomic weapon was used in anger was 1945. Isn't it safe to assume that we've developed techniques for sidestepping the apocalypse by now?"

"Law of accumulating catastrophe," Jack said. "Static builds toward a discharge. Look at all the little wars: Korea, Vietnam, the Near East, South Africa, Indonesia—"

"Mongolia and Paraguay," Shirley offered.

"Yes. On the average, one minor war every seven or eight years. Each one creating sequences of reflexive response that help to motivate the next, because everybody's eager to put into practice the lessons of the last war. Building up a mounting intensity that's bound to explode into the Final War. Which is due to begin and end on January 1, 2000."

"Do you believe this?" I asked.

"Myself? Not really," Jack said. "I'm simply stating the theory. I don't detect any signs of imminent holocaust in the world, though I admit that all I know is what comes over the screen. Nevertheless, the Apocalyptists catch the imagination. Shirley, run those tapes of the Chicago riot, will you?"

She slipped a capsule into the slot. The entire rear wall of the room blossomed with color as the playback of the telecast began. I saw the towers of Lake Shore Drive and Michigan Boulevard; I saw bizarre figures spilling out over the highway, onto the beach, cavorting beside the icy lake. Most of them were painted in gaudy stripes like mummers on the loose. Most were partly naked, and this was not the innocent, natural nudity of Jack and Shirley on a hot day, but something ugly and raw and deliberately obscene, a wanton flaunting of jiggling breasts and paint-daubed buttocks. This was a display calculated to shock: Hieronymus Bosch grotesques set loose, waggling their nakedness in the face of a world regarded as doomed. I had not paid attention to the movement before. I was startled to see a girl hardly adolescent rush before the camera, whirl, flip up her skirt, crouch and urinate in the face of another reveler who had fallen in stupor. I watched the open fornication, the grotesque tangles of bodies, the complex couplings that were more accurately triplings and quadruplings. An immensely fat old woman waddled across the beach, cheering the younger rioters on. A mountain of furniture went up in flames. Policemen, bewildered, sprayed foam on the mob but did not enter it.

"Mere anarchy is loosed upon the world," I muttered. "How long has this been going on?"

"Since July, Leo," said Shirley quietly. "You didn't know?"

"I've been very busy."

Jack said, "There's a distinct crescendo. At first it was a movement of crackpots in the Midwest—around '93, '94— a thousand members or so, convinced that they'd better pray hard because Doomsday was less than a decade away. They got the proselytizing bug and started to preach doom, only this time the message came across. And the movement got out of hand. For the last six months the idea has been building that it's foolish to waste time in anything but fun, because there's not much time left."

I shuddered. "Universal madness?"

"Quite so. On every continent the profound conviction that the bombs fall a year from January 1. Eat, drink, and be merry. It's spreading. I hate to think of what the hysteria will be like a year from now in the supposed final week of the world. We three may be the only survivors, Leo."

I stared at the screen for a few moments more, appalled.

"Shut that thing off," I said at length.

Shirley chuckled. "How could you not have heard of this, Leo?"

"I've been out of touch with everything." The screen darkened. The painted demons of Chicago still leaped obscenely through my brain. The world is going mad, I thought, and I have not noticed it. Shirley and Jack saw how rocked I was by this revelation of the Apocalyptist apocalypse, and they deftly shifted the subject, talking of the ancient Indian ruins they had discovered in the desert a few miles away. Long before midnight I showed my weariness and they saw me to bed. Shirley returned to my room a few minutes later; she had undressed, and her bare body glowed like a holiday candle in the doorway.

"Can I get you anything, Leo?"

"I'm fine," I told her.

"Merry Christmas, darling. Or have you forgotten that too? Tomorrow's Christmas Day."

"Merry Christmas, Shirley."

I blew her a kiss, and she turned out my light. While I slept, Vornan-19 entered our world six thousand miles away, and nothing would be quite the same for any of us, ever again.

## * THREE *

I AWOKE LATE on Christmas morning. Jack and Shirley had clearly been up for hours. There was a bitter taste in my mouth and I did not want company, not even theirs; as was my privilege, I went into the kitchen and silently programmed my breakfast. They sensed my mood and stayed away. Orange juice and toast came from the output panel of the autochef. I devoured them, punched for black coffee, then dumped the dishes in the cleaner, started the cycle, and went out. I walked by myself for three hours. When I returned I felt purged. It was too cool a day for sunbathing or gardening; Shirley showed off some of her sculptures, Jack read me a little of his poetry, and I spoke hesitantly about the obstacle to my work. That evening we dined magnificently on roast turkey and chilled Chablis.

The days that followed were soothing ones. My nerves uncoiled. Sometimes I walked alone in the desert; sometimes they came with me. They took me to their Indian ruin. Jack knelt to show me the potsherds in the sand: triangular wedges of white pottery marked by black bars and dots. He indicated the sunken contours of a pit-dwelling; he showed me the fragmentary foundations of a building wall made of rough stone mortared with mud.

"Is this Papago stuff?" I asked.

"I doubt it. I'm still checking, but I'm sure it's too good for the Papagos. My guess is that it's a colony of ancestral Hopis, say a thousand years back, coming downstate out of Kayenta. Shirley's supposed to bring me some tapes on

34

archaeology next time she goes into Tucson. The data library doesn't have any of the really advanced texts."

"You could request them," I said. "It wouldn't be hard for the Tucson library to transfer facsims to the dataphone people and shoot them right out to you. If Tucson doesn't have the right books, they can scoop them from L.A. The whole idea of this data network is that you can get what you need at home, right away, when—"

"I know," Jack said gently. "But I didn't want to start too much of a fuss. The next thing you know, I might have a team of archaeologists out here. We'll get our books the old-fashioned way, by going to the library."

"How long have you known about this site?"

"A year," he said. "There's no hurry."

I envied him his freedom from all normal pressures. How had these two done it, finding a life like this for themselves in the desert? For one jealous moment I wished it were possible for me to do the same. But I could hardly stay permanently with them, though they might not object, and the idea of living by myself in some other corner of the desert was not appealing. No. My place was at the University. So long as I had the privilege of escaping to the Bryants when the need arrived, I could seek solace in my work. And at that thought I felt a surge of joy; after only two days here, I was beginning to think hopefully of my work again!

Time flowed easily by. We celebrated the advent of 1999 with a little party at which I got mildly drunk. My tensions eased. A burst of summer warmth hit the desert during the first week in January, and we stretched naked in the sun, mindlessly happy. A winter-flowering cactus in their garden produced a cascade of yellow blooms, and bees appeared from somewhere. I let a great furry bumblebee with thighs swollen with pollen alight on my arm, and twitching only slightly, made no effort to shoo him. After a moment he flew to Shirley and explored the warm valley between her breasts; then he vanished. We laughed. Who could fear such a fat bumblebee?

Almost ten years had gone by, now, since Jack had resigned from the University and taken Shirley into the desert. The turning of the year brought the usual reflections on the passage of time, and we had to admit that we had changed very little. It seemed as if a kind of stasis had settled over us all in the late 1980's. Though I was past 50, I had the appearance and health of a much younger man, and my hair was still black, my face unlined. For that I gave thanks, but I had paid a steep price for my preservation: I was no further along in my work this first week of 1999 than I had been the first week of 1989. I still sought ways of confirming my theory that the flow of time is two-directional and that at least on the subatomic level it can be reversed. For a full decade I had moved in roundabout ways, getting nowhere, while my fame grew willy-nilly and my name was often mentioned for the Nobel. Take it as Garfield's Law that when a theoretical physicist becomes a public figure, something has gone awry with his career. To journalists I was a glamorous wizard who would someday give the world a time machine; to myself I was a futile failure trapped in a maze of detours.

The ten years had flecked the edges of Jack's temples with gray, but otherwise time's metamorphosis had been a positive one for him. He was more muscular, a brawny man who had utterly shed that indoor pallor; his body rippled with strength and he moved with an easy grace that belied his vanished awkwardness. Exposure to the sun had darkened his skin for good. He seemed confident, potent, assured, where once he had been wary and tentative.

Shirley had gained most of all. The changes in her were slight but all to the good. I remembered her as lean, coltish, too ready to giggle, too slender in the thigh for the fullness of her breasts. The years had adjusted those minor

36

flaws. Her golden-tan body was magnificent in its proportions now, and that made her seem all the less naked when she was nude, for she was like some Aphrodite of Phidias walking about under the Arizona sun. Ten pounds heavier than in the California days, yes, but every ounce of it placed perfectly. She was flawless, and, like Jack, she had that deep reservoir of strength, that total self-assurance, which guided her every move and every word. Her beauty was still ripening. In two or three more years she would be blinding to behold. I did not wish to think about her as she one day would be, withered and shrunken. It was hard to imagine that these two—and especially she—were condemned to the same harsh sentence under which we all must live.

To be with them was joy. I felt whole enough, in the second week of my visit, to discuss the problems of my work with Jack in some detail. He listened sympathetically, following with an effort, and seemed not to understand much. Was it true? Could a mind as fine as his have lost contact so thoroughly with physics? At any rate he listened to me, and it did me good. I was groping in darkness; I felt as though I was more distant from my goal now than I had been five or eight years before. I needed a listener, and I found him in Jack.

The difficulty lay in the annihilation of antimatter. Move an electron back in time and its charge changes; it becomes a positron and immediately seeks its antiparticle. To find is to perish. A billionth of a second and the tiny explosion comes, and a photon is released. We could sustain our time-reversal thrust only by sending our particle back into a matter-free universe.

Even if we could find enough power to hurl larger particles—protons and neutrons and even alphas—backward in time, we would still enter the same trap. Whatever we sent to the past would be annihilated so swiftly that it would be the merest microevent on our tracking scanner. The newstapes to the contrary, there was no chance at all of true time travel; a man sent back in time would be a superbomb, assuming that a living thing could survive the transition into antimatter in the first place. Since this part of our theory seemed incontestable, we had been exploring the notion of a matter-free universe, seeking some pocket of nothingness into which we could thrust our backward-going traveler, containing it while we monitored it. But here we were beyond our depth.

Jack said, "You want to open up a synthetic universe?"

"Essentially."

"Can you do it?"

"In theory we can. On paper. We set up a strain pattern that breaches the wall of the continuum. Then we thrust our backward-moving electron through the breach."

"But how can you monitor it?"

"We can't," I said. "That's where we're stuck."

"Of course," Jack murmured. "Once you introduce anything but the electron into the universe, it's no longer matter-free, and you get the annihilation that you don't want. But then you've got no way of observing your own experiment."

"Call it Garfield's Uncertainty Principle," I said faintly. "The act of observing the experiment queers it instantaneously. Do you see why we're hung up?"

"Have you made any efforts at opening this adjoining universe of yours?"

"Not yet. We don't want to go to the expense until we're sure we can do something with it. For that matter, we've got a little further checking to do before we dare try it. You don't go about ripping space-time open until you've run a mock-up of every possible consequence."

He came over to me and punched me lightly in the shoulder. "Leo, Leo, Leo, don't you ever wish you had decided to become a barber instead?"

"No. But there are times I wish physics were a little easier."

"Then you might as well have been a barber."

We laughed. Together we walked to the sundeck, where Shirley lay reading. It was a bright, crisp January afternoon, the sky a metallic blue, great slabs of clouds poised on the tips of the mountains, the sun big and warm. I felt very much at ease. In my two weeks here I had succeeded in externalizing my work problem, so that it seemed almost to belong to someone else. If I could get far enough outside it, I might find some daring new way to slice through the obstacles once I went back to Irvine.

The trouble was that I no longer thought in daring new ways. I thought in clever combinations of the old ways, and that was not good enough. I needed an outsider to examine my dilemma and show me with a quick intuitive flash which way the solution might be reached. I needed Jack. But Jack had retired from physics. He had chosen to disconnect his superb mind.

On the sundeck Shirley rolled over, sat up, grinned at us. Her body glistened with beads of perspiration. "What brings you two outdoors?"

"Despair," I said. "The walls were closing in."

"Sit down and warm up, then." She tapped a button that cut off the radio outlet. I had not even noticed that the radio was on until the sound died away. Shirley said, "I've just been listening to the latest on the man from the future."

"Who's that?" I asked.

"Vornan-19. He's coming to the United States!"

"I don't think I know anything about—"

Jack shot a tense glance at Shirley, the first time I had ever seen him reprove her. Instantly my interest was engaged. Was this something they were keeping from me?

"It's just nonsense," Jack said. "Shirley shouldn't have bothered you with it."

"Will you tell me what you're talking about?"

Shirley said, "He's the living answer to the Apocalyptists. He claims to have come back from the year 2999, as a sort of tourist, you know. He showed up in Rome, stark naked on the Spanish Stairs, and when they tried to arrest him, he knocked a policeman out with a touch of his fingertips. Since then he's been causing all sorts of confusion."

"A stupid hoax," Jack said. "Obviously some moron is tired of pretending that the world is coming to an end next January, and decided to pretend that he was a visitor from a thousand years from now. And people are believing him. It's the times we live in. When hysteria's a way of life, you follow every lunatic who comes along."

"Suppose he *is* a time traveler, though!" Shirley said.

"If he is, I'd like to meet him," I put in. "He might be able to answer a few questions I've got about time-reversal phenomena." I chuckled. Then I stopped chuckling. It wasn't funny at all. I stiffened and said, "You're right, Jack. He's nothing but a charlatan. Why are we wasting all this time talking about him?"

"Because there's a possibility he's real, Leo." Shirley got to her feet and shook out the long golden hair rippling to her shoulders. "The interviews make him out to be very strange. He talks about the future as though he's been there. Oh, maybe he's only clever, but he's entertaining. He's a man I'd like to meet."

"When did he appear?"

"Christmas Day," said Shirley.

"While I was here? And you didn't mention it?"

She shrugged. "We assumed you were following the newscasts and didn't find it an interesting topic."

"I haven't been near the screen since I came."

"Then you ought to do some catching up," she said.

Jack looked displeased. It was unusual to see this rift between them, and he had looked notably cross when Shirley had expressed a wish to meet the time traveler.

Odd, I thought. With his interest in the Apolcalyptists, why should he discriminate against the latest manifestation of irrationality?

My own feeling about the man from the future was a neutral one. The business of time travel amused me, of course; I had broken my soul to prove its practical impossibility, and I was hardly likely to accept cheerfully the claim that it had been accomplished. No doubt that was why Jack had tried to shield me from this item of news, believing that I needed no distorted parodies of my own work to remind me of the problems I had fled from just before Christmas. But I was getting free of my depression; time-reversal no longer triggered bleakness in me. I was in the mood to find out more about this fraud. The man seemed to have charmed Shirley via television, and anything that charmed Shirley was of interest to me.

One of the networks ran a documentary on Vornan-19 that evening, preempting an hour of prime time usually taken up by one of the kaleidoscope shows. That in itself revealed the depth and extent of public interest in the story. The documentary was aimed at Robinson Crusoes like myself who had neglected to follow the developments thus far, and so I was able to bring myself up to date all at once.

We floated on pneumochairs before the wall screen and outlasted the commercials. Finally a resonant voice said, "What you are about to see is in part a computer simulation." The camera revealed the Piazza di Spagna on Christmas morning, with a sprinkling of figures posed on the Stairs and in the piazza as though the computer simulating them had been programmed by Tiepolo. Into this neatly reconstructed frieze of casual bystanders came the simulated image of Vornan-19 descending on a shining arc from the heavens. The computers do this sort of thing so well today. It does not really matter that a camera's eye fails to record some sudden major event, for it can always be hauled from time's abyss by a cunning re-creation. I

41

wonder what future historians will make of these simulations . . . if the world survives past the first of next month, of course.

The descending figure was nude, but the simulators ducked the problem of the conflicting testimony of the nuns and the others by showing us only a rear view. There was no prudishness about that, I'm sure; the television coverage of the Apocalyptist revelry that Shirley and Jack had shown me had been quite explicitly revealing of the flesh, and apparently it is now a standard ploy of the networks to work anatomy into the newscasts whenever such displays fall under the protection of the Supreme Court decision on legitimate journalistic observation. I have no objection to this coverage of uncoverage; the nudity taboos are long overdue for discard, and I suppose that anything encouraging a well-informed citizenry is desirable, even pandering in the newscasts. But there is always cowardice an inch behind the façade of integrity. Vornan-19's loins went unsimulated because three nuns had sworn he had been covered by a misty nimbus, and it was easier to sidestep the issue than to risk offending the devout by contradicting the testimony of the holy sisters.

I watched Vornan-19 inspecting the piazza. I saw him mount the Spanish Stairs. I smiled as the excited policeman rushed up, proffered his cloak, and was knocked to the ground by an unseen thunderbolt.

The colloquy with Horst Klein followed. This was done most cleverly, for Klein himself was used, conversing with a dubbed simulation of the time traveler. The young German reconstructed his own conversation with Vornan, while the computer played back what Klein recalled the visitor to have said.

The scene shifted. Now we were indoors, in a high room with congruent polygons inscribed on the walls and ceiling, and with the smooth, even glow of thermoluminescence illuminating the faces of a dozen men. Vornan-19 was in custody, voluntarily, for no one could touch him without being smitten by that electric-eel voltage of his. He was being interrogated. The men about him were skeptical, hostile, amused, angered in turn. This, too, was a simulation; no one had bothered to make a record at the time.

Speaking in English, Vornan-19 repeated what he had told Horst Klein. The interrogators challenged him on various points. Aloof, tolerant of their hostility, Vornan parried their thrusts. Who was he? A visitor. Where was he from? The year 2999. How had he come here? By time transport. Why was he here? To view the medieval world at first hand.

Jack snickered. "I like that. We're medievals to him!"

"It's a convincing touch," said Shirley.

"The simulators dreamed it up," I pointed out. "So far we haven't heard an authentic word."

But shortly we did. Bridging the events of the past ten days in a few words, the program's narrator described how Vornan-19 had moved into the most imposing suite of an elegant hotel on the Via Veneto, how he was holding court there for all interested comers, how he had obtained a wardrobe of fine contemporary clothes by requesting one of Rome's costliest tailors to attend to his needs. The whole problem of credibility had seemingly been by-passed. What astonished me was the ease with which Rome appeared to accept his story at face value. Did they really believe he came from the future? Or was the Roman attitude a huge joke, a self-indulgent romp?

The screen showed us shots of Apocalyptist pickets outside his hotel, and suddenly I understood why the hoax was succeeding. Vornan-19 did have something to offer a troubled world. Accept him, and one accepted the future. The Apocalyptists were attempting to deny the future. I watched them: the grotesque masks, the painted bodies, the wanton capers, the signs held high, crying, REJOICE! THE END IS NEAR! In fury they shook their fists at the hotel and cast sacks of living light at the building, so that trickles of gleaming red and blue pigment streamed down the weathered masonry. The man from the future was the nemesis of their cult. An epoch racked by fears of imminent extinction turned to him easily, naturally, and hopefully. In an apocalyptic age all wonders are welcome.

"Last night in Rome," said the narrator, "Vornan-19 held his first live press conference. Thirty reporters representing the major global news services questioned him."

Abruptly the screen dissolved into a swirl of colors, out of which came the replay of the news conference. Not a simulation this time. Vornan himself, live, appeared before my eyes for the first time.

I was shaken.

I can use no other word. In view of my later involvement with him, let me make it quite clear that at this time I regarded him as nothing but an ingenious fraud. I felt contempt for his pretensions and despised those who, for whatever motives, were choosing to play his silly game. Nevertheless my first sight of the purported visitor had a wholly unexpected impact. He peered outward from the screen, relaxed and poised, and the effect of his presence was something more than merely three-dimensional.

He was a slim man of less than middle height, with narrow sloping shoulders, a slender feminine neck, and a finely modeled head held proudly erect. The planes of his face were pronounced: sharp cheek-bones, angular temples, a strong chin, a prominent nose. His skull was slightly too large for his frame; it was high-vaulted, longer than it was broad, and the bone structure in back would have been of interest to a phrenologist, for his skull was curiously prolonged and ridged. Its unusual features, though, fell within the range of what one might expect to find on the streets of any large city.

His hair was close-cropped and gray. His eyes, too, were gray. He might have been of any age from thirty to sixty. His skin was unlined. He wore a pale blue tunic that had the simplicity of high style, and at his throat was a neatly gathered foulard, in cerise, providing the only touch of color about him. He looked cool, graceful, alert, intelligent, charming, and somewhat disdainful. I was reminded forcefully of a sleek bluepoint Siamese cat I had once known. He had the ambivalent sexuality of a superb tom, for there is something sinuously feminine even about most male cats, and Vornan projected that same quality, that well-groomed look of pantherish grace. I don't mean to say that he was epicene in the sense of being sexless, but rather that he was androgynous, omnisexual, capable of finding and giving pleasure with anyone or anything. I stress the point that this was my instant impression, and not something that I am projecting backward out of what I later discovered about Vornan-19.

Character is defined mainly by the eyes and the mouth. Vornan's power centered there. His lips were thin, his mouth somewhat too wide, his teeth flawless, his smile dazzling. He flashed the smile like a beacon, radiating an immense warmth and concern, and just as swiftly cut it off, so that the mouth became a nullity and the center of attention shifted to the chilly, penetrating eyes. Those were the two most conspicuous sides of Vornan's personality: the instant capacity to demand and seize love, represented by the irresistible blaze of the smile; and the quick withdrawal to calculating aloofness, represented by the moonstone gleam of the eyes. Charlatan or not, he was plainly an extraordinary man, and despite my scorn for such charades as this, I felt impelled to watch him in action. The simulated version shown a few moments before, under interrogation by the bureaucrats, had had the same features, but the power was missing. The first instant's view of the live Vornan carried an immediate magnetism absent from the computerized zombie.

The camera lingered on him for perhaps thirty seconds, long enough to register his curious ability to command attention. Then it panned around the room, showing the newsmen. Remote as I am from the heroes of the screen, I recognized at least half a dozen of them, and the fact that Vornan had been thought worthy of the time of the world's star reporters was important in itself, testimony to the effect he had already had on the world while Jack and Shirley and I lazed in the desert. The camera continued around, revealing all the gimmicks of our gadgety era: the power core of the recording instruments, the dull snout of the computer input, the boom from which the sound equipment dangled, the grid of depth-sensors that kept the three dimensions of the telecast from wandering, and the small cesium laser that provided the spotlighting. Usually all these devices are carefully kept out of sight, but for this production they had been obtrusively thrust forward—props, one might say, to demonstrate that we medievals knew a thing or two.

The press conference began with a voice saying in clipped London tones, "Mr. Vornan, would you kindly describe your assertions concerning your presence here?"

"Certainly. I have come across time to gain insight into the life processes of early technological man. My starting point was the year you reckon as 2999. I propose to tour the centers of your civilization and carry back with me a full account for the delight and instruction of my contemporaries."

He spoke smoothly and with no discernible hesitation. His English was scrubbed free of accent; it was the sort of English I have heard computers speaking, a speech cobbled together from chaste isolated phonemes and thus missing any regional taint. The robotic quality of his timbre and enunciation clearly conveyed the notion that this man was speaking a language he had learned *in vacuo,* from some sort of teaching machine; but of course a twentieth-century Finn or Basque or Uzbek who had learned English via tape would have sounded much the same way. Vornan's voice itself was flexible and well modulated, pleasant to hear.

A questioner said, "How come you speak English?"

"It seemed the most useful medieval language for me to learn."

"Isn't it spoken in your time?"

"Only in a greatly altered form."

"Tell us a little about the world of the future."

Vornan smiled—the charm again—and said patiently, "What would you like to know?"

"The population."

"I'm not sure. Several billions, at least."

"Have you reached the stars yet?"

"Oh, yes, of course."

"How long do people live in 2999?"

"Until they die," said Vornan amiably. "That is, until they choose to die."

"What if they don't so choose?"

"I suppose they'd keep on living. I'm really not sure."

"What are the leading nations of 2999?"

"We have no nations. We have the Centrality, and then there are the decentralized settlements. That is all."

"What's the Centrality?"

"A voluntary association of citizens in a single area. A city, in a sense, but something more than a city."

"Where is it?"

Vornan-19 frowned delicately. "On one of the major continents. I forget your names for the continents."

Jack looked up at me. "Shall I turn it off? He's obviously a phony. He can't even fake the details convincingly!"

"No, leave it," Shirley said. She seemed entranced. Jack tensed again, and I quickly said, "Yes, let's watch a little more. It's amusing."

". . . only one city, then?"

"Yes," Vornan replied. "Composed of those who value communal life. There's no economic need for us to cluster

47

together, you know. We're each quite self-sufficient. What fascinates me is the need you folk have to keep your hands in each other's pockets. This business of money, for example. Without it, a man starves, a man goes naked. Am I right? You lack independent means of production. Am I right in believing that energy conversion is not yet an accomplished fact?"

A harsh American voice said, "Depends what you mean by energy conversion. Mankind's had ways of getting energy since the first fires were kindled."

Looking perturbed, Vornan said, "I mean *efficient* energy conversion. The full use of the power stored within a single—ah, a single atom. You lack this?"

I glanced sideways at Jack. He was gripping the float of his pneumochair in sudden anguish, and his features were distorted with tension. I looked away again as though I had intruded on something terribly private, and I realized that a decade-old question had been answered at least in part.

Vornan was no longer discussing energy conversion when I was able to return my attention to the screen.

". . . a tour of the world. I wish to sample the full range of experience available in this era. And I will begin in the United States of America."—

"Why?"

"One likes to see the processes of decadence in motion. When one visits a crumbling culture, one does best to explore its most powerful component first. My impression is that the chaos that will come upon you will radiate outward from the United States, and therefore I wish to search for the symptoms there first." He said this with a kind of bland impersonality, as though it should be quite self-evident that our society was collapsing and that no offense could possibly be given by remarking on something so obvious. Then he flashed the smile just long enough to stun his audience into ignoring the underlying darkness of his words.

48

The press conference trickled to an anticlimactic end. Random questions about Vornan's world and about the method by which he had come to our time were met with such vague generalities that he seemed clearly to be mocking his questioners. Occasionally he implied that he might provide further details on some point another time; mostly he declared that he simply did not know. He was particularly evasive on all efforts to get from him a sharp description of world events in our immediate future. I gathered that he had no high regard for our attainments and was a trifle surprised to discover that we had electricity and atomic energy and space travel at our early stage in the stream of history. He made no attempt to hide his disdain, but the odd thing was that his cockiness failed to be infuriating. And when the editor of a Canadian facsimsheet said, "Just how much of all this do you really expect us to believe?" he replied quite pleasantly, "Why, feel free to believe none of it. I'm sure it makes no difference to me."

When the program was over, Shirley turned to me and said, "Now you've seen the fabulous man from tomorrow, Leo. What do you think of him?"

"I'm amused."

"Convinced?"

"Don't be silly. This is nothing but a very clever publicity dodge that's working out magnificently for somebody. But give the devil credit: he's got charm."

"He does indeed," Shirley said. She looked toward her husband. "Jack, darling, would you mind very much if I arrange to sleep with him when he comes to the States? I'm sure they've invented a few new wrinkles in sex in the next thousand years, and maybe he could teach me something."

"Very funny," Jack said.

His face was black with rage. Shirley recoiled as she saw it. It startled me that he would overreact in this way to her innocently wanton suggestion. Surely their marriage was secure enough so that she could play at infidelity without angering him. And then it struck me that he was not reacting at all to her talk of sleeping with Vornan, that he was still locked in his earlier anguish. That talk of total energy conversion—of a decentralized world in which each man was an economically self-sufficient unit—

"Do you mind?" he said, and left the room.

Shirley and I exchanged troubled glances. She bit her lip, tugged at her hair, and said softly, "I'm sorry, Leo. I know what's eating him, but I can't explain."

"I think I can guess."

"Yes, you probably would be the one who could."

She opened the circuit that opaqued the side window. I saw Jack on the sundeck, gripping the rail, hulking forward and staring into the darkened desert. Lightning forked across the summits of the mountains in the west, and then came the instant fury of a winter rainstorm. Sheets of water cascaded across the glass paneling. Jack remained there, a statue more than a man, and let the storm unleash its force upon him. Beneath my feet I felt the purr of the house's life-system as the storage pumps sucked the rainwater into the cisterns for later use. Shirley came up beside me and put her hand on my arm. "I'm afraid," she whispered. "Leo, I'm afraid."

* FOUR *

"COME OUT INTO the desert with me," Jack said. "I'd like to talk to you, old man."

Two days had passed since the telecast of Vornan-19's press conference. We had not turned the wallscreen on again, and the tension had ebbed from the house. I was planning to return to Irvine the following day. My work was calling me, and I felt also that I should leave Shirley and Jack in privacy while they dealt with whatever gulfs were opening in their lives. Jack had said little during the two days; he appeared to be making a conscious effort to conceal the pain he had felt that night. I was surprised and pleased by his invitation.

"Will Shirley go?" I asked.

"She doesn't need to. Just the two of us."

We left her sunbathing in the noon light, her eyes closed, her supple body upturned, her loveliness bare to the sun's caress. Jack and I walked more than a mile from the house, taking a path we rarely used. The sand was still dimpled from the heavy rainfall, and the scrubby plants were erupting in violent greenery.

Jack halted at a place where three high mica-encrusted monoliths formed a kind of natural Stonehenge, and crouched down before one of the boulders to tug at a clump of sage growing by its base. When he had succeeded in pulling the hapless plant free, he cast it aside and said, "Leo, did you ever wonder why I left the University?"

"You know I did."

"What was the story I gave you?"

"That you were at a dead end in your work," I said. "That you were bored with it, that you had lost faith in yourself and in physics, that you simply wanted to get away to your love-nest with Shirley and stay there and write and meditate."

He nodded. "It was a lie."

"I know."

"Well, partly a lie. I did want to come away here and live apart from the world, Leo. But the bit about being at a dead end: it wasn't true at all. My problem was quite the opposite. I was *not* at a dead end. God knows I wanted to be. But I saw my way clearly to the culmination of my thesis. The answers were in sight, Leo. All the answers."

Something twitched in my left cheek. "And you could stop, knowing that it was all in your grasp?"

"Yes." He scuffed at the base of the boulder, knelt, scooped sand, sifted it through his fingers. He did not look at me. At length he said, "Was it an act of moral grandeur, I wonder, or just an act of cowardice? What do you think, Leo?"

"You tell me."

"Do you know where my work was heading?"

"I think I knew it before you," I said. "But I wasn't going to point it out. I had to let you make all the decisions. You never once indicated that you saw any of the larger implications at all, Jack. As far as I could tell, you thought you were dealing with the atomic binding forces in a vacuum of theory."

"I was. For the first year and a half."

"And then?"

"I met Shirley, remember? She didn't know much about physics. Sociology, history, those were her fields. I described my work to her. She didn't understand, so I put it in simpler terms, and then still simpler terms. It was good discipline for me, verbalizing what had really been just a bunch of equations. And finally I said that what I was doing was finding out what holds atoms together internally. And she said, 'Does that mean we'd be able to take them apart without blowing things up?' 'Yes,' I said. 'Why, we could take any atom at all and liberate enough energy to run a house on it, I suppose.' Shirley gave me a queer look and said, 'That would be the end of our whole economic structure, wouldn't it?' "

"It had never occurred to you before?"

"Never, Leo. Never. I was that skinny kid from M.I.T., yes? I didn't worry about applied technology. Shirley turned me upside down. I started calculating, then got on the phone to the library and had the computer run off some engineering texts for me, and Shirley gave me a little lecture on elementary economics. Then I saw, yes, by damn, somebody could take my equations and figure out a way of liberating unlimited energy. It was $E = MC^2$ all over again. I panicked. I couldn't assume the responsibility for overturning the world. My first impulse was to go to you and ask what you thought I should do."

"Why didn't you?"

He shrugged. "It was the cheap way out. Loading the burden onto you. Anyway, I realized that you probably saw the problem already, and that you would have said something about it to me unless you felt I ought to work out the moral part by myself. So I asked for that sabbatical, and spent my time fooling around at the accelerator while I thought things over. I looked up Oppenheimer and Fermi and the rest of the boys who built the atomic bomb, and asked myself what I would have done in their place. They worked in wartime, to help humanity against a really filthy enemy, and even *they* had their doubts. I wasn't doing anything that would save humanity from clear and present danger. I was simply whipping up a gratuitous bit of research that would smash the world's money structure. I saw myself as an enemy of mankind."

"With real energy conversion," I said quietly, "there'd be no more hunger, no more greed, no more monopolies—"

"There'd also be a fifty-year upheaval while the new order of things was taking shape. And the name of Jack Bryant would be accursed. Leo, I couldn't do it. I wasn't able to take the responsibility. At the end of that third year, I packed myself in. I walked away from my own work and came out here. I committed a crime against knowledge to avoid committing a worse crime."

"And you feel guilty about it?"

"Of course I do. I feel that my whole life for the past decade has been a penance for running away. Have you ever wondered about the book I've been writing, Leo?"

"Many times."

"It's a kind of autobiographical essay: an *apologia pro vita sua*. In it I explain what I was working on at the

University, how I came to realize its true nature, why I halted work, and what my attitude toward my own withdrawal has been. The book's an examination of the moral responsibilities of science, you could say. By way of an appendix, I include the complete text of my thesis."

"As it was the day you stopped work?"

"No," Jack said. "The *complete* text. I told you the answers were in sight when I quit. I finished my work five years ago. It's all there in the manuscript. With a billion dollars and a decently equipped laboratory any reasonably alert corporation could translate my equations into a fully functioning power system the size of a walnut that would run forever on an input of sand."

Just then it seemed to me as if the Earth wobbled a little on its axis. I said after a long moment, "Why did you wait this long to bring the subject up?"

"That stupid newscast the other night gave me the push. The so-called man from 2999, with his idiot talk of a decentralized civilization in which every man is self-sufficient because he's got full energy conversion. It was like having a vision of the future—a future that I helped to shape."

"Surely you don't believe—"

"I don't know, Leo. It's a load of nonsense to imagine a man dropping in on us from a thousand years ahead. I was as convinced as you were that the man was all phony . . . until he started describing the decentralization thing."

"The idea of complete liberation of atomic energy has been around for a long time, Jack. This fellow's clever enough to grab it up and use it. It doesn't necessarily mean that he really is from the future and that your equations have actually gone into use. Forgive me, Jack, but I think you're overestimating your own uniqueness. You've taken an idea out of the floating pool of futuristic dreams and turned it into reality, yes, but no one except you and Shirley knows that, and you mustn't let his random shot fool you into thinking—"

54

"But suppose it *is* true, Leo?"

"If you're really worried about it, why don't you burn your manuscript?" I suggested.

He looked as shocked as if I had proposed self-mutilation.

"I couldn't do that."

"You'd protect mankind against the upheaval that you seem to feel advance guilt for causing."

"The manuscript's safe enough, Leo."

"Where?"

"Downstairs. I've built a vault for it and rigged up a deadfall in the house reactor. If anyone tries to enter the vault improperly, the safeties come out of the reactor and the house blows sky high. I don't need to destroy what I've written. It'll never fall into the wrong hands."

"Yet you assume it *has* fallen into the wrong hands, somewhere in the next thousand years; so that by the time Vornan-19 is born, the world is already living on your power system. Right?"

"I don't know, Leo. The whole thing is crazy. I think I'm going crazy myself."

"Let's say for argument's sake that Vornan-19 is genuine and that such a power system is in use in A.D. 2999. Yes? Okay, but we don't know that it's the system you devised. Suppose you burn your manuscript. The act of doing that would change the future so that the economy described by Vornan-19 would never have come into existence. He himself might wink out of existence the moment your book went into the incinerator. And that way you'd know that the future was saved from the terrible fate you had created for it."

"No, Leo. Even if I burned the manuscript, *I'd* still be here. I could recreate my equations from memory. The menace is in my brain. Burning the book would prove nothing."

"There are memory-washing drugs—"

He shuddered. "I couldn't trust those."

I looked at him in horror. With a sensation like that of falling through a trapdoor, I made contact with Jack's paranoia for the first time; and the healthy, tanned extrovert of these desert years vanished forever. To think that he had come to this! Tied in knots over the possibility that a shrewd but implausible fraud represented a veritable ambassador from a distant future shaped by Jack's own suppressed creation!

"Is there anything I can do to help you?" I said softly.

"There is, Leo. One thing."

"Anything."

"Find some way to meet Vornan-19 yourself. You're an important scientific figure. You can pull the right strings. Sit down and talk with him. Find out if he's really a faker."

"Of course he is."

"Find it out, Leo."

"And if he's really what he says he is?"

Jack's eyes blazed with unsettling intensity. "Question him about his own era, then. Get him to tell you more about this atomic energy thing. Get him to tell you when it was invented—by whom. Maybe it didn't come up until five hundred years from now—an independent rediscovery, nothing to do with my work. Wring the truth out of him, Leo. I have to know."

What could I say?

Could I tell him, Jack, you've gone skully? Could I beg him to enter therapy? Could I offer a quick amateur diagnosis of paranoia? Yes, and lose forever my dearest friend. But to become a partner in psychosis by solemnly quizzing Vornan-19 this way was distasteful to me. Assuming I could ever get access to him, assuming there was some way of obtaining an individual audience, I had no wish to stain myself by treating the mountebank even for a moment as though his pretensions should be taken seriously.

56

I could lie to Jack. I could invent a reassuring conversation with the man.

But that was treachery. Jack's dark, tormented eyes begged for honest aid. I'll humor him, I thought.

"I'll do what I can," I promised.

His hand clasped mine. We walked quietly back to the house.

The next morning, as I packed, Shirley came into my room. She wore a clinging, pearly iridescent wrap that miraculously enhanced the contours of her body. I who had grown callously accustomed to her nakedness was reminded anew that she was beautiful, and that my uncle-like love for her incorporated a nugget of repressed though irrepressible lust.

She said, "How much did he tell you out there yesterday?"

"Everything."

"About the manuscript? About what he's afraid of?"

"Yes."

"Can you help him, Leo?"

"I don't know. He wants me to get hold of the man from 2999 and check everything out with him. That may not be so easy. And it probably won't do much good even if I can."

"He's very disturbed, Leo. I'm worried about him. You know, he looks so healthy on the outside, and yet this thing has been burning through him year after year. He's lost all perspective."

"Have you thought of getting professional help for him?"

"I don't dare," she whispered. "It's the one thing not even I can suggest. This is the great moral crisis of his life, and I've got to take it that way. I can't suggest that it's a sickness. At least not yet. Perhaps if you came back here able to convince him that this man's a hoax, that would help Jack start letting go of his obsession. Will you do it?"

"Whatever I can, Shirley."

Suddenly she was in my arms. Her face was thrust into the hollow between my cheek and my shoulder; the globes of her breasts, discernible through the thin wrap, crushed themselves against my chest, and her fingertips dug into my back. She was trembling and sobbing. I held her close, until I began to tremble for another reason, and gently I broke the contact between us. An hour later I was bumping over the dirt road, heading for Tucson and the transportation pod that was waiting to bring me back to California.

I reached Irvine at nightfall. A thumb to the doorplate and my house opened for me. Sealed for three weeks, climateproofed, it had a musty, tomblike odor. The familiar litter of papers and spools everywhere was reassuring. I went in just as a light rain began to fall. Wandering from room to room, I felt that sense of an ending that I used to know on the day after the last day of summer; I was alone again, the holiday was over, the Arizona brightness had given way to the misty dark of California winter. I could not expect to find Shirley scampering spritelike about the house, nor Jack uncoiling some characteristically involuted idea for my consideration. The homecoming sadness was even sharper this time, for I had lost the strong, sturdy Jack I had depended on for so many years, and in his place there had appeared a troubled stranger full of irrational doubts. Even golden Shirley stood revealed as no goddess but a worried wife. I had gone to them with a sickness in my own soul and had come home healed of that, but it had been a costly visit.

I cut out the opaquers and peered outside at the Pacific's surging surf, at the reddish strip of beach, at the white swirls of fog invading the twisted pines that grew where sand yielded to soil. The staleness in the house gave way as that piney salt air was sucked through the vents. I slipped a music cube into the scanner, and the thousands of tiny speakers embedded in the walls spun a skein of Bach for me. I allowed myself a few ounces of cognac. For a while I sat quietly sipping, letting the music cocoon me, and gradually I felt a kind of peace come over me. My hopeless work awaited me in the morning. My friends were in anguish. The world was convulsed by an apocalyptic cult and now was beset by a self-appointed emissary from the epochs ahead. Yet there had always been false prophets loose in the land, men had always struggled with problems so heavy they strained their souls, and the good had always been plagued with shattering doubts and turmoils. Nothing was new. I need feel no pity for myself. Live each day for itself, I thought, meet the challenges as they arise, brood not, do your best, and hope for a glorious resurrection. Fine. Let the morrow come.

After a while I remembered to reactivate my telephone. It was a mistake.

My staff knows that I am incommunicado when I am in Arizona. All incoming calls are shunted to my secretary's line, and she deals with them as she sees fit, never consulting me. But if anything of major importance comes up, she rings it into the storage cell of my home telephone so that I'll find out about it right away when I return. The instant I brought my phone to life, the storage cell disgorged its burden; the chime sounded and automatically I nudged the output switch. My secretary's long, bony face appeared on the screen.

"I'm calling on January fifth, Dr. Garfield. There have been several calls for you today from a Sanford Kralick of the White House staff. Mr. Kralick wants to speak to you urgently and insisted a number of times that he be put through to Arizona. He pushed me quite hard, too. When I finally got it across to him that you couldn't be disturbed, he asked me to have you call him at the White House as soon as possible, any hour of the day or night.

He said it was on a matter vital to national security. The number is—"

That was all. I had never heard of Mr. Sanford Kralick, but of course Presidential aides come and go. This was perhaps the fourth time the White House had called me in the past eight years, since I had inadvertently become part of the available supply of learned pundits. A profile of me in one of the weekly journals for the feeble-minded had labeled me as a man to be watched, an adventurer on the frontiers of thought, a dominant force in American physics, and since then I had been manipulated to the status of a star scientist. I was occasionally asked to lend my name to this or that official statement on the National Purpose or on the Ethical Structure of Humanity; I was called to Washington to guide beefy Congressmen through the intricacies of particle theory when appropriations for new accelerators were under discussion; I was dragooned as part of the backdrop when some bold explorer of space was being awarded the Goddard Prize. The foolishness even spread to my own profession, which should have known better; occasionally I keynoted an annual meeting of the A.A.A.S., or tried to explain to a delegation of oceanographers or archaeologists what was taking place out on my particular frontier of thought. I admit hesitantly that I came to welcome this nonsense, not for the notoriety it provided, but simply because it supplied me with a virtuous-sounding excuse for escaping from my own increasingly less rewarding work. Remember Garfield's Law: star scientists usually are men in a private creative bind. Having ceased to produce meaningful results, they go on the public-appearance circuit and solace themselves with the reverence of the ignorant.

Never once, though, had one of these Washington summonses been couched in such urgent terms. "Vital to national security," Kralick had said. Really? Or was he one of those Washingtonians for whom hyperbole is the native tongue?

60

My curiosity was piqued. It was dinnertime in the capital just now. Call at any hour, Kralick had said. I hoped I would interrupt him just as he sat down to supreme de volaille at some absurd restaurant overlooking the Potomac. Hastily I punched out the White House number. The Presidential seal appeared on my screen and a ghostly computerized voice asked me my business.

"I'd like to talk to Sanford Kralick," I said.

"One moment, please."

It took more than one moment. It took about three minutes while the computer hunted up a relay number for Kralick, who was out of his office, called it, and had him brought to the phone. In time my screen showed me a somber-looking young man, surprisingly ugly, with a tapering wedge of a face and bulging orbital ridges that would have been the pride of some Neanderthal. I was relieved; I had expected one of those collapsible plastic yes-men so numerous in Washington. Whatever else Kralick might be, he at least had not been stamped from the usual mold. His ugliness was in his favor.

"Dr. Garfield," he said at once. "I've been hoping you'd call! Did you have a good vacation?"

"Excellent."

"Your secretary deserves a medal for loyalty, professor. I practically threatened to call out the National Guard if she wouldn't put me through to you. She refused anyway."

"I've warned my staff that I'll vivisect anyone who lets my privacy be broken, Mr. Kralick. What can I do for you?"

"Can you come to Washington tomorrow? All expenses paid."

"What is it this time? A conference on our chances of surviving into the twenty-first century?"

Kralick grinned curtly. "Not a conference, Dr. Garfield. We need your services in a very special way. We'd like to co-opt a few months of your time and put you to work on a job that no one else in the world can handle."

"A few *months?* I don't think I can——"

"It's essential, sir. I'm not just making governmental noises now. This is big."

"May I have a detail or two?"

"Not over the phone, I'm afraid."

"You want me to fly to Washington on no day's notice to talk about something you can't tell me about?"

"Yes. If you prefer, I'll come to California to discuss it. But that would mean even more delay, and we've already forfeited so much time that——"

My hand hovered over the cutoff knob, and I made sure Kralick knew it. "Unless I get at least a clue, Mr. Kralick, I'm afraid I'll have to terminate this discussion."

He didn't look intimidated. "One clue, then."

"Yes?"

"You're aware of the so-called man from the future who arrived a few weeks ago?"

"More or less."

"What we have in mind involves him. We need you to question him on certain topics. I——"

For the second time in three days I felt that sensation of dropping through a trapdoor. I thought of Jack begging me to talk to Vornan-19; and now here was the government commanding me to do the same. The world had gone mad.

I cut Kralick off by blurting, "All right. I'll come to Washington tomorrow."


* FIVE *

THE TELEPHONE SCREEN deceives. Kralick in the screen had looked engagingly lithe and agile; Kralick in the flesh turned out to be six feet seven or so, and that look of intellectuality that made his ugly face interesting was wholly engulfed by the impression of massiveness he projected. He met me at the airport; it was a little before noon, Washington time, when I arrived.

*   *   *

As we sped along the autotrack to the White House, he insistently stressed the importance of my mission and his gratitude for my cooperation. He offered no details of what he wanted from me. We took the downtown shunt of the track and rolled smoothly through the White House's private bypass gate. Somewhere in the bowels of the earth I was duly scanned and declared acceptable, and we ascended into the venerable building. I wondered if the President himself would do the briefing. As it turned out, I never caught sight of the man. I was shown into the Situation Room, which bristled preposterously with communications gear. In a crystal capsule on the main table was a Venusian zoological specimen, a purplish plasmoid that tirelessly sent forth its amoebalike projections in a passable imitation of life. An inscription on the base of the capsule said that it had been found on the second expedition. I was surprised: I had not thought we had discovered so many that we could afford to leave them lying around like paperweights in the dens of the bureaucracy.

A brisk little man with cropped gray hair and a flamboyant suit entered the room, almost at a trot. His shoulders were padded like a fullback's and a row of glittering chromed spines jutted from his jacket like vertebrae gone berserk. Obviously this was a man who believed very much in being up to date.

"Marcus Kettridge," he said. "Special Assistant to the President. Glad you're with us, Dr. Garfield."

Kralick said, "What about the visitor?"

"He's been in Copenhagen. The relay came in half an hour ago. Would you like to see it before the briefing?"

"It might be an idea."

Kettridge opened his hand; a tape capsule lay on his palm, and he inserted it. A screen I had not noticed before came to life. I saw Vornan-19 strolling through the baroque fancifulness of the Tivoli Gardens, domed against the weather and showing not a trace of the Danish winter. Patterns of flashing lights stained the sky. He moved like a dancer, controlling every muscle for maximum impetus. By his side walked a blonde giantess, perhaps nineteen years old, with a corona of dazzling hair and a dreamy look on her face. She wore crotch-high shorts and a skimpy bandeau across immense breasts; she might as well have been naked. Yards of flesh showed. Vornan put his arm around her and idly touched the tip of a finger to each of the deep dimples above her monumental buttocks.

Kettridge said, "The girl's a Dane named Ulla Something that he collected yesterday at the Copenhagen Zoo. They spent the night together. He's been doing that everywhere, you know—like an emperor, summoning girls into his bed by royal command."

"Not only girls," rumbled Kralick.

"True. True. In London there was that young hairdresser."

I watched Vornan-19's progress through Tivoli. A curious throng attended him; and in his immediate presence were a dozen brawny Danish police officers with neural whips, a few people who seemed to be government officials, and half a dozen individuals who obviously were reporters. I said, "How do you keep the journalists at bay?"

"It's a pool," Kettridge snapped. "Six reporters represent all the media. They change every day. It was Vornan's idea; he said he liked publicity but he hated to have a mob around him."

64

The visitor had come to a pavilion where Danish youngsters were dancing. The honkings and skreeings of the band unfortunately were reproduced in perfect clarity, and the boys and girls moved in jerky discontinuity, arms and legs flailing. It was one of those places where the floor is a series of interlocking revolving slidewalks, so that as you stand in place, going through the gyrations of the dance, you are swept on an orbit through the entire hall, confronting partner after partner. Vornan stood watching this in seeming wonder for a while. He smiled that wonderful smile of his and signaled to his bovine consort. They stepped out onto the dance floor. I saw one of the officials put coins in the slot; clearly Vornan did not deign to handle money himself, and it was necessary for someone to follow after him, paying the bills.

Vornan and the Danish girl took places facing one another and caught the rhythm of the dance. There was nothing difficult about it: blatant pelvic thrusts combined with a pattern of stomping and clutching, just like all the other dances of the past forty years. The girl stood with feet flat, knees flexed, legs far apart, head tipped back; the giant cones of her breasts rose toward the faceted mirrors of the ceiling. Vornan, clearly enjoying himself, adopted the knees-in, elbows-out posture of the boys about him and started to move. He picked up the knack of it easily, after only a brief preliminary moment of uncertainty, and off he went, whirled through the hall by the mechanism beneath the floor, facing now this girl, now that, and performing the explicit erotic movements expected of him.

Nearly all the girls knew who he was, it appeared. Their gasps and expressions of awe made that apparent. The fact that a global celebrity was moving in the throng created a certain amount of confusion, throwing the girls off their pace; one simply stopped moving and stared in rapture at Vornan for the whole period of ninety seconds or so that he was her partner. But there was no serious

65

trouble for the first seven or eight turns. Then Vornan was dancing with a plumply pretty dark-haired girl of about sixteen who became totally catatonic with terror. She froze and twisted jerkily and managed to step backward beyond the electronic guard signal at the rear of her moving strip. A buzzer sounded to warn her, but she was beyond any such guidance, and a moment later she had one foot on each of two strips heading in opposite directions. She went down, her short skirt flipping upward to reveal pudgy pink thighs, and in her fright she grabbed at the legs of the boy nearest her.

He toppled too, and in another moment I had a graphic demonstration of the domino effect, because dancers were losing their balance all over the room. Nearly everyone was on more than one strip at once and was clutching at someone else for support. A wave of collapse rippled across the great hall. And there was Vornan-19, still upright, watching the catastrophe in high good humor. His Junoesque paramour was also on her feet, 180 degrees away from him; but then a groping hand caught her ankle, and she went down like a felled oak, careening into two or three other dancers as she dropped. The scene was straight from the pit: writhing figures everywhere, arms and legs in the air, no one able to rise. The machinery of the dance pavilion finally crunched to a halt. The untangling took long minutes. Many girls were crying. Some had skinned knees or abraded rumps; one had somehow contrived to lose her skirt in the melee and was crouched in a fetal huddle. Where was Vornan? Vornan was already at the rim of the hall, safely extricating himself the instant the floor stopped moving. The blonde goddess was beside him.

"He's got an immense talent for disruption," said Kettridge.

Kralick, laughing, said, "This isn't as bad as the business yesterday at the smorgasbord place in Stockholm,

66

when he punched the wrong button and got the whole table revolving."

The screen darkened. An unsmiling Kettridge turned to me. "This man will be the guest of the United States three days from now, Dr. Garfield. We don't know how long he's staying. We intend to monitor his movements closely and try to head off some of the confusion that he's been known to cause. What we have in mind, Professor, is appointing a committee of 'five or six leading scholars as—well, guides for the visitor. Actually they'll also be overseers, watchdogs, and . . . spies."

"Does the United States officially believe that he's a visitor from 2999?"

"Officially, yes," said Kettridge. "That is, we're going to treat him as if he's kosher."

"But—" I spluttered.

Kralick put in, "Privately, Dr. Garfield, we think he's a hoaxer. At least I do, and I believe Mr. Kettridge does. He's an extremely sharp-witted and enterprising phony. However, for purposes of public opinion, we choose to accept Vornan-19 at face value until there's some reason to think otherwise."

"For God's sake, *why?*"

"You know of the Apocalyptist movement, Dr. Garfield?" asked Kralick.

"Well, yes. I can't say I'm an expert, but—"

"So far, Vornan-19 hasn't done anything much more harmful than mesmerizing a roomful of Danish schoolgirls into falling on their butts. The Apocalyptists do real damage. They riot, they loot, they destroy. They're the force of chaos in our society. We're attempting to contain them before they rip everything apart."

"And by embracing this self-appointed ambassador from the future," I said, "you explode the chief selling point of the Apocalyptists, which is that the world is supposed to come to an end next January 1."

"Exactly."

"Very good," I said. "I had already suspected it. Now you confirm it as official policy. But is it proper to meet mass insanity with deliberate dishonesty?"

Kettridge said ponderously, "Dr. Garfield, the job of government is to maintain the stability of the governed society. When possible, we like to adhere to the Ten Commandments in so doing. But we reserve the right to meet a threat to the social structure in any feasible way, up to and including the mass annihilation of hostile forces, which I think you will regard as a more serious action than a little fibbing, and which this government has resorted to on more than one occasion. In short, if we can ward off the Apocalyptist lunacy by giving Vornan-19 a seal of approval, it's worth a bit of moral compromise."

"Besides," said Kralick, "we don't actually *know* he's a fraud. If he isn't, we're not committing any act of bad faith."

"The possibility must be very soothing to your souls," I said.

I regretted my flippancy at once. Kralick looked hurt, and I didn't blame him. *He* hadn't set this policy. One by one, the frightened governments of the world had decided to short-circuit the Apocalyptists by proclaiming Vornan to be the real thing, and the United States was merely falling in line. The decision had been taken on high; Kralick and Kettridge were merely implementing it, and I had no call to impugn their morality. As Kralick had said, it might just turn out that hailing Vornan this way would be not only useful but even correct.

Kettridge fussed with the spines of his ornate costume and did not look at me as he said, "We can understand, Dr. Garfield, that in the academic world people tend to view moral issues in the abstract, but nevertheless—"

"All right," I said wearily, "I suppose I was wrong. I had to put myself on record, that's all. Let's go past that point. Vornan-19 is coming to the United States, and

68

we're going to roll out the red carpet for him. Fine. Now—what do you want from me?"

"Two things," said Kralick. "First: you're widely regarded, sir, as the world's ranking authority on time-reversal physics. We'd like you to provide us with your opinion as to whether it's theoretically possible for a man to travel backward in time as Vornan-19 claims to have done, and how, in your appraisal, it might have been accomplished."

"Well," I said, "I have to be skeptical, because so far we've succeeded only in sending individual electrons backward in time. This converts them into positrons—the antiparticle of the electron, identical in mass but opposite in charge—and the effect is one of virtually instant annihilation. I see no practical way to sidestep the conversion of matter into antimatter during time-reversal, which means that to account for the purported time trip of Vornan-19, we must first explain how so much mass can be converted, and then why it is that although presumably composed of antimatter he does not touch off the annihilation effect when—"

Kralick politely cleared his throat. I stopped talking. Kralick said, "I'm sorry that I didn't make myself quite clear. We don't want an immediate reply from you. We'd like a position paper, Dr. Garfield, which you can file in the next forty-eight hours or thereabouts. We'll provide any necessary secretarial assistance. The President is quite anxious to read what you have to say."

"All right. The other thing you wanted?"

"We'd like you to serve on the committee that will guide Vornan-19 when he gets here."

·"Me? Why?"

"You're a nationally known scientific figure associated in the public's mind with time travel," said Kettridge. "Isn't that reason enough?"

"Who else is going to be on this committee?"

"I'm not at liberty to reveal names, even to you,"

69

Kralick told me. "But I give you my word that they're all figures whose stature in the scientific or scholarly world is equal to your own."

"Meaning," I said, "that not one of them has said yes yet, and you're hoping to bulldoze them all."

Kralick looked hurt again. "Sorry," I said.

Kettridge, unsmiling, declared, "It was our belief that by putting you in close contact with the visitor, you would find some means of extracting information from him about the time-travel process he employed. We believed that this would be of considerable interest to you as a scientist, as well as of major value to the nation."

"Yes," I said. "True. I'd like to pump him on the subject."

"And then," said Kralick, "why should you be hostile to the assignment? We've chosen a leading historian to find out the pattern of events in our future, a psychologist who will attempt to check on the genuineness of Vornan's story, an anthropologist who'll look for cultural developments, and so on. The committee will simultaneously be examining the legitimacy of Vornan's credentials and trying to get from him anything that may be of value to us, assuming that he's what he says he is. I can't imagine any work that could be of greater significance to the nation and to humanity at this time."

I closed my eyes a moment. I felt properly chastened. Kralick was sincere in his earnest way, and so was Kettridge in his fast-talking though heavy-handed style. They needed me, honestly. And was it not true that I had reasons of my own for wanting to peer behind Vornan's mask? Jack had begged me to do it, never dreaming that it would be so easy for me to manage.

Why was I balking, then?

I saw why. It had to do with my own work and the minute possibility that Vornan-19 was a genuine traveler in time. The man who is trying to invent the wheel is not really eager to learn the details of a five-hundred-mile-per-hour turbine car. Here was I, piddling around for half a lifetime with my reversed electrons, and here was Vornan-19, telling tales of vaulting across the centuries; in the depths of my soul I preferred not to think about him at all. However, Kralick and Kettridge were right: I was the man for this committee.

I told them I would serve.

They expressed their gratitude profusely, and then seemed to lose interest in me, as though they didn't plan to waste any emotion on someone who was already signed up. Kettridge disappeared, and Kralick gave me an office somewhere in the underground annex of the White House. Little blobs of living light floated in a tank on the ceiling. He told me that I had full access to the executive mansion's secretarial services, and showed me where the computer outputs and inputs were. I could make any phone calls I wanted, he said, and use any assistance I required in order to prepare my position paper on time travel for the President.

"We've arranged accommodations for you," Kralick told me. "You're in a suite right across the park."

"I thought I might go back to California this evening to wind up my affairs."

"That wouldn't be satisfactory. We have only seventy-two hours, you know, before Vornan-19 arrives in New York. We need to spend that time as efficiently as possible."

"But I had only just returned from vacation!" I protested. "I was in and out again. I need to leave instructions for my staff—to make arrangements for the laboratory—"

"That can all be done by phone, can't it, Dr. Garfield? Don't worry about the phone expense. We'd rather have you spend two or three hours on the line to California than lose all the time of having you make another round trip in the short time remaining."

He smiled. I smiled.

"All right?" he asked.

"All right," I said.

It was very clear. My options had expired the moment I had agreed to serve on the committee. I was now part of the Vornan Project, with no independent scope for action. I would have only as much freedom as the Government could spare, until this thing was over. The odd part was that I didn't resent it, I who had always been the first to sign any petition attacking infringement of liberties, I who had never regarded myself as an organization man but rather as a free-lance scholar loosely affiliated with the University. Without a murmur I let myself be pressed into service. I suppose it was all a subliminal way of dodging the unpleasantness that awaited me when I finally did get back into my laboratory to struggle with my unanswered questions.

The office they had given me was cozy. The floor was bouncy sponge glass, the walls were silvered and reflective, and the ceiling was aglow with color. It was still early enough to call California and find someone in the laboratory. I notified the University proctor, first, that I'd been called into Government service. He didn't mind. Then I spoke to my secretary and said I'd have to extend my absence indefinitely. I made arrangements for staff work and for monitoring my pupils' research projects. I discussed the question of mail delivery and maintenance of my house with the local data utility, and over the screen came a detailed authorization form. I was supposed to check off the things I wished the utility to do for me and the things I did not. It was a long list:

> Mow lawn
> Survey sealing and climateproofing
> Relay mail and messages
> Gardening
> Monitor storm damage

> Notify sales organizations
> Pay bills

And so on. I checked off nearly everything and billed the service to the United States Government. I had learned something from Vornan-19 already: I didn't plan to pay a bill of my own until I was released from this job.

When I had tidied up my personal affairs, I put through a call to Arizona. Shirley answered. She looked taut and edgy, but she seemed to loosen a little when she saw my face on her screen. I said, "I'm in Washington."

"What for, Leo?"

I told her. She thought I was joking at first, but I assured her that I was telling the truth.

"Wait," she said. "I'll get Jack."

She walked away from the phone. The perspective changed as she retreated, and instead of the usual head-and-shoulders view the screen showed me the tiny image of all of Shirley, a three-quarters view. She stood in the doorway, back to camera, leaning against the doorframe so that one ripe globe of a breast showed under her arm. I knew that government flunkies were monitoring my call, and it infuriated me that they should be getting this free view of Shirley's loveliness. I moved to cut off the vision, but it was too late; Shirley was gone and Jack was on screen.

"What's this?" he asked. "Shirley said—"

"I'm going to be talking to Vornan-19 in a few days."

"You shouldn't have bothered, Leo. I've been thinking about that conversation we had. I feel damned foolish about it. I said a lot of, well, unstable things, and I never dreamed that you'd drop everything and go running off to Washington to—"

"It didn't exactly happen that way, Jack. I got drafted to come out here. Vital to national security, that sort of thing. But I just wanted to tell you that as long as I'm here, I'll try to help you in what you discussed."

"I'm grateful, Leo."

"That's all. Try to relax. Maybe you and Shirley need to get away from the desert for a while."

"Maybe later on," he said. "Let's see how things work out."

I winked at him and broke the contact. He wasn't fooling me at all with his feigned cheeriness. Whatever had been boiling and bubbling inside him a few days ago was still there, even though he was trying to apologize it away as foolishness. He needed help.

One more job, now. I opened up the input and started to dictate my position paper on time-reversal. I didn't know how much copy they wanted, but I figured that it didn't really matter. I began to talk. A bright dot of green light danced along the ground-glass screen of the computer's output, typing out my words as I spoke them. Working entirely from memory and not bothering to summon from the data tanks the texts of my own publications, I reeled off a quick, nontechnical précis of my thoughts on time-reversal. The gist of it was that while time-reversal on the subatomic level had already been achieved, it did not in terms of any physical theory I understood seem possible for a human being to travel backward in time and arrive at his destination alive, regardless of the power source used to transport him. I bolstered this with a few thoughts on accumulative temporal momentum, the extension of mass into an inverted continuum, and the annihilation of antimatter. And I wound it up by concluding in almost those words that Vornan-19 was plainly a fake.

Then I spent a few moments contemplating my glowing words in the vibrant but temporary green gleam on the screen. I brooded on the fact that the President of the United States, by executive decision, had chosen to look upon Vornan-19's claims as convincing ones. I pondered the efficacy of telling the President to his face that he was party to a fraud. I debated whether to forfeit my own integrity for the sake of keeping the top man's conscience from twinging, and then I said to hell with it and told the computer to print what I had dictated and transfer it to the Presidential data files.

A minute later my personal copy bounced out of the output slot, typed, justified on both margins, and neatly stitched. I folded it, put it in my pocket, and called Kralick.

"I'm finished," I said. "I'd like to get out of here, now."

He came for me. It was very late afternoon, which is to say it was a bit past midday on the time system my metabolism was accustomed to, and I was hungry. I asked Kralick about lunch. He looked a little puzzled until he realized the time-zone problem. "It's almost dinnertime for me," he said. "Look, why don't we go across the street and have a drink together, and then I'll show you to your suite in the hotel. Then I can arrange some dinner for you, if that's all right. An early dinner instead of a late lunch."

"Good enough," I told him.

Like Virgil in reverse, he guided me upward out of the maze beneath the White House, and we emerged in the open air at twilight. The city had had a light snowfall while I had been underground, I saw. Melting coils were humming in the sidewalks, and robot sweepers drifted dreamily through the streets, sucking up the slush with their long, greedy hoses. A few flakes were still falling. In the shining towers of Washington the lights glittered like jewels against the blue-black afternoon sky. Kralick and I left the White House grounds by a side gate and cut across Pennsylvania Avenue in a knight's move that brought us into a small, dim cocktail lounge. He folded his long legs under the table with difficulty.

It was one of the automatic places that had been so

popular a few years back: a control console at each table, a computerized mixologist in the back room, and an elaborate array of spigots. Kralick asked me what I'd have, and I said filtered rum. He punched it into the console and ordered Scotch and soda for himself. The credit plate lit up; he pushed his card into the slot. An instant later the drinks gurgled from the spigots.

"Drink high," he said.

"The same."

I let the rum slip down my gullet. It went down easily, landing on no solid food to speak of, and began to infiltrate my nervous system. Shamelessly I asked for a refill while Kralick was still unwinding himself on his first. He tossed me a thoughtful look, as if telling himself that nothing in my dossier had indicated I was an alcoholic. But he got me the drink.

"Vornan has gone on to Hamburg," Kralick said abruptly. "He's studying night life along the Reepersbahn."

"I thought that was closed down years ago."

"They run it as a tourist attraction, complete with imitation sailors who come ashore and get into brawls. God knows how he ever heard of it, but you can bet there'll be a fine brawl there tonight." He glanced at his watch. "It's probably going on now. Six hours ahead of us. Tomorrow he's in Brussels. Then Barcelona for a bullfight. And then New York."

"God help us."

"God," said Kralick, "is bringing the world to an end in eleven months and—what is it?—sixteen days?" He laughed thickly. "Not soon enough. Not soon enough. If He'd do the job tomorrow, we wouldn't have to put up with Vornan-19."

"Don't tell me you're a crypto-Apocalyptist!"

"I'm a cryptoboozer," he said. "I started on this stuff at lunchtime and my head's spinning, Garfield. Do you know, I was a lawyer once? Young, bright, ambitious, a

76

decent practice. Why did I want to go into the Government?"

"You ought to punch for an antistim," I said guardedly.

"You know, you're right."

He ordered himself a pill, and then, as an afterthought, ordered a third rum for me. My earlobes felt a little thick. Three drinks in ten minutes? Well, I could always have an antistim too. The pill arrived and Kralick swallowed it; he grimaced as his metabolism went through the speedup that would burn the backlog of alcohol out of it. For a long moment he sat there shivering. Then he pulled himself together.

"Sorry. It hit me all at once."

"Feel better?"

"Much," he said. "Did I say anything classified?"

"I doubt it. Except you were wishing the world would end tomorrow."

"Strictly a mood. Nothing religious about it. Do you mind if I call you Leo?"

"I'd prefer it."

"Good. Leo, look, I'm sober now, and what I'm saying is the straight orbit. I've handed you a lousy job, and I'm sorry about it. If there's anything I can do to make your life more comfortable while you're playing nursemaid to this futuristic quack, just ask me. It's not my money I'll be spending. I know you like your comforts, and you'll have them."

"I appreciate that—ah, Sanford."

"Sandy."

"Sandy."

"For instance, tonight. You came in on short notice, and I don't suppose you've had a chance to contact any friends. Would you like a companion for dinner . . . and afterward?"

That was thoughtful of him. Ministering to the needs of the aging bachelor scientist. "Thanks," I said, "but I think

I'll manage by myself tonight. Get caught up with my thoughts, get coordinated to your time-zone—"

"It won't be any trouble."

I shrugged the matter aside. We nibbled small algae crackers and listened to the distant hiss of the speakers in the bar's sound system. Kralick did most of the talking. He mentioned the names of a few of my fellow members of the Vornan committee, among them F. Richard Heyman, the historian, and Helen McIlwain, the anthropologist, and Morton Fields of Chicago, the psychologist. I nodded sagely. I approved.

"We checked everything carefully," said Kralick. "I mean, we didn't want to put two people on the committee who had had a feud or something of that sort. So we searched the entire data files to trace the relationships. Believe me, it was a job. We had to reject two good candidates because they'd been involved in, well, rather irregular incidents with one of the other members of the committee, and that was a disappointment."

"You keep files on fornication among the learned?"

"We try to keep files on everything, Leo. You'd be surprised. But anyway we put a committee together, finally, finding replacements for those who wouldn't serve, and replacements for those who turned up incompatible with the others on the data check, and arranging and rearranging—"

"Wouldn't it have been simpler to write Vornan off as a hoax and forget about him?"

Kralick said, "There was an Apocalyptist rally in Santa Barbara last night. Did you hear about it?"

"No."

"A hundred thousand people gathered on the beach. In the course of getting there they did two million dollars worth of property damage, estimated. After the usual orgies they began to march into the sea like lemurs."

"Lemmings."

"Lemmings." Kralick's thick fingers hovered over the
78

bar console a moment, then withdrew. "Picture a hundred thousand chanting Apocalyptists from all over California marching stark naked into the Pacific on a January day. We're still getting the figures on the drownings. Over a hundred, at least, and God knows how much pneumonia, and ten girls were trampled to death. They do things like that in Asia, Leo. Not here. Not here. You see what we're up against? Vornan will smash this movement. He'll tell us how it is in 2999, and people will stop believing that The End Is Nigh. The Apocalyptists will collapse. Another rum?"

"I think I ought to get to my hotel."

"Right." He uncoiled himself and we went out of the bar. As he walked around the edges of Lafayette Park, Kralick said, "I think I ought to warn you that the information media know you're in town and will start to bombard you with interview requests and whatnot. We'll screen you as well as we can, but they'll probably get through to you. The answer to all questions is—"

"No comment."

"Precisely. You're a star, Leo."

Snow was falling again, somewhat more actively than the melting coils were programmed to handle. Thin crusts of white were forming here and there on the pavement, and it was deeper in the shrubbery. Pools of newly melted water glistened. The snow twinkled like starlight as it drifted down. The stars themselves were hidden; we might have been alone in the universe. I felt a great loneliness. In Arizona now the sun was shining.

As we entered the grand old hotel where I was staying, I turned to Kralick and said, "I think I'll accept that offer of a dinner companion after all."

# SIX

I SENSED THE real power of the United States Government for the first time when the girl came to my suite about seven that evening. She was a tall blonde with hair like spun gold. Her eyes were brown, not blue, her lips were full, her posture was superb. In short, she looked astonishingly like Shirley Bryant.

Which meant that they had been keeping tabs on me for a long time, observing and recording the sort of women I usually chose, and producing one of exactly the right qualifications on a moment's notice. Did that mean that they thought Shirley was my mistress? Or that they had drawn an abstract profile of all my women, and had come up with a Shirley-like girl because I had (unconsciously!) been picking Shirley-surrogates all along?

This girl's name was Martha. I said, "You don't look like a Martha at all. Marthas are short and dark and terribly intense, with long chins. They smell of cigarettes all the time."

"Actually," Martha said, "I'm a Sidney. But the government didn't think you'd go for a girl named Sidney."

Sidney, or Martha, was an ace, a star. She was too good to be true, and I suspected that she had been created golemlike in a government laboratory to serve my needs. I asked her if that was so, and she said yes. "Later on," she said, "I'll show you where I plug in."

"How often do you need a recharge?"

"Two or three times a night, sometimes. It depends."

She was in her early twenties, and she reminded me forcibly of the co-eds around the campus. Perhaps she was a robot, perhaps she was a call girl; but she acted like neither—more like a lively, intelligent, mature human being who just happened to be willing to make herself

80

available for duties like this. I didn't dare ask her if she did things of this sort all the time.

Because of the snow, we ate in the hotel dining room. It was an old-fashioned place with chandeliers and heavy draperies, head waiters in evening clothes and an engraved menu a yard long. I was glad to see it; the novelty of using menu cubes had worn off by now, and it was graceful to read our choices from a printed card while a live human being took down our wishes with a pad and pencil, just as in bygone times.

The government was paying. We ate well. Fresh caviar, oyster cocktails, turtle soup, Chateaubriand for two, very rare. The oysters were the delicate little Olympias from Puget Sound. They have much to commend them, but I miss the true oysters of my youth. I last ate them in 1976 at the Bicentennial Fair—when they were five dollars a dozen, because of the pollution. I can forgive mankind for destroying the dodo, but not for blotting out bluepoints.

Much satiated, we went back upstairs. The perfection of the evening was marred only by a nasty scene in the lobby when I was set upon by a few of the media boys looking for a story.

"Professor Garfield—"

"—is it true that—"

"—words on your theory of—"

"—Vornan-19—"

"No comment." "No comment." "No comment." "No comment."

Martha and I escaped into the elevator. I slapped a privacy seal on my door—old-fashioned as this hotel is, it has modern conveniences—and we were safe. She looked at me coquettishly, but her coyness didn't last long. She was long and smooth, a symphony in pink and gold, and she wasn't any robot, although I found where she plugged in. In her arms I was able to forget about men from 2999, drowning Apocalyptists, and the dust gathering on my laboratory desk. If there is a heaven for

Presidential aides, let Sandy Kralick ascend to it when his time comes.

In the morning we breakfasted in the room, took a shower together like newlyweds, and stood looking out the window at the last traces of the night's snow. She dressed; her black plastic mesh sheath seemed out of place in the morning's pale light, but she was still lovely to behold. I knew I would never see her again.

As she left, she said, "Someday you must tell me about time-reversal, Leo."

"I don't know a thing about it. So long, Sidney."

"Martha."

"You'll always be Sidney to me."

I resealed the door and checked with the hotel switchboard when she was gone. As I expected, there had been dozens of calls, and all had been turned away. The switchboard wanted to know if I'd take a call from Mr. Kralick. I said I would.

I thanked him for Sidney. He was only a bit puzzled. Then he said, "Can you come to the first committee meeting at two, in the White House? A get-together session."

"Of course. What's the news from Hamburg?"

"Bad. Vornan caused a riot. He went into one of the tough bars and made a speech. The essence of it was that the most lasting historic achievement of the German people was the Third Reich. It seems that's all he knows about Germany, or something, and he started praising Hitler and getting him mixed up with Charlemagne, and the authorities yanked him out of there just in time. Half a block of nightclubs burned down before the foam tanks arrived." Kralick grinned ingenuously. "Maybe I shouldn't be telling you this. It still isn't too late for you to pull out."

I sighed and said, "Oh, don't worry, Sandy. I'm on the team for keeps now. It's the least I can do for you ... after Sidney."

"See you at two. We'll pick you up and take you across via tunnel because I don't want you devoured by the media madmen. Stay put until I'm at your door."

"Right," I said. I put down the phone, turned, and saw what looked like a puddle of green slime gliding across my threshold and into the room.

It wasn't slime. It was a fluid audio pickup full of monomolecular ears. I was being bugged from the corridor. Quickly I went to the door and ground my heel into the puddle. A thin voice said, "Don't do that, Dr. Garfield. I'd like to talk to you. I'm from Amalgamated Network of—"

"Go away."

I finished grinding my heel. I wiped up the rest of the mess with a towel. Then I leaned close to the floor and said to any remaining ears sticking to the woodwork, "The answer is still No Comment. Go away."

I got rid of him, finally. I adjusted the privacy seal so that it wouldn't be possible even to slide a single molecule's thickness of anything under the door, and waited out the morning. Shortly before two Sandy Kralick came for me and smuggled me into the underground tunnel leading to the White House. Washington is a maze of subterranean connections. I'm told you can get from anywhere to anywhere if you know the routes and have the right access-words handy when the scanners challenge you. The tunnels go down layer after layer. I hear there's an automated brothel six layers deep below the Capitol, for Congressional use only; and the Smithsonian is supposed to be carrying on experiments in mutagenesis somewhere below the Mall, spawning biological monstrosities that never see the light of day. Like everything else you hear about the capital, I suppose these stories are apocryphal; I suppose that the truth, if it were ever known, would be fifty times as ghastly as the fables. This is a diabolical city.

Kralick led me to a room with walls of anodized bronze

somewhere beneath the West Wing of the White House. Four people were in it already. I recognized three of them. The upper levels of the scientific establishment are populated by a tiny clique, inbred, self-perpetuating. We all know one another, through interdisciplinary meetings of one kind or another. I recognized Lloyd Kolff, Morton Fields, and Aster Mikkelsen. The fourth person rose stiffly and said, "I don't believe we've met, Dr. Garfield. F. Richard Heyman."

"Yes, of course. *Spengler, Freud, and Marx,* isn't it? I remember it very fondly." I took his hand. It was moist at the fingertips, and I suppose moist at the palms too, but he shook hands in that peculiarly untrusting Central European manner by which the suspicious one seizes the fingers of the other in a remote way, instead of placing palm next to palm. We exchanged noises about how pleased we were to make the other's acquaintance.

Give me full marks for insincerity. I did not think much of F. Richard Heyman's book, which struck me as both ponderous and superficial at once, a rare feat; I did not care for the occasional reviews he wrote for the general magazines, which inevitably turned out to be neat eviscerations of his colleagues; I did not like the way he shook hands; I did not even like his name. What was I supposed to call an "F. Richard" when we had to use names? "F?" "Dick?" What about "my dear Heyman?" He was a short stocky man with a cannonball head, a fringe of coarse red hair along the back half of his skull, and a thick reddish beard curling down over his cheeks and throat to hide what I'm sure was a chin as round as the top of his head. A thin-lipped sharklike mouth was barely visible within the foliage. His eyes were watery and unpleasant.

The other members of the committee I had no hostilities toward. I knew them vaguely, was aware of their high standings in their individual professions, and had never come to any disagreement with them in the scientific forums where we encountered one another. Morton Fields

84

of the University of Chicago was a psychologist, affiliated with the new so-called cosmic school, which I interpreted to be a kind of secular Buddhism. They sought to unravel the mysteries of the soul by placing it in rapport with the universe as a totality, which has a pretentious sound to it. In person Fields looked like a corporation executive on the way up, say, a comptroller: lean athletic frame, high cheekbones, sandy hair, tight downturned mouth, prominent chin, pale questioning eyes. I could imagine him feeding data into a computer four days a week and spending his weekends slamming a golf ball mercilessly about the fairways. Yet he was not as pedantic as he looked.

Lloyd Kolff, I knew, was the doyen of philologists: a massive thick-bodied man, well along in his sixties, with a seamed, florid face and the long arms of a gorilla. His base of operations was Columbia, and he was a favorite among graduate students because of his robust earthiness; he knew more Sanskrit obscenities than any man of the last thirty centuries, and used them all vividly and frequently. Kolff's sideline was erotic verse, all centuries, all languages. He supposedly wooed his wife—also a philologist—by murmuring scorching endearments in Middle Persian. He would be an asset to our group, a valuable counterbalance to the stuffed shirt that I suspected F. Richard Heyman to be.

Aster Mikkelsen was a biochemist from Michigan State, part of the group involved in the life-synthesis project. I had met her at last year's A.A.A.S. conference in Seattle. Though her name has a Scandinavian ring to it, she was not one of those Nordic Junos of whom I am so scandalously fond, however. Dark-haired, sharp-boned, slender, she gave an appearance of fragility and timidity. She was hardly more than five feet tall; I doubt that she weighed a hundred pounds. I suppose she was about forty, though she looked younger. Her eyes held a wary sparkle; her features were elegant. Her clothes were defiantly chaste, modeling her boyish figure as if to advertise the fact that

85

she had nothing to offer the voluptuary. Through my mind there speared the incongruous image of Lloyd Kolff and Aster Mikkelsen in bed together, the beefy folds of his heavy, hairy body thrust up against her slim frail form, her lean thighs and tapering calves straining in agony to contain his butting form, her ankles dug deep into his copious flesh. The mismatch of physiques was so monstrous that I had to close my eyes and look away. When I dared to open them, Kolff and Aster were standing side by side as before, the ziggurat of flesh beside the dainty nymph, and both were peering at me in alarm.

"Are you all right?" Aster asked. Her voice was high and piping, a reedy girlish sound. "I thought you were going to faint!"

"I'm a bit tired," I bluffed. I could not explain why that sudden image had come to me, nor why it left me so dazed. To cover my confusion I turned to Kralick and asked him how many other members our committee would have. One, he said: Helen McIlwain, the famed anthropologist, who was due at any moment. As though on cue, the door slid open and the divine Helen herself strode into the room.

Who has not heard of Helen McIlwain? What more can be said about her? The apostle of cultural relativism, the lady anthropologist who is no lady, the dogged student of puberty rites and fertility cults who has not hesitated to offer herself as tribeswoman and blood sister? She who pursued the quest for knowledge into the sewers of Ouagadougu to partake of skewered dog, she who wrote the basic text on the techniques of masturbation, she who had learned at first hand how virgins are initiated in the frozen wastes of Sikkim? It seemed to me that Helen had always been with us, going from one outrageous exploit to another, publishing books that in another era would have had her burned at the stake, solemnly informing the television audience of matters that might shock hardened scholars. Our paths had crossed many times, although not

86

lately. I was surprised to see how youthful she looked; she had to be at least fifty.

She was dressed—well—flamboyantly. A plastic bar encircled her shoulders, and from it descended a black fiber cunningly designed to look like human hair. Perhaps it *was* human hair. It formed a thick cascade reaching to mid-thigh, a fetishist's delight, long and silken and dense. There was something fierce and primordial about this tent of hair in which Helen was encased; all that was missing was the bone through the nose and the ceremonial scarifications on the cheeks. Beneath the mass of hair she was nude, I think. As she moved across the room, one caught sight of glints of pinkness peeping through the hairy curtain. I had the momentary illusion that I was seeing the tip of a rosy nipple, the curve of a smooth buttock. Yet so cohesive was the sensual sweep of the long, sleek, satin-smooth strands of hair that it cloaked her body almost entirely, granting us only those fleeting views which Helen intended us to have. Here graceful, slender arms were bare. Her neck, swanlike, rose triumphantly out of the hirsuteness, and her own hair, auburn and glossy, did not suffer by comparison with her garment. The effect was spectacular, phenomenal, awesome, and absurd. I glanced at Aster Mikkelsen as Helen made her grand entrance, and saw Aster's lips flicker briefly in amusement.

"I'm sorry I was late," Helen boomed in that magnificent contralto of hers. "I've been at the Smithsonian. They've been showing me a *magnificent* set of ivory circumcision knives from Dahomey!"

"And letting you practice with them?" Lloyd Kolff asked.

"We didn't get that far. But after this silly meeting, Lloyd, darling, if you'd like to come back there with me, I'd be delighted to demonstrate my technique. On you."

"It is sixty-three years too late for that," Kolff rumbled, "as you should know. I'm surprised your memory is so short, Helen."

"Oh, yes, darling! Absolutely right! A thousand apologies. I quite forgot!" And she rushed over to Kolff, hairy garment aflutter, to kiss him on his broad cheek. Sanford Kralick bit his lip. Obviously that was something his computer had missed. F. Richard Heyman looked uncomfortable, Fields smiled, and Aster seemed bored. I began to see that we were in for a lively time.

Kralick cleared his throat. "Now that we're all here, if I could have your attention a moment . . ."

He proceeded to brief us on our job. He used screens, data cubes, sonic synthesizers, and a battery of other up-to-the-minute devices by way of conveying to us the urgency and necessity of our mission. Basically, we were supposed to help make Vornan-19's visit to 1999 more rewarding and enjoyable; but also we were under instructions to keep a close watch on the visitor, tone down his more outrageous behavior if possible, and determine secretly to our own satisfaction whether he was genuine or a clever fraud.

It turned out that our own group was split on that last point. Helen McIlwain believed firmly, even mystically, that Vornan-19 *had* come from 2999. Morton Fields was of the same opinion, although he wasn't so vociferous about it. It seemed to him that there was something symbolically appropriate about having a messiah-figure come out of the future to aid us in our time of travail; and since Vornan fit the criteria, Fields was willing to accept him. On the other side, Lloyd Kolff thought the idea of taking Vornan seriously was too funny for words, while F. Richard Heyman seemed to grow purple in the face at the mere thought of embracing any notion so irrational. I likewise was unable to buy Vornan's claims. Aster Mikkelsen was neutral, or perhaps agnostic is the better word. Aster had true scientific objectivity: she wasn't going to commit herself on the time traveler until she'd had a chance to see him herself.

Some of this genteel academic bickering took place

under Kralick's nose. The rest occurred at dinner that night. Just the six of us at the table in the White House, with noiseless servants gliding in and out to ply us with delicacies at the taxpayer's expense. We did a lot of drinking. Certain polarities began to expose themselves in our ill-assorted little band. Kolff and Helen clearly had slept together before and meant to do so again; they were both so uninhibited about their lustiness that it plainly upset Heyman, who seemed to have a bad case of constipation from his cranial vault clear to his insteps. Morton Fields apparently had some sexual interest in Helen too, and the more he drank the more he tried to express it, but Helen wasn't having any; she was too involved with that fat old Sanskrit-spouting Falstaff, Kolff. So Fields turned his attention to Aster Mikkelsen, who, however, seemed as sexless as the table, and deflected his heavy-handed advances with the cool precision of a woman long accustomed to such tasks. My own mood was a detached one, an old vice: I sat there, the disembodied observer, watching my distinguished colleagues at play. This was a group carefully selected to eliminate personality conflicts and other flaws, I thought. Poor Sandy Kralick believed he had assembled six flawless savants who would serve the nation with zealous dedication. We hadn't been convened for eight hours yet, and already the lines of cleavage were showing up. What would happen to us when we were thrust into the presence of the slick, unpredictable Vornan-19? I feared much.

The banquet ended close to midnight. A row of empty wine bottles crisscrossed the table. Government flunkies appeared and announced that they would conduct us to the tunnels.

It turned out that Kralick had distributed us in hotels all around town. Fields made a boozy little scene about seeing Aster to her place, and she sidestepped him somehow. Helen and Kolff went off together, arm in arm; as they got into the elevator I saw his hand slide deep under the shroud of hair that enveloped her. I walked back to my hotel. I did not turn on the screen to find out what Vornan-19 had been up to this evening in Europe. I suspected, quite justly, that I'd get enough of his antics as the weeks unrolled, and that I could do without tonight's news.

I slept poorly. Helen McIlwain haunted my dreams. I had never before dreamed that I was being circumcised by a redheaded witch garbed in a cloak of human hair. I trust I don't have that dream again . . . ever.

## * SEVEN *

AT NOON THE next day the six of us—and Kralick—boarded the intercity tube for New York, nonstop. An hour later we arrived, just in time for an Apocalyptist demonstration at the tube terminal. They had heard that Vornan-19 was due to land in New York shortly, and they were doing a little preliminary cutting up.

We ascended into the vast terminal hall and found it a sea of sweaty, shaggy figures. Banners of living light drifted in the air, proclaiming gibberish slogans or just ordinary obscenities. Terminal police were desperately trying to keep order. Over everything came the dull boom of an Apocalyptist chant, ragged and incoherent, a cry of anarchy in which I could make out only the words "doom . . . flame . . . doom . . ."

Helen McIlwain was enthralled. Apocalyptists were at least as interesting to her as tribal witch doctors, and she tried to rush out to the terminal floor to soak up the experience at close range. Kralick asked her to come back, but it was too late; she rushed toward the mob. A bearded prophet of doom clutched at her and ripped the network of small plastic disks that was her garment this morning. The disks popped in every direction, baring a swath of

90

Helen eight inches wide down the front from throat to waist. One bare breast jutted into view, surprisingly firm for a woman her age, surprisingly well developed for a woman of her lean, lanky build. Helen looked glassy-eyed with excitement; she clutched at her new swain, trying to extract the essence of Apocalyptism from him as he shook and clawed and pummeled her. Three burly guards went out there at Kralick's insistence to rescue her. Helen greeted the first one with a kick in the groin that sent him reeling away; he vanished under a tide of surging fanatics and we did not see him reappear. The other two brandished neural whips and used them to disperse the Apocalyptists. Howls of outrage went up; there were sharp shrill cries of pain, riding over the undercurrent of "doom . . . flame . . . doom . . ." A troop of half-naked girls, hands to hips, paraded past us like a chorus line, cutting off my view; when I could see into the mob again, I realized that the guards had cut an island around Helen and were bringing her out. She seemed transfigured by the experience. "Marvelous," she kept saying, "marvelous, marvelous, such orgasmic frenzy!" The walls echoed with "doom . . . flame . . . doom . . ."

Kralick offered Helen his jacket, and she waved it away, not caring about the bare flesh or perhaps caring very much to keep it in view. Somehow they got us out of there. As we hustled through the door, I heard one terrible cry of pain rising above everything else, the sound that I imagine a man would make as he was being drawn before quartering. I never found out who screamed that way, or why.

"... doom ..." I heard, and we were outside.

Cars waited. We were taken to a hotel in mid-Manhattan. On the 125th floor we had a good view of the downtown renewal area. Helen and Kolff shamelessly took a double room; the rest of us received singles. Kralick supplied each of us with a thick sheaf of tapes dealing with suggested methods of handling Vornan. I filed mine without playing anything. Looking down into the distant street, I saw figures moving in a frantic stream on the pedestrian level, patterns forming and breaking, occasionally a collision, gesticulating arms, the movements of angry ants. Now and then a flying wedge of rowdies came roaring down the middle of the street. Apocalyptists, I assumed. How long had this been going on? I had been out of touch with the world; I had not realized that at any given moment in any given city one was vulnerable to the impact of chaos. I turned away from my window.

Morton Fields came into the room. He accepted my offer of a drink, and I punched the programming studs on my room service board. We sat quietly sipping filtered rums. I hoped he wouldn't babble at me in psychology jargon. But he wasn't the babbling kind: direct, incisive, sane, that was his style.

"Like a dream, isn't it?" he asked.

"This man from the future thing?"

"This whole cultural environment. The *fin de siècle* mood."

"It's been a long century, Fields. Maybe the world is happy to see it out. Maybe all this anarchy around us is a way of celebration, eh?"

"You could have a point," he conceded. "Vornan-19's a sort of Fortinbras, come to set the time back into joint."

"You think so?"

"It's a possibility."

"He hasn't acted very helpful so far," I said. "He seems to stir up trouble wherever he goes."

"Unintentionally. He's not attuned to us savages yet, ·and he keeps tripping over tribal taboos. Give him some time to get to know us and he'll begin to work wonders."

"Why do you say that?"

Fields solemnly tugged his left ear. "He has charismatic

powers, Garfield. *Numen.* The divine power. You can see it in that smile of his, can't you?"

"Yes. Yes. But what makes you think he'll use that charisma rationally? Why not have some fun, stir up the mobs? Is he here as a savior or just as a tourist?"

"We'll find that out ourselves, in a few days. Mind if I punch another drink?"

"Punch three," I said airily. "I don't pay the bills."

Fields regarded me earnestly. His pale eyes seemed to be having trouble focusing, as though he were wearing a pair of corneal compressors and didn't know how to use them yet. After a long silence he said, "Do you know anyone who's ever been to bed with Aster Mikkelsen?"

"Not really. Should I?"

"I was just wondering. She might be a Lesbian."

"I doubt it," I said, "somehow. Does it matter?"

Fields laughed thinly. "I tried to seduce her last night."

"So I noticed."

"I was quite drunk."

"I noticed that too."

Fields said, "Aster told me an odd thing while I was trying to get her into bed. She said she didn't go to bed with men. She put it in a kind of flat declarative uninflected way, as though it ought to be perfectly obvious to anyone but a damned idiot. I was just wondering if there was something about her I ought to know and didn't."

"You might ask Sandy Kralick," I suggested. "He's got a dossier on all of us."

"I wouldn't do that. I mean—it's a little unworthy of me—"

"To want to sleep with Aster?"

"No, to go around to that bureaucrat trying to pick up tips. I'd rather keep the matter between us."

"Between us professors?" I amplified.

"In a sense." Fields grinned, an effort that must have cost him something. "Look, old fellow, I didn't mean to push my concerns onto you. I just thought—if you know anything about—about her—"

"Her proclivities?"

"Her proclivities."

"Nothing at all. She's a brilliant biochemist," I said. "She seems rather reserved as a person. That's all I can tell you."

Fields finally went away after a while. I heard Lloyd Kolff's lusty laughter roaring through the hallways. I felt like a prisoner. What if I phoned Kralick and asked him to send me Martha/Sidney at once? I stripped and got under the shower, letting the molecules do their buzzing dance, peeling away the grime of my journey from Washington. Then I read for a while. Kolff had given me his latest book, an anthology of metaphysical love lyrics he had translated from the Phoenician texts found at Byblos. I had always thought of Phoenicians as crisp Levantine businessmen, with no time for poetry, erotic or otherwise; but this was startling stuff, raw, fiery. I had not dreamed there were so many ways of describing the female genitalia. The pages were festooned with long streamers of adjectives: a catalog of lust, an inventory of stock-in-trade. A little of it went a very long way. I wondered if he had given a copy to Aster Mikkelsen.

I must have dozed. About five in the afternoon I was awakened by a few sheets sliding out of the data slot in the wall. Kralick was sending around Vornan-19's itinerary. Standard stuff: the New York Stock Exchange, the Grand Canyon, a couple of factories, an Indian reservation or two, and—pencilled in as tentative—Luna City. I wondered if we were expected to accompany him to the Moon if he went there. Probably.

At dinner that evening Helen and Aster went into a long huddle about something. I found myself stranded next to Heyman, and was treated to a discourse on Spenglerian interpretations of the Apocalyptist movement. Lloyd Kolff told scabrous tales in several languages to

94

Fields, who listened dolefully and drank a good deal once again. Kralick joined us for dessert to say that Vornan-19 was boarding a rocket for New York the following morning and would be among us by noon, local time. He wished us luck.

We did not go to the airport to meet Vornan. Kralick expected trouble there, and he was right; we stayed at the hotel, watching the scene of the arrival on our screens. Two rival groups had gathered at the airport to greet Vornan. There was a mass of Apocalyptists, but that was not surprising; these days there seemed to be a mass of Apocalyptists everywhere. What was a little more unsettling was the presence of a group of a thousand demonstrators whom, for lack of a better word, the announcer called Vornan's "disciples." They had come to worship. The camera played lovingly over their faces. They were not bedizened lunatics like the Apocalyptists; no, they were very middle class, most of them, very tense, under tight control, not Dionysian revelers at all. I saw the pinched faces, the clamped lips, the sober mien—and I was frightened. The Apocalyptists represented the froth of society, the drifters, the rootless. These who had come to bow the knee to Vornan were the dwellers in small suburban apartments, the depositors in savings institutions, the goers to sleep at early hours, the backbone of American life. I remarked on this to Helen McIlwain.

"Of course," she said. "It's the counterrevolution, the coming reaction to Apocalyptist excess. These people see the man from the future as the apostle of order restored." Fields had said much the same thing.

I thought of falling bodies and pink thighs in a Tivoli dance hall. "They're likely to be disappointed," I said, "if they think that Vornan's going to help them. From what I've seen, he's strictly on the side of entropy."

"He may change when he sees what power he can wield over them."

95

Of all the many frightening things I saw and heard those first days, Helen McIlwain's calm words were, as I look back, the most terrifying of all.

Of course, the government had had long experience in importing celebrities. Vornan's arrival was announced for one runway, and then he came in on another, at the far end of the airport, while a dummy rocket sent up for the purpose from Mexico City glided in for a landing where the man from 2999 was supposed to come down. The police contained the mob fairly well, considering. But as the two groups rushed forth onto the field, they coalesced, the Apocalyptists mingling with the disciples of Vornan, and then, abruptly, it was impossible to know which group was which. The camera zeroed in on one throbbing mass of humanity and retreated just as quickly upon the discovery that a rape was in progress beneath all the confusion. Thousands of figures swarmed about the rocket, whose dull blue sides gleamed temptingly in the feeble January sunlight; meanwhile Vornan was quietly being extracted from the true rocket a mile away. Via helicopter and transportation pod he came to us, while tanks of foam were emptied on the strugglers surrounding the blue rocket. Kralick phoned ahead to let us know that they were bringing Vornan to the hotel suite that was serving as our New York headquarters.

I felt a moment of sudden blinding panic as Vornan-19 approached the room.

How can I convey the intensity of that feeling in words? Can I say that for an instant the moorings of the universe seemed to loosen, so that the Earth was drifting free in the void? Can I say that I felt myself wandering in a world without reason, without structure, without coherence? I mean this quite seriously: it was a moment of utter fear. My various ironic, wry, mocking, detached poses deserted me; and I was left without the armor of cynicism, naked in a withering gale, facing the prospect that I was about to meet a wanderer out of time.

96

The fear I felt was the fear that abstraction was turning to reality. One can talk a great deal about time-reversal, one can even shove a few electrons a brief distance into the past, and yet it all remains essentially abstract. I have not seen an electron, nor can I tell you where one finds the past. Now, abruptly, the fabric of the cosmos had been ripped apart and a chilly wind blew upon me out of the future; though I tried to recapture my old skepticism, I found it was impossible. God help me, I believed that Vornan was authentic. His charisma preceded him into the room, converting me in advance. What price hardheadedness? I was jelly before he appeared. Helen McIlwain stood enraptured. Fields fidgeted; Kolff and Heyman looked troubled; even Aster's icy shield was penetrated. Whatever I was feeling, they were feeling it too.

Vornan-19 entered.

I had seen him on the screens so often in the past two weeks that I felt I knew him; but when he came among us, I found myself in the presence of a being so alien that he was unknowable. And traces of that feeling lingered during the months that followed, so that Vornan was always something apart.

He was even shorter than I had expected him to be, no more than an inch or two taller than Aster Mikkelsen. In a room of big men he looked overwhelmed, with towering Kralick at one side and mountainous Kolff at the other. Yet he was in perfect command. He drew his eyes over all of us in one smooth gesture and said, "This is most kind of you, to take this trouble for me. I am flattered."

God help me. I *believed*.

We are each of us the summaries of the events of our time, the great and the small. Our patterns of thought, our clusters of prejudices, these things are determined for us by the distillate of happenings that we inhale with our every breath. I have been shaped by the small wars of my lifetime, by the detonations of atomic weapons in my childhood, by the trauma of the Kennedy assassination, by the extinction of the Atlantic oyster, by the words my first woman spoke to me in her moment of ecstasy, by the triumph of the computer, by the tingle of Arizona sunlight on my bare skin, and much else. When I deal with other human beings, I know that I have a kinship with them, that they have been shaped by some of the events that fashioned my soul, that we have at least certain points of common reference.

What had shaped Vornan?

None of the things that had shaped me. I found grounds for awe in that. The matrix from which he came was wholly different from mine. A world that spoke other languages, that had had ten centuries of further history, that had undergone unimaginable alterations of culture and motive—that was the world from which he came. Through my mind flashed an imagined view of Vornan's world, an idealized world of green fields and gleaming towers, of controlled weather and vacations in the stars, of incomprehensible concepts and inconceivable advances; and I knew that whatever I imagined would fall short of the reality, that I had no points of reference to share with him at all.

I told myself that I was being a fool to give way to such fear.

I told myself that this man was of my own time, a clever manipulator of his fellow mortals.

I fought to recover my defensive skepticism. I failed.

We introduced ourselves to Vornan. He stood in the middle of the room, faintly supercilious, listening as we recited our scientific specialties to him. The philologist, the biochemist, the anthropologist, the historian, and the psychologist announced themselves in turn. I said, "I'm a physicist specializing in time-reversal phenomena," and waited.

Vornan-19 replied, "How remarkable. You've discovered time-reversal so early in civilization! We must talk about this some time soon, Sir Garfield."

Heyman stepped forward and barked, "What do you mean, 'so early in civilization'? If you think we're a pack of sweaty savages, you——"

"Franz," Kolff muttered, catching Heyman's arm, and I found out what the *F.* in "F. Richard Heyman" stood for. Heyman subsided stonily. Kralick scowled at him. One did not welcome a guest, however suspect a guest, by snarling defiance.

Kralick said, "We've arranged for a tour of the financial district for tomorrow morning. The rest of this day, I thought, could be spent at liberty, just relaxing. Does that sound all——"

Vornan was paying no attention. He had moved in a curious gliding way across the room and was eye-to-eye with Aster Mikkelsen. Quite softly he said, "I regret that my body is soiled from long hours of traveling. I wish to cleanse myself. Would you do me the honor of bathing with me?"

We gaped. We were all braced for Vornan's habit of making outrageous requests, but we hadn't expected him to try anything so soon, and not with Aster. Morton Fields went rigid and swung around like a man of flint, clearly groping for a way to rescue Aster from her predicament. But Aster needed no rescuing. She accepted Vornan's invitation to share a bathroom with him gracefully and with no sign of hesitation. Helen grinned. Kolff winked. Fields spluttered. Vornan made a little bow—flexing his knees as well as his spine, as though he did not really know how bows were accomplished—and ushered Aster briskly from the room. It had happened so fast that we were totally stunned.

Fields managed to say finally, "We can't let him do that!"

"Aster didn't object," Helen pointed out. "It was her decision."

Heyman pounded his hand into his fist. "I resign!" he boomed. "This is an absurdity! I withdraw entirely!"

Kolff and Kralick turned to him at once. "Franz, keep your temper," Kolff roared, and Kralick said simultaneously, "Dr. Heyman, I beg of you—"

"Suppose he had asked *me* to take a bath with him?" Heyman demanded. "Are we to grant him every whim? I refuse to be a party to this idiocy!"

Kralick said, "No one's asking you to yield to obviously excessive requests, Dr. Heyman. Miss Mikkelsen was under no pressure to agree. She did it for the sake of harmony, for—well, for scientific reasons. I'm proud of her. Nevertheless, she didn't *have* to say yes, and I don't want you to feel that you—"

Helen McIlwain cut in serenely, "I'm sorry you chose to resign this quickly, Franz, love. Wouldn't you have wanted to discuss the shape of the next thousand years with him? You'll never get a chance, now. I doubt that Mr. Kralick can let you interview him as you wish if you don't cooperate, and of course there are so many other historians who'd be happy to take your place, aren't there?"

Her ploy was devilishly effective. The thought of letting some despised rival get first crack at Vornan left Heyman devastated; and soon he was muttering that he hadn't really resigned, he had only *threatened* to resign. Kralick let him wiggle on that hook for a while before agreeing to forget the whole unhappy incident, and in the end Heyman promised none too gracefully to take a more temperate attitude toward the assignment.

. Fields, during all this, kept looking toward the door through which Aster and Vornan had vanished. At length he said edgily, "Don't you think you ought to find out what they're doing?"

"Taking a bath, I imagine," said Kralick.

"You're very calm about it!" Fields said. "But what if you've sent her off with a homicidal maniac? I detect certain signs in that man's posture and facial expression that lead me to believe he's not to be trusted."

Kralick lifted a thick eyebrow. "Really, Dr. Fields? Would you care to dictate a report on that?"

"Not just yet," he said sullenly. "But I think Miss Mikkelsen ought to be protected. It's too early for us to begin assuming that this future-man is motivated in any way by the mores and taboos of our society, and—"

"That's right," said Helen. "It may be his custom to sacrifice a dark-haired virgin every Thursday morning. The important thing for us to remember is that he doesn't think like us, not in any of the big ways nor in the small ones."

It was impossible to tell from her deadpan tone whether she meant it, although I suspected she didn't. As for Fields' distress, that was simple enough to explain: having been frustrated in his own designs on Aster, he was upset to find Vornan spiriting her away so readily. He was so upset, in fact, that he triggered an exasperated Kralick into revealing something that he had plainly not intended to tell us.

"My staff is monitoring Vornan at all times," Kralick snapped at the psychologist. "We've got a complete audio, video, and tactile pickup on him, and I don't believe he knows it, and I'll thank you not to *let* him know it. Miss Mikkelsen is in no danger whatever."

Fields was taken aback. I think we all were.

"Do you mean your men are *watching* them—right now?"

"Look," said Kralick in obvious annoyance. He snatched up the house phone and dialed a transfer number. Instantly the room's wallscreen lit up with a relay of what his pickup devices were seeing. We were given a view in full color and three dimensions of Aster Mikkelsen and Vornan-19.

They were stark naked. Vornan's back was to the camera; Aster's was not. She had a lean, supple, narrow-hipped body and the breasts of a twelve-year-old.

They were under a molecular shower together. She was scrubbing his back.

They appeared to be having a fine time.

## * EIGHT *

THAT EVENING KRALICK had arranged to have Vornan-19 attend a party in his honor at the Hudson River mansion of Wesley Bruton, the utilities tycoon. Bruton's place had been completed only two or three years back; it was the work of Albert Ngumbwe, the brilliant young architect who is now designing the Pan-African capital city in the Ituri Forest. It was so much of a showplace that even I had heard of it in my California isolation: the outstanding representative of contemporary design, it was said. My curiosity was piqued. I spent most of the afternoon going over a practically opaque book by one of the architectural critics, setting the Bruton house in its context—my homework, so to say. The helicopter fleet would depart at 6:30 from the heliport atop our hotel, and we'd travel under the tightest of security arrangements. The problem of logistics was going to be a severe one in this tour, I could see, and we would have to be infiltrated from place to place like contraband. Several hundred reporters and other media pests attempted to follow Vornan everywhere, even though it was agreed that coverage would be restricted to the daily pool of six journalists. A cloud of angry Apocalyptists trailed Vornan's movements, shouting their disbelief in him. And now there was the additional headache of a gathering force of disciples, a countermob of the sleek and respectable not-quite-middle-class burghers who saw in him the apostle of law and order, and who trampled on law and order in their hectic desire to worship him. With all these to contend with, we had to move swiftly.

Toward six we began to collect in our main suite. I found Kolff and Helen there when I arrived. Kolff was dressed in high style, and he was awesome to behold: a shimmering tunic enfolded his monumental bulk, sparkling in a whole spectrum of colors, while a gigantic cummerbund in midnight blue called attention to his jutting middle. He had slicked his straggly white hair across his dome of a skull. On his vast breast were mounted a row of academic medals conferred by many governments. I recognized only oné, which I also have been awarded: France's Legion des Curies. Kolff flourished a full dozen of the silly things.

Helen seemed almost restrained by comparison. She wore a sleek flowing gown made of some coy polymer that was now transparent, now opaque; viewed at the proper angle, she seemed nude, but the view lasted only an instant before the long chains of slippery molecules changed their orientation and concealed her flesh. It was cunning, attractive, and even tasteful in its way. Around her throat she wore a curious amulet, blatantly phallic, so much so that it negated itself and ultimately seemed innocent. Her makeup consisted of a green lipglow and dark halos around her eyes.

Fields entered shortly, wearing an ordinary business suit, and then came Heyman, dressed in a tight evening outfit at least twenty years out of style. Both of them looked uneasy. Not long afterward Aster stepped into the room, clad in a simple thigh-length robe, and adorned by a row of small tourmalines across her forehead. Her arrival stirred tension in the room.

I jerked about guiltily, hardly able to meet her eyes. Like all the rest, I had spied on her; even though it had not been my idea to switch on that espionage pickup and peer at her in the shower, I had looked with all the others, I had put my eye to the knothole and stolen a peek. Her tiny breasts and flat, boyish buttocks were no secret to me now. Fields went rigid once again, clenching his fists; Heyman flushed and scuffed at the sponge-glass floor. But Helen, who did not believe in such concepts as guilt or shame or modesty, gave Aster a warm, untroubled. greeting, and Kolff, who had transgressed so often in a long life that he had no room left for a minor bit of remorse over some unintentional voyeurism, boomed happily, "Did you enjoy your clean-getting?"

Aster said quietly, "It was amusing."

She offered no details. I could see Fields bursting to know if she had been to bed with Vornan-19. It seemed a moot point to me; our guest had already demonstrated a remarkable and indiscriminate sexual voracity, but on the other hand Aster appeared well able to guard her chastity even from a man she had bathed with. She looked cheerful and relaxed and not at all as though she had suffered any fundamental violation of her personality in the last three hours. I rather hoped she *had* slept with him; it might have been a healthy experience for her, cool and isolated woman that she was.

Kralick arrived a few minutes later, Vornan-19 in tow. He led us all to the roof heliport, where the copters were waiting. There were four of them: one for the six members of the news pool, one for the six of us and Vornan, one for a batch of White House people, and one for our security guard. Ours was the third to take off. With a quiet whir of turbines it launched itself into the night sky and sped northward. We could not see the other copters at any time during the flight. Vornan-19 peered with interest through his window at the glowing city beneath.

"What is the population of this city, please?" he asked.

"Including the surrounding metropolitan area, about thirty million people," said Heyman.

"All of them human?"

The question baffled us. After a moment Fields said, "If you mean, do any of them come from other worlds, no. We don't have any beings from other worlds on Earth.

We've never discovered any intelligent life forms in this solar system, and we don't have any of our star probes back yet."

"No," said Vornan, "I am not talking about other-worlders. I speak of natives to Earth. How many of your thirty million here are full-blood human, and how many are servitors?"

"Servitors? Robots, you mean?" Helen asked.

"In the sense of synthetic life-forms, no," said Vornan patiently. "I refer to those who do not have full human status because they are genetically other than human. You have no servitors yet? I have trouble finding the right words to ask. You do not build life out of lesser life? There are no——no——" He faltered. "I cannot say. There are no words."

We exchanged troubled glances. This was practically the first conversation any of us had had with Vornan-19, and already we were wallowing in communication dilemmas. Once again I felt that chill of fear, that awareness that I was in the presence of something strange. Every skeptical rationalist atom in my being told me that this Vornan was nothing but a gifted con-man, and yet when he spoke in this random way of an Earth populated by humans and less-than-humans, there was powerful conviction in his groping attempts to explain what he meant. He dropped the subject. We flew onward. Below us the Hudson wound sluggishly to the sea. In a while the metropolitan zone ebbed and we could make out the dark areas of the public forests, and then we were descending toward the private landing strip of Wesley Bruton's hundred-acre estate, eighty miles north of the city. Bruton owned the largest tract of undeveloped privately held land east of the Mississippi, they said. I believed it.

The house was radiant. We saw it from a distance of a quarter of a mile as we left the helicopters; it breasted a rise overlooking the river, shining with an external green light that sent streams of brightness toward the stars. A covered glidewalk carried us up the grade, through a winter garden of sculptured ice, tinted fantasies done by a master hand. Coming closer, we could make out Ngumbwe's structural design: a series of concentric translucent shells comprising a peaked pavilion taller than any of the surrounding trees. Eight or nine overlapping arches formed the roof, revolving slowly so that the shape of the house continually changed. A hundred feet above the highest arch hung a great beacon of living light, a vast yellow globe that turned and writhed and swirled on its tenuous pedestal. We could hear music, high-pitched, vibrant, coming from festoons of tiny speakers draped along the icy limbs of gaunt, monumental trees. The glidewalk guided us toward the house; a door yawned like a mouth, gaping sideways to engulf us. I caught a glimpse of myself mirrored in the glassy surface of the door, looking solemn, a bit plump, ill at ease.

Within the house chaos reigned. Ngumbwe clearly was in league with the powers of darkness; no angle was comprehensible, no line met another. From the vestibule where we stood dozens of rooms were visible, branching in every direction, and yet it was impossible to discern any pattern, for the rooms themselves were in motion, constantly rearranging not only their individual shapes but their relation to one another. Walls formed, dissolved, and were reincarnated elsewhere. Floors rose to become ceilings while new rooms were spawned beneath them. I had a sense of colossal machinery grinding and clanking in the bowels of the earth to achieve these effects, but all was done smoothly and noiselessly. In the vestibule itself the structure was relatively stable, but the oval alcove had pink, clammy walls of skinlike material which swooped down at a sharp declivity, rising again just beyond where we stood, and twisting in midair so that the seamless surface was that of a Möbius strip. One could walk that wall, pass the turnover point, and leave the room for another, yet there were no apparent exits. I had to laugh. A madman had designed this house, another madman lived in it; but one had to take a certain perverse pride in all this misplaced ingenuity.

"Remarkable!" Lloyd Kolff boomed. "Incredible! What do you think of it, eh?" he asked Vornan.

Vornan smiled palely. "Quite amusing. Does the therapy work well?"

"Therapy?"

"This is a house for the curing of the disturbed? A bedlam, is that the word?"

"This is the home of one of the world's wealthiest men," Heyman said stiffly, "designed by the talented young architect Albert Ngumbwe. It's considered a landmark of artistic accomplishment."

"Charming," said Vornan-19 devastatingly.

The vestibule rotated and we moved along the clammy surface until abruptly we were in another room. The party was in full swing. At least a hundred people were clustered in a diamond-shaped hall of immense size and unfathomable dimensions; the din they made was fearful, although by some clever prank of acoustical engineering we had not heard a thing until we had passed the critical zone of the Möbius strip. Now we were among a horde of elegant guests who clearly had been celebrating the night's event long before the arrival of the guest of honor. They danced, they sang, they drank, they puffed clouds of multi-hued smoke. Spotlights played upon them. I recognized dozens of faces in one dazzled sweep across the room: actors, financiers, political figures, playboys, spacemen. Bruton had cast a wide net through society, capturing only the distinguished, the lively, the remarkable. It surprised me that I could put names to so many of the faces, and I realized that it was a measure of Bruton's success that he could gather under one multiplicity of roofs so many individuals that a cloistered professorial sort like myself could recognize.

A torrent of sparkling red wine flowed from a vent high on one wall and ran in a thick, bubbly river diagonally across the floor like water in a pig trough. A dark-haired girl clad only in silver hoops stood under it, giggling as it drenched her. I groped for her name and Helen said, "Deona Sawtelle. The computer heiress." Two handsome young men in mirror-surface tuxedos tugged at her arms, trying to pull her free, and she eluded them to frolic in the flowing wine. In a moment they joined her. Nearby a superb dark-skinned woman with jeweled nostrils screamed happily in the grip of a titanic metal figure that was rhythmically clutching her to its chest. A man with a shaven and polished skull lay stretched full length on the floor while three girls scarcely out of their teens sat astride him and, I think, tried to undo his trousers. Four scholarly gentlemen with dyed beards sang raucously in a language unknown to me, and Lloyd Kolff strode across to greet them with whoops of mysteriously expressed pleasure. A woman with golden skin wept quietly at the base of a monstrous whirling construction of ebony, jade, and brass. Through the smoky air soared mechanical creatures with clanking metal wings and peacock tails, shrieking stridently and casting glittering droppings upon the guests. A pair of apes chained with loops of interlocked ivory gaily copulated near the intersection of two acute angles of the wall. This was Nineveh; this was Babylon. I stood dazzled, repelled by the excess of it all and yet delighted, as one is delighted by cosmic audacity of any kind. Was this a typical Wesley Bruton party? Or had it all been staged for the benefit of Vornan-19? I could not imagine people behaving like this under normal circumstances. They all seemed quite natural, though; it would take only some layers of dirt and a change of scene, and this could be an Apocalyptist riot, not a gathering of the elite. I caught sight of Kralick—appalled. He stood to one side of the vanished entrance, huge and bleak-faced, his ugly features no longer looking charming as dismay filtered through his flesh. He had not intended to bring Vornan into such a place.

Where was our visitor, anyway? In the first shock of our plunge into the madhouse we had lost sight of him. Vornan had been right: this was bedlam. And there he was in the midst of it. I saw him now, alongside the river of wine. The girl in the silver hoops, the computer heiress, rose on her knees, body stained deep crimson, and ran her hand lightly down her side. The hoops opened to the gentle command and dropped away. She offered one to Vornan, who accepted it gravely, and hurled the rest into the air. The mechanical birds snapped them up in midflight and began to devour them. The computer heiress, wholly bare now, clapped her hands in delight. One of the young men in the mirror tuxedos produced a flask from his pocket and sprayed the girl's breasts and loins, leaving a thin plastic coating. She thanked him with a curtsy, and turning again to Vornan-19, scooped up wine with her hands and offered him a drink. He sipped. The whole left half of the room went into a convulsion, the floor rising twenty feet to reveal an entirely new group of revelers emerging from a cellar somewhere. Kralick, Fields, and Aster were among those of our group who vanished from view in this rotation of the main floor. I decided I should keep close to Vornan, since no other member of our committee was assuming the responsibility. Kolff was in paroxysms of laughter with his four bearded savants; Helen stood as if in a daze, trying to record every aspect of the scene; Heyman went swirling away in the arms of a voluptuous brunette with talons affixed to her fingers. I shouldered my way across the floor. A waxen young man seized my hand and kissed it. A tottering dowager sent a swirl of vomit within six inches of my shoes, and a buzzing gold-en-hued metallic beetle a foot in diameter emerged from the floor to clean the mess, emitting satisfied clicks; I saw the gears meshing beneath its wings when it scuttled away. A moment later I was beside Vornan.

His lips were smeared with wine, but his smile was still magnificent. As he caught sight of me, he disengaged himself from the Sawtelle girl, who was trying to pull him into the rivulet of wine, and said to me, "This is excellent, Sir Garfield. I am having a splendid evening." His forehead furrowed. "Sir Garfield is the wrong form of address, I remember. You are Leo. It is a splendid evening, Leo. This house—it is comedy itself!"

All around us the bacchanal raged more furiously. Blobs of living light drifted at eye level; I saw one distinguished guest capture one and eat it. A fist-fight had begun between the two escorts of a bloated-looking woman who was, I realized in awe and distaste, a beauty queen of my youth. Near us two girls rolled on the floor in a vehement wrestling match, ripping away handfuls of each other's clothing. A ring of onlookers formed and clapped rhythmically as the zones of bare flesh were revealed; suddenly pink buttocks flashed and the quarrel turned into an uninhibited sapphic embrace. Vornan seemed fascinated by the flexed legs of the girl beneath, by the thrusting pelvis of her conqueror, by the moist sucking sounds of their joined lips. He inclined his head to get a better view. Yet at the same moment a figure approached us and Vornan said to me, "Do you know this man?" I had the unsettling impression that Vornan had been looking in two directions at once, taking in a different quadrant of the room with each of his eyes. Was it so?

The newcomer was a short, chunky man no taller than Vornan-19, but at least twice as wide. His immensely powerful frame was the support for a massive dolichocephalic head that rose, without virtue of a neck, from his enormous shoulders. He had no hair, not even eyebrows or lashes, which made him look far more naked than the various nude and seminude caperers reeling about in our vicinity. Ignoring me, he pushed a vast paw at Vornan-19 and said, "So you're the man from the future? Pleased to know you. I'm Wesley Bruton."

"Our host. Good evening." Vornan gave him a variant of the smile, less dazzling, more urbane, and almost at once the smile flicked away and the eyes came into play: keen, cool, penetrating. Nodding gently in my direction he said, "You know Leo Garfield, of course?"

"Only by reputation," Bruton roared. His hand was still outstretched. Vornan had not taken it. The look of expectancy in Bruton's eyes slowly curdled into bewildered disappointment and barely suppressed fury. Feeling I had to do something, I seized the hand myself, and as he mangled me I shouted, "So good of you to invite us, Mr. Bruton. It's a miraculous house." I added in a lower voice, "He doesn't understand all of our customs. I don't think he shakes hands."

The utilities magnate looked mollified. He released me and said, "What do *you* think of the place, Vornan?"

"Delightful. Lovely in its delicacy. I admire the taste of your architect, his restraint, his classicism."

I couldn't be sure whether that was meant as sincere praise or as derision. Bruton appeared to take the compliments at face value. He seized Vornan by one wrist, clamped his other hand about me, and said, "I'd like to show you some of the behind-the-scenes stuff, fellows. This ought to interest you, Professor. And I know Vornan here will go for it. Come on!"

I feared that Vornan would make use of that shock technique he had demonstrated on the Spanish Stairs and send Bruton flying a dozen yards for having dared to lay hands on him. But, no, our guest let himself be manhandled. Bruton bulled his way through the swirling chaos of the party, towing us in his wake. We reached a dais in the center of the room. An invisible orchestra sounded a terrifying chord and burst forth with a symphony I had never heard before, bringing loops of sound spurting from every corner of the room. A girl in the garb of an Egyptian princess was dancing atop the dais. Bruton clamped one hand on each of her bare thighs and lifted her out of the way as though she were a chair. We mounted the dais beside him; he signaled and we sank abruptly through the floor.

"We're two hundred feet down," Bruton announced. "This is the master control room. Look!"

He waved his arms grandly. All about us were screens relaying images of the party. The action unfolded kaleidoscopically in a dozen rooms at once. I saw poor Kralick wobbling unsteadily while some femme fatale climbed on his shoulders. Morton Fields was coiled in a compromising position about a portly woman with a broad, flat nose; Helen McIlwain was·dictating notes into the amulet at her throat, a task that required her to give a good imitation of the fellative act, while Lloyd Kolff was enjoying the act itself not far away, laughing cavernously as a wide-eyed girl crouched before him. I could not find Heyman at all. Aster Mikkelsen stood in the midst of a room with moist, palpitating walls, looking serene as the frenzy raged about her. Tables laden with food moved seemingly of their own will through each room; I watched the guests seizing tidbits, stuffing themselves, hurling tender morsels at one another. There was a room in which spigots of (I presume) wine or liquor dangled from the ceiling for anyone to grasp and squeeze and draw comfort from; there was a room that was in total darkness, but not unoccupied; there was a room in which the guests took turns donning the headband of some sensory-disruptive device.

"Watch this!" Bruton cried.

Vornan and I watched, he with mild interest, I in distress, as Bruton yanked switches, closed contacts, tapped out computer orders in maniacal glee. Lights flickered on and off in the upper rooms; floors and ceilings changed places; small artificial creatures flew insanely among the shrieking, laughing guests. Shattering sounds too terrifying to be called music resounded through the building. I thought the Earth itself would erupt in protest, and molten lava engulf us all.

"Five thousand kilowatts an hour," Bruton proclaimed.

He splayed his hands against a counterbalanced silvery globe a foot in diameter and nudged it forward on a jeweled track. Instantly one wall of the control room folded out of sight, revealing the giant shaft of a magnetohydrodynamic generator descending into yet another subbasement. Monitor needles did a madman's dance; dials flashed green and red and purple at us. Perspiration rolled down Wesley Bruton's face as he recited, almost hysterically, the engineering specifications of the power plant on which his palace was founded. He sang us a wild song of kilowatts. He set his grip on thick cables and massaged them in frank obscenity. He beckoned us down to see the core of his generator, and we followed, led ever deeper into the pit by this gnomish tycoon. Wesley Bruton, I remembered vaguely, had put together the holding company that distributed electricity across half the continent, and it was as though all the generating capacity of that incomprehensible monopoly were concentrated here, beneath our feet, harnessed for the sole purpose of maintaining and sustaining the architectural masterpiece of Albert Ngumbwe. The air was fiercely hot at this level. Sweat rolled down my cheeks. Bruton ripped open his jacket to bare a hairless chest banded by thick cords of muscle. Vornan-19 alone remained untroubled by the heat; he danced along beside Bruton, saying little, observing much, quite uninfected by the feverish mood of his host.

We reached the bottom. Bruton fondled the swelling flank of his generator as though it were a woman's haunch. Suddenly it must have dawned on him that Vornan-19 was less than ecstatic over this parade of wonders. He whirled and demanded, "Do you have anything like this where you come from? Is there a house that can match my house?"

"I doubt it," said Vornan gently.

"How do people live up there? Big houses? Small?"

"We tend toward simplicity."

"So you've never seen a place like mine! Nothing to equal it in the next thousand years!" Bruton paused. "But —doesn't my house still exist in your time?"

"I am not aware of that."

"Ngumbwe promised me it would last a thousand years! Five thousand! No one would tear a place like this down! Listen, Vornan, stop and think. It must be there somewhere. A monument of the past—a museum of ancient history—"

"Perhaps it is," said Vornan indifferently. "You see, this area lies outside the Centrality. I have no firm information on what may be found there. However, I believe the primitive barbarity of this structure might have been offensive to those who lived in the Time of Sweeping, when many things changed. Much perished then through intolerance."

"Primitive—barbarity—" Bruton muttered. He looked apoplectic. I wished I had Kralick on hand to get me out of this.

Vornan went on planting barbs in the billionaire's unexpectedly thin hide. "It would have been charming to retain a place like this," he said. "To stage festivals in it, curious ceremonies in honor of the return of spring." Vornan smiled. "We might even have winters again, if only so we could experience the return of spring. And then we would dance and frolic in your house, Sir Bruton. But I think it is lost. I think it has gone, hundreds of years ago. I am not sure. I am not sure."

"Are you making fun of me?" Bruton bellowed. "Laughing at my house? Am I just a savage to you? Do—"

I cut in quickly. "As an expert on electricity, Mr. Bruton, perhaps you'd like to know something about power sources in Vornan-19's era. At one of his interviews a few weeks ago he said a few things about self-contained power sources involving total energy-conversion, and possibly he'd elaborate, now, if you'd care to question him."

Bruton forgot at once that he was angry. He used his arm to wipe away the sweat that was trickling into his browless eyes and grunted, "What's this? Tell me about this!"

Vornan put the backs of his hands together in a gesture that was as communicative as it was alien. "I regret that I know so little about technical matters."

"Tell me something, though!"

"Yes," I said, thinking of Jack Bryant in his agony and wondering if this was my moment to learn what I had to learn. "This system of self-sufficient power, Vornan. When did it come into use?"

"Oh . . . very long ago. In my day, that is."

"*How* long ago?"

"Three hundred years?" he asked himself. "Five hundred? Eight hundred? It is so difficult to calculate these things. It was long ago . . . very long ago."

"What was it?" Bruton demanded. "How big was each generating unit?"

"Quite small," said Vornan evasively. He put his hand lightly against Bruton's bare arm. "Shall we go upstairs? I am missing your so-interesting party."

"You mean it eliminated the need for power transmission altogether?" Bruton could not let go. "Everybody generated his own? Just as I'm doing down here?"

We mounted a catwalk, spidery and intricate, that swung us to an upper level. Bruton continued to pepper Vornan with questions as we threaded our route back to the master control room. I tried to interject queries that would pin down the point in time at which this great changeover had come about, hoping to be able to ease Jack's soul by telling him it had happened far in our future. Vornan danced gaily about our questions, saying little of substance. His lighthearted refusal to meet any request for information squarely aroused my suspicions once more. How could I help but swing on a pendulum, now gravely grilling Vornan about the events of future history, now cursing myself for a gullible fool as I realized he was a fraud? In the control room Vornan chose a simple method to relieve himself of the burden of our inquisitiveness. He strode to one of the elaborate panels, gave Bruton a smile of the highest voltage, and said, "This is deliciously amusing, this room of yours. I admire it greatly." He pulled three switches and depressed four buttons; then he turned a wheel ninety degrees and yanked a lengthy lever.

Bruton howled. The room went dark. Sparks flew like demons. From far above came the cacophonous wail of disembodied musical instruments and the sounds of crashing and colliding. Below us, two movable catwalks clanged together; an eerie screech rose from the generator. One screen came to life again, showing us by its pale glow the main ballroom with the guests dumped into a disheveled heap. Red warning lights began to flash. The entire house was awry, rooms orbiting rooms. Bruton was madly clawing at the controls, pressing this and twisting that, but each further adjustment he made seemed only to compound the disruption. Would the generator blow, I wondered? Would everything come crashing down on us? I listened to a stream of curses that would have put Kolff into ecstasy. Machinery still gnashed both above and below us. The screen presented me with an out-of-focus view of Helen McIlwain riding piggyback on the shoulders of a distressed Sandy Kralick. There were the sounds of alarums and excursions. I had to move on. Where was Vornan-19? I had lost sight of him in the dark. Fitfully I edged forward, looking for the exit from the control room. I spied a door; it was in paroxysms, moving along its socket in arythmic quivering jerks. Crouching, I counted five complete cycles and then, hoping I had the timing at least approximately correct, leaped through just in time to avoid being crushed.

"Vornan!" I yelled.

A greenish mist drifted through the atmosphere of the room I entered now. The ceiling tilted at unlikely angles. Bruton's guests lay slumped on the floor, some unconscious, a few injured, at least one couple locked in a passionate embrace. I thought I caught sight of Vornan in a room vaguely visible to my left, but I made the mistake of leaning against a wall, and a panel responded to my pressure and pivoted, thrusting me into a different room. I had to squat here; the ceiling was perhaps five feet high. Scuttling across it, I pushed open a folding screen and found myself in the main ballroom. The waterfall of wine had become a fountain, spurting its bubbly fluid toward the dazzling ceiling. Guests milled vacantly, grabbing at one another for comfort and reassurance. Underfoot buzzed the mechanical insects that cleared away debris; half a dozen of them had caught one of Bruton's metal birds and were rending it with tiny beaks. None of our group could be seen. A high whining sound now came from the fabric of the house.

I prepared myself for death, thinking it properly absurd that I should perish in the home of one lunatic at the whim of another while I was engaged on this lunatic mission. But still I fought my way onward through the smoke and noise, through the tangled, screaming figures of the elegant guests, through the sliding walls and collapsing floors. Once more it seemed to me I saw Vornan moving ahead of me. With maniacal persistence I went after him, feeling that it was somehow my duty to find him and lead him out of the building before it demolished itself in one final expression of petulance. But I came to a barrier beyond which I could not pass. Invisible yet impermeable, it held me fast. "Vornan!" I shouted, for now I saw him plainly. He was chatting with a tall, attractive woman of middle years who seemed wholly undisturbed by what had happened. "Vornan! It's me, Leo Garfield!" But he could hear nothing. He gave the woman his arm, and they strolled away, sauntering in an irregular course through the chaos. I hammered with my fists against the invisible wall.

"That's no way to get out," said a husky feminine voice. "You couldn't smash that in a million years."

I turned. A vision in silver had appeared behind me: a slender girl, no older than nineteen, whose entire form gleamed in whiteness. Her hair had a silken glitter; her eyes were silver mirrors; her lips were silvered; her body was encased in a silver gown. I looked again and realized it was no gown, but merely a layer of paint; I detected nipples, a navel, twin muscle-ridges up the flat belly. From throat to toes she wore the silver spray, and by the ghostly light she seemed radiant, unreal, unattainable. I had not seen her before at the party.

"What happened?" she asked.

"Bruton took us on a tour of the control room. Vornan pressed some buttons when we weren't watching him. I think the house is going to explode."

She touched her silvery hand to her silvery lips. "No, it won't go up. But we'd better get out anyway. If it's going through random changes, it might squeeze everybody flat before things settle down. Come with me."

"You know how to get out?"

"Of course," she said. "Just follow along! There's an exit pouch three rooms from here . . . unless it's moved."

Mine not to reason why. She darted through a hatch that yawned suddenly, and mesmerized by the view of her dainty silvered rump, I followed. She led me along until I gasped with fatigue. We leaped over thresholds that undulated like serpents; we burrowed through heaps of giddy inebriates; we soared past impediments that came and went in mindless palpitations. I had never seen anything so beautiful as this burnished statue come to life, this girl of silver, nude and sleek and swift, moving purposefully through the dislocations of the house. She halted by a quivering strip of wall and said, "In here."

"Where?"

"There." The wall yawned wide. She thrust me inside and got in after me; then with a quick pirouette she moved around me, pressed on something, and we were outside the house.

The blast of January wind struck us like a whirling sword.

I had forgotten about the weather; we had been wholly shielded from it throughout the evening. Suddenly we were exposed to it, I in my light evening clothes, the girl in nudity covered only by a molecule-thick layer of silver paint. She stumbled and went down in a snowbank, rolling over as though aflame; I tugged her to her feet. Where could we go? Behind us the house churned and throbbed like a cephalopod gone berserk. Until this moment the girl had seemed to know what to do, but the frigid air numbed and stunned her, and now she trembled in paralysis, frightened and pathetic.

"The parking lot," I said.

We raced for it. It lay at least a quarter of a mile away, and we did not travel on any covered glidewalk now; we ran over frozen ground made hazardous by mounds of snow and rivers of ice. I was so stoked by excitement that I hardly noticed the cold, but it punished the girl brutally. She fell several times before we reached the lot. There it was at last. The vehicles of the rich and mighty were neatly arranged under a protective shield. Somehow we erupted through; Bruton's parking attendants had gone out of control in the general failure of power, and they made no attempt to stop us. They circled in buzzing bewilderment, flashing their lights on and off. I dragged the girl to the nearest limousine, pulled open its door, thrust her inside, and dropped down beside her.

Within it was warm and womblike. She lay gasping,

shivering, congealed. "Hold me!" she cried, "I'm freezing! For God's sake, hold me!"

My arms wrapped tight around her. Her slim form nestled against mine. In a moment her panic was gone; she was warm again, and as self-possessed as she had been when she led us from the house. I felt her hands against me. Willingly I surrendered to her silvered lure. My lips went to hers and came away tasting of metal; her cool thighs encircled me; I felt as though I were making love to some artfully crafted engine, but the silver paint was no more than skin deep, and the sensation vanished as I reached warm flesh beneath it. In our passionate struggles her silver hair revealed itself as a wig; it slipped away, displaying an unsilvered skull, bald as porcelain, below. I knew her now: she must be Bruton's daughter. His gene for hairlessness bred true. She sighed and drew me down into oblivion.

## * NINE *

KRALICK SAID, "We lost control of events. We have to keep a tighter grip on things next time. Which one of you was with Vornan when he got hold of the controls?"

"I was," I said. "There was absolutely no way of preventing what took place. He moved quickly. Neither Bruton nor I suspected that he might do any such thing."

"You can't ever let yourself get off guard with him," Kralick said in anguish. "You have to assume at any given moment that he's capable of doing the most outrageous thing imaginable. Haven't I tried to get that point across to you before?"

"We are basically rational people," said Heyman. "We do not find it easy to adjust to the presence of an irrational person."

A day had passed since the debacle at Wesley Bruton's wondrous villa. Miraculously, there had been no fatalities; Kralick had signaled for Government troops, who had pulled all the guests from the throbbing, swaying house in time. Vornan-19 had turned up standing outside the house, watching calmly as it went through its antics. The damage to the house, I heard Kralick mutter, had been several hundred thousand dollars. The Government would pay. I did not envy Kralick his job of calming Wesley Bruton down. But at least the utilities magnate could not say that he had suffered unjustly. His own urge to lionize the man from the future had brought this trouble upon him. Bruton surely had seen the reels of Vornan's trip through the capitals of Europe, and was aware that unpredictable things took place around and about Vornan. Yet Bruton had insisted on giving the party, and had insisted too on taking Vornan to the control room of his mansion. I could not feel very sorry for him. As for the guests who had been interrupted in their revelry by the cataclysm, they deserved little pity either. They had come to stare at the time traveler and to make fools of themselves. They had done both, and what harm was it if Vornan had chosen to make fools of them in return?

Kralick was right to be displeased with us, though. It was our responsibility to keep such things from happening. We had not discharged that responsibility very well on our first outing with the man from the future.

A little grimly, we prepared to continue the tour.

Today we were visiting the New York Stock Exchange. I have no idea how that came to be on Vornan's itinerary. Certainly he did not request it; I suspect that some bureaucrat in the capital decided arbitrarily that it would be a worthy propaganda move to let the futuristic sightseer have a look at the bastion of the capitalistic system. For my part I felt a little like a visitor from some alien environment myself, since I had never been near the Stock Exchange nor had any dealings with it. This is not the

121

snobbery of the academic man, please understand. If I had time and inclination, I would gladly have joined the fun of speculating in Consolidated System Mining and United Ultronics and the other current favorites. But my salary is a good one and I have a small private income besides, ample for my needs; since life is too short to allow us to sample every experience, I have lived within my income and devoted my energy to my work, rather than to the market. In a kind of eager ignorance, then, I readied myself for our visit. I felt like a grade-school boy on an outing.

Kralick had been called back to Washington for conferences. Our governmental shepherd for the day was a taciturn young man named Holliday, who looked anything but happy at having drawn this assignment. At eleven that morning we headed downtown, traveling en masse: Vornan, the seven of us, an assortment of official hangers-on, the six members of today's media pool, and our guards. By prearrangement the Stock Exchange gallery would be closed to other visitors while we were there. Traveling with Vornan was complex enough without having to share a visitors' balcony.

Our motorcade of glossy limousines halted grandly before the immense building. Vornan looked politely bored as we were ushered inside by Exchange officials. He had said next to nothing all day; in fact, we had heard little from him since the grim homeward ride from the Bruton fiasco. I feared his silence. What mischief was he storing up? Right now he seemed wholly disconnected; neither the shrewd, calculating eyes nor the all-conquering smile were at work. Blank-faced, withdrawn, he seemed no more than a slight, ordinary man as we filed toward the visitors' gallery.

The scene was stupendous. Beyond doubt this was the home of the moneychangers.

We looked down into a room at least a thousand feet on each side, perhaps a hundred fifty feet from floor to ceiling. In the middle of everything was the great masculine shaft of the central financial computer: a glossy column twenty yards in diameter, rising from the floor and disappearing through the ceiling. Every brokerage house in the world had its direct input to that machine. Within its polished depths existed who knew how many clicking and chattering relays, how many memory cores of fantastic smallness, how many phone links, how many data tanks? With one swift bolt of a laser cannon it would be possible to sever the communications network that held together the financial structure of civilization. I looked warily at Vornan-19, wondering what deviltry he had in mind. But he seemed calm, aloof, only faintly interested in the floor of the Exchange.

About the central rod of the computer shaft were situated smaller cagelike structures, some thirty or forty of them, each with its cluster of excited, gesticulating brokers. The open space between these booths was littered with papers. Messenger boys scurried frantically about, kicking the discarded papers into clouds. Overhead, draped from one wall to the other, ran the gigantic yellow ribbon of the stock ticker, reeling off in magnified form the information that the main computer was transmitting everywhere. It seemed odd to me that a computerized stock exchange would have all this bustle and clutter on its floor, and that there would be so much paper lying about, as though the year were 1949 instead of 1999. But I did not take into account the force of tradition among these brokers. Men of money are conservative, not necessarily in ideology but certainly in habit. They want everything to remain as it has always been.

Half a dozen Stock Exchange executives came out to greet us—crisp, gray-haired men, attired in neat old-fashioned business suits. They were unfathomably rich, I suppose; and why, given such riches, they chose to spend the days of their lives in this building I could not and cannot understand. But they were friendly. I suspect they would give the same warm, open-handed greeting to a touring delegation from the socialist countries that have not yet adopted modified capitalism—say, a pack of touring zealots from Mongolia. They thrust themselves upon us, and they seemed almost as delighted to have a gaggle of touring professors on their balcony as they did to have a man claiming to come from the far future.

The President of the Stock Exchange, Samuel Norton, made us a brief, courtly speech. He was a tall, well-groomed man of middle years, easy of manner, obviously quite pleased with his place in the universe. He told us of the history of his organization, gave us some weighty statistics, boasted a bit about the current Stock Exchange headquarters, which had been built in the 1980's, and closed by saying, "Our guide will now show you the workings of our operations in detail. When she's finished, I'll be happy to answer any general questions you may have—particularly those concerning the underlying philosophy of our system, which I know must be of great interest to you."

The guide was an attractive girl in her twenties with short, shiny red hair and a gray uniform artfully designed to mask her feminine characteristics. She beckoned us forward to the edge of the balcony and said, "Below us you see the trading floor of the New York Stock Exchange. At the present time, four thousand one hundred twenty-five common and preferred stocks are traded on the Exchange. Dealings in bonds are handled elsewhere. In the center of the floor you see the shaft of our main computer. It extends thirteen stories into the basement and rises eight stories above us. Of the hundred floors in this building, fifty-one are used wholly or in part for the operations of this computer, including the levels for programming, decoding, maintenance, and record storage. Every transaction that takes place on the floor of the Exchange or on any of the subsidiary exchanges in other cities and countries is noted with the speed of light within this computer. At present there are eleven main subsidiary exchanges: San Francisco, Chicago, London, Zurich, Milan, Moscow, Tokyo, Hong Kong, Rio de Janeiro, Addis Ababa, and—ah—Sydney. Since these span all time zones, it is possible to carry out securities transactions twenty-four hours a day. The New York Exchange, however, is open only from ten in the morning to half past three, the traditional hours, and all 'off-the-floor' transactions are recorded and analyzed for the pre-opening session the following morning. Our daily volume on the main trading floor is about three hundred fifty million shares, and roughly twice that many shares are traded each day on the subsidiary exchanges. Only a generation ago such figures would have been regarded as fantastic.

"Now, how does a securities transaction take place?

"Let us say that you, Mr. Vornan, wish to purchase one hundred shares of XYZ Space Transit Corporation. You have seen in yesterday's tapes that the market price is currently about forty dollars a share, so you know that you must invest approximately four thousand dollars. Your first step is to contact your broker, which of course can be done by a touch of your finger to your telephone. You place your order with him, and he immediately relays it to the trading floor. The particular data bank in which XYZ Space Transit transactions are recorded takes his call and notes your order. The computer conducts an auction, just as has been done in listed securities on the Exchange since 1792. The offers to sell XYZ Space Transit are matched against the offers to buy. At the speed of light it is determined that one hundred shares are available for sale at forty, and that a buyer exists. The transaction is closed and your broker notifies you. A small commission is his only charge to you; in addition there is a small fee for the computer services of the Exchange. A portion of this goes to the retirement fund of the so-called specialists who formerly handled the matching of buy and sell orders on the trading floor.

"Since everything is handled by computer, you may wonder what is taking place elsewhere on the trading floor. What you see represents a delightful Stock Exchange tradition: although not strictly necessary any longer, we maintain a staff of brokers who buy and sell securities for their own accounts, exactly as in the old days. They are following the precomputer process. Let me trace the course of a single transaction for you. . . ."

In clean, precise tones she showed us what all the mad scurrying on the floor was about. I was startled to realize that it was done purely as a charade; the transactions were unreal and at the end of each day all accounts were canceled. The computer actually handled everything. The noise, the discarded papers, the intricate gesticulations—these were reconstructions of the archaic past, performed by men whose lives had lost their purpose. It was fascinating and depressing: a ritual of money, a running-down of the capitalistic clock. Old brokers who would not retire took part in this daily amusement, I gathered, while alongside them the monstrous shaft of the computer, which had unmanned them a decade previously, gleamed as the erect symbol of their impotence.

Our guide droned on and on, telling us of the stock ticker and the Dow-Jones averages, deciphering the cryptic symbols that drifted dreamily by on the screen, talking of bulls and bears, of short sellers, of margin requirements, of many another strange and wonderful things. As the climax of her act she switched on a computer output and allowed us to have a squint at the boiling madhouse within the master brain, where transactions took place at improbable speeds and billions of dollars changed hands within moments.

I was awed by the awesomeness of it all. I who had never played the market felt the urge to phone my broker, if I could find one, and get plugged into the great data banks. Sell a hundred GFX! Buy two hundred CCC! Off a point! Up two! This was the core of life; this was the

126

essence of being. The mad rhythm of it caught me completely. I longed to rush toward the computer shaft, spread my arms wide, embrace its gleaming vertical bulk. I envisioned its lines reaching out through the world, even unto the reformed socialist brethren in Moscow, threading a communion of dollars from city to city, and extending perhaps to the Moon, to our coming bases on the planets, to the stars themselves ... capitalism triumphant!

The guide faded away. President Norton of the Stock Exchange stepped forward again, beaming pleasantly, and said, "Now, if I can help you with any further problems—"

"Yes," said Vornan mildly. "What is the purpose, please, of a stock exchange?"

The executive reddened and showed signs of shock. After all this detailed explication ... to have the esteemed guest ask what the whole thing was about? We looked embarrassed ourselves. None of us had thought that Vornan had come here ignorant of the basic uses of this enterprise. How had he let himself be taken to the Exchange without knowing what it was he was going to see? Why had he not asked before this? I realized once again that if he were genuine, Vornan must view us as amusing apes whose plans and schemes were funny to watch for their own sake; he was not so much interested in visiting a thing called a Stock Exchange as he was in the fact that our Government earnestly desired him to visit that thing.

"Well," said the Stock Exchange man, "am I to understand, Mr. Vornan, that in the time that you—that you come from there is no such thing as a securities exchange?"

"Not that I know of."

"Perhaps under some other name?"

"I can think of no equivalent."

Consternation. "But how do you manage to transfer units of corporate ownership, then?"

Blankness. A shy, possibly mocking smile from Vornan-19.

"You *do* have corporate ownership?"

"Pardon," Vornan said. "I have studied your language carefully before making my journey, but there are many gaps in my knowledge. Perhaps if you could explain some of your basic terms—"

The executive's easy dignity began to flee. Norton's cheeks were mottled, his eyes were flickering like those of a beast trapped in a cage. I had seen something of the same look on Wesley Bruton's face when he had learned from Vornan that his magnificent villa, built to endure through the ages like the Parthenon and the Taj Mahal, had vanished and been forgotten by 2999, and would have been retained only as a curiosity, a manifestation of baroque foolishness, if it had survived. The Stock Exchange man could not comprehend Vornan's incomprehension, and it unnerved him.

Norton said, "A corporation is a—well, a company. That is, a group of individuals banded together to do something for profit. To manufacture a product, to perform a service, to—"

"A profit," said Vornan idly. "What is a profit?"

Norton bit his lip and dabbed at his sweaty forehead. After some hesitation he said, "A profit is a return of income above costs. A surplus value, as they say. The corporation's basic goal is to make a profit that can be divided among its owners. Thus it must be efficiently productive, so that the fixed costs of operation are overcome and the unit cost of manufacturing is lower than the market price of the product offered. Now, the reason why people set up corporations instead of simple partnerships is—"

"I do not follow," said Vornan. "Simpler terms, please. The object of this corporation is profit, to be divided among owners, yes? But what is an owner?"

"I was just coming to that. In legal terms—"

"And what use is this profit that the owners should want it?"

I sensed that a deliberate baiting was going on. I looked in worry at Kolff, at Helen, at Heyman. But they seemed hardly to be perturbed. Holliday, our government man, was frowning a bit, but perhaps he thought Vornan-19's questions more innocent than they seemed to me.

The nostrils of the Stock Exchange man flickered ominously. His temper seemed to be held under tight restraint. One of the media men, alive to Norton's discomfiture, moved close to flash a camera in his face. He glowered at it.

"Am I to understand," Norton asked slowly, "that in your era the concept of the corporation is unknown? That the profit motive is extinct? That money itself has vanished from use?"

"I would have to say yes," Vornan replied pleasantly. "At least, as I comprehend those terms, we have nothing equivalent to them."

"This has happened *in America?*" Norton asked in incredulity.

"We do not precisely have an America," said Vornan. "I come from the Centrality. The terms are not congruous, and in fact I find it hard to compare even approximately—"

"America's gone? How could that be? When did it happen?"

"Oh, during the Time of Sweeping, I suppose. Many things changed then. It was long ago. I do not remember an America."

F. Richard Heyman saw an opportunity to scrape a little history out of the maddeningly oblique Vornan. He swung around and said, "About this Time of Sweeping that you've occasionally mentioned. I'd like to know—"

He was interrupted by a geyser of indignation from Samuel Norton.

"America gone? Capitalism extinct? It just couldn't happen! I tell you——"

One of the executive's aides moved hurriedly to his side and urgently murmured something. The great man nodded. He accepted a violet-hued capsule from the other and touched its ultrasonic snout to his wrist. There was a quick whirr, an intake of what I suppose was some kind of tranquilizing drug. Norton breathed deeply and made a visible effort to collect himself.

More temperately, the Stock Exchange leader said to Vornan, "I don't mind telling you that I find all this hard to believe. A world without America in it? A world that doesn't use money? Tell me this, will you, please: *Has the whole world gone Communist where you come from?*"

There ensued what they call a pregnant silence, during which cameras and recorders were busy catching tense, incredulous, angry, or disturbed facial expressions. I sensed impending disaster. At length Vornan said, "It is another term I do not understand. I apologize for my extreme ignorance. I fear that my world is much unlike yours. However"——at this point he produced his glittering smile, drawing the sting from his words——"it is your world, and not mine, that I have come here to discuss. Please do tell me the use of this Stock Exchange of yours."

But Norton could not shake his obsession with the contours of Vornan-19's world. "In a moment. If you'll tell *me,* first, how you make purchases of goods——a hint or two of your economic system——"

"We each have all that any person would require. Our needs are met. And now, this idea of corporation ownership——"

Norton turned away in despair. Vistas of an unimaginable future stretched before us: a world without economics, a world in which no desire went unfulfilled. Was it possible? Or was it all the oversimplified shrugging-away of details that a mountebank did not care to simulate for us?

One or the other, I was beguiled. But Norton was derailed. He gestured numbly to one of the other Stock Exchange men, who came forward brightly to say, "Let's start right at the beginning. We've got this company that makes things. It's owned by a little group of people. Now, in legal terms there's a concept known as liability, meaning that the owners of a company are responsible for anything their company might do that's improper or illegal. To shift liability, they create an imaginary entity called a corporation, which bears the responsibility for any action that might be brought against them in their business capacity. Now, since each member of the owning group has a share in the ownership of this corporation, we can issue *stock*, that is, certificates representing proportional shares of beneficial interest in the . . ."

And so on and on. A basic course in economics.

Vornan beamed. He let the whole thing run its route, right to the point where the man was explaining that when an owner wished to sell his share in the company, he found it expedient to work through a central auction system that would put his stock up for the highest bidder, when Vornan quietly and devastatingly admitted that he still couldn't quite grasp the concepts of ownership, corporations, and profit, let alone the transfer of stock interests. I'm sure he said it just to annoy and goad. He was playing the part now of the man from Utopia, eliciting long explanations of our society and then playfully giving the structure itself a shove by registering ignorance of its underlying assumptions, implying that the underlying assumptions were transient and insignificant. There was a distressed huddle among the offended but stonily reserved Stock Exchange officials. It had never occurred to them that anyone might take this mock-innocent attitude. Even a child knew what money was and what corporations did, even if the concept of limited liability remained elusive.

I felt no great impulse to get mixed up in the awkwardness. My eyes roved idly here and there. Looking toward the great yellow blowup of the stock ticker, I saw:

STOCK EXCHANGE PLAYS HOST TO MAN FROM 2999

And then:

VORNAN-19 ON VISITORS GALLERY NOW

The tape began then to tell of stock transactions and of fluctuating averages. But the damage was done. Action on the trading floor came to a halt. The counterfeit buying and selling stopped, and a thousand faces were upturned to the balcony. Great shouts arose, incoherent, unintelligible. The brokers were waving and cheering. They flowed together, swirling around the trading posts, pointing, waving, crying out mysterious booming noïses. What did they want? The Dow-Jones industrial averages for January, 2999? The laying-on of hands? A glimpse of the man from the future? Vornan was at the rim of the balcony, now, smiling, holding up his hands as though delivering a benediction upon capitalism. The last rites, perhaps ... extreme unction for the financial dinosaurs.

Norton said, "They're acting strangely. I don't like this."

Holliday' reacted to the note of alarm in his voice. "Let's get Vornan out of here," he murmured to a guard standing just by my elbow. "There's the look of a riot starting."

Tickertape floated through the air. The churning brokers seized long streamers of it, danced around with it, sent it coiling upward toward the balcony. I heard a few shouts against the background of noise: they wanted Vornan to come down among them. Vornan continued to acknowledge their homage.

The ticker declared:

An exodus from the trading floor had begun. The brokers were coming upstairs to find Vornan! Our group dissolved in confusion. I was growing accustomed now to making quick exits; Aster Mikkelsen stood beside me, so I seized her by the hand and whispered hoarsely, "Come on, before the trouble starts! Vornan's done it again!"

"But he hasn't done anything!"

I tugged at her. A door appeared, and we slipped quickly through it. I looked back and saw Vornan following me, surrounded by his security guards. We passed down a long glittering corridor that coiled tubelike around the entire building. Behind us came shouts, muffled and inchoate. I saw a door marked NO ADMITTANCE and opened it. I was on another balcony, this one overlooking what could only have been the gut of the master computer. Snaky strands of data leaped convulsively from tank to tank. Girls in short smocks rushed back and forth, thrusting their hands into enigmatic openings. What looked like an intestine stretched across the ceiling. Aster laughed. I pulled her after me and we went out again, into the corridor. A robotruck came buzzing up toward us. We sidestepped it. What did the tape say now? FLOOR BROKERS RUN AMOK?

"Here," Aster said. "Another door!"

We found ourselves at the lip of a dropshaft and stepped blithely into it. Down, down, down . . .

. . . and out. Into the warm arcade of Wall Street. Sirens wailed behind us. I paused, gasping, taking my bearings, and saw that Vornan was still behind me, with Holliday and the media crew right in back of him.

"Into the cars!" Holliday ordered.

We made our escape successfully. Later in the day we learned that the Dow-Jones averages had suffered a decline of 8.51 points during our visit to the Exchange, and that two elderly brokers had perished from derangement of their cardiac pacemakers during the excitement. As we sped out of New York City that night, Vornan said idly to Heyman, "You must explain capitalism to me again some time. It seems quite thrilling, in its fashion."

* TEN *

WE HAD A simpler time of things at the automated brothel in Chicago. Kralick was a little leery of letting Vornan visit the place, but Vornan requested it himself, and such a request could hardly be denied without risking explosive consequences. At any rate, since such places are legal and even fashionable, there was no reason for refusing, short of lingering puritanism.

Vornan was no puritan himself. That much was clear. He had lost little time commandeering the sexual services of Helen McIlwain, as Helen bragged to us on the third night of our stewardship. There was at least a fair chance that he had had Aster too, though of course neither he nor Aster was saying anything about it. Having demonstrated an insatiable curiosity for our sexual mores, Vornan could not be kept away from the computerized bordello; and, he slyly told Kralick, it would be part of his continuing education in the mysteries of the capitalistic system. Since Kralick had not been with us at the New York Stock Exchange, he failed to see the joke.

I was delegated to be Vornan's guide. Kralick seemed embarrassed to ask it of me. But it was unthinkable to let him go anywhere without a watchdog, and Kralick had come to know me well enough to realize that I had no objections to accompanying him to the place. Neither, for that matter, had Kolff, but he was too boisterous himself for such a task, and Fields and Heyman were unfit for it on grounds of excessive morality. Vornan and I set out together through the erotic maze early on a dark afternoon, hours after we had podded into Chicago from New York.

The building was at once sumptuous and chaste: an ebony tower on the Near North Side, at least thirty stories, windowless, the façade decorated with abstract inlays. There was no indication of the building's purpose on its door. With great misgivings I ushered Vornan through the climate field, wondering what kind of chaos he would contrive to create inside.

I had never been to one of these places myself. Permit me the mild boast of saying that it had never been necessary for me to purchase sexual companionship; there had always been an ample supply available to me for no other *quid pro quo* than my own services. I wholeheartedly approved of the enabling law that had permitted their establishment, though. Why should sex not be a commodity as easily purchased as food and drink? Is it not as essential to human well-being, or nearly so? And is there not considerable revenue to be captured by licensing a public utility of eroticism, carefully regulated and heavily taxed? In the long run it was the national revenue need that had triumphed over our traditional puritanism; I wonder if the brothels would ever have come into being but for the temporary exhaustion of other tax avenues.

I did not try to explain the subtleties of all this to Vornan-19. He seemed baffled enough by the mere concept of money, let alone the idea of exchanging money for sex, or of taxing such transactions for the benefit of society as a whole. As we entered, he said pleasantly, "Why do your citizens require such places?"

"To satisfy their sexual needs."

"And they give money for this satisfaction, Leo? Money which they have obtained by performing other services?"

"Yes."

"Why not perform the services directly in return for sexual satisfaction?"

I explained briefly the role of money as a medium of exchange, and its advantages over barter. Vornan smiled. He said, "It is an interesting system. I will discuss it at great length when I get home. But why must money be paid in exchange for sexual pleasure? That seems unfair. The girls one hires here get money, and they get sexual pleasure too, so they are being paid twice."

"They don't get sexual pleasure," I said. "Just money."

"But they engage in the sexual act. And so they receive a benefit from the men who come here."

"No, Vornan. They just let themselves be used. There's no transaction of pleasure. They make themselves available to anyone, you see, and somehow that cancels out any physical pleasure in what they do."

"But surely pleasure comes when one body is joined to another, regardless of motive!"

"That isn't so. Not among us. You have to understand—"

I stopped. His expression was one of disbelief. Worse, of shock. At that moment Vornan seemed more authentically a man of another time than ever before. He was genuinely jarred by this revelation of our sexual ethos; his façade of mild amusement dropped away, and I saw the real Vornan-19, stunned and repelled by our barbarity. Lost in confusion, I could not begin to extricate myself by tracing the evolution of our way of life. Instead I suggested blurredly that we begin our tour of the building.

Vornan agreed. We moved forward across a vast internal plaza of yielding purple tile. Before us stretched a shining blank wall broken only by reception cubicles. I had been briefed on what was expected of us. Vornan entered one cubicle; I took a seat in the cubicle to the left of his.

A small output screen lit up the moment I crossed the

threshold. It said, *Please reply to all questions in a clear, loud voice.* A pause. *If you have read and understood this instruction, indicate your understanding with the word yes.*

"Yes," I said. Suddenly I wondered if Vornan were capable of comprehending written instructions. He spoke English fluently, but he did not necessarily have any knowledge of the written language. I thought of going to his aid; but the brothel computer was saying something to me, and I kept my eyes on the screen.

It was quizzing me about my sexual preferences.

*Female?*

"Yes."

*Under thirty?*

"Yes." After some thought.

*Preferred color of hair?*

I hesitated. "Red," I said, just for the sake of variety.

*Preferred physical type: Choose one by pressing button beneath the screen.*

The screen showed me three feminine contours: fashionably thin and boyish, middle-of-the-road girl-next-door curvaceousness, and hypermammiferous steroid-enhanced ultra-voluptuousness. My hand wandered across the buttons. It was a temptation to go for the fleshiest, but reminding myself that I was seeking variety, I opted for the boyish figure, which in outline reminded me of Aster Mikkelsen's.

Now the computer began to grill me about the sort of lovemaking I wished to enjoy. It informed me crisply that there were extra charges for specific enumerated deviant acts. It listed the additional fee for each, and I noted in a certain chilly fascination that sodomy was five times as expensive as fellatio, and that supervised sadism was considerably costlier than masochism. But I passed up the whips and boots, and also chose to do without the use of the nongenital orifices. Let other men take their pleasure in navel or ear, I thought. I am a conservative in such matters.

The next sequence to pass across the screen was choice of positions, since I had opted for regulation congress. Something like a scene out of the *Kama Sutra* came in view: twenty-odd male and female stick figures, coupling in extravagantly imaginative ways. I have seen the temples of Konarak and Khajurao, those monuments to bygone Hindu exuberance and fertility, covered over with virile men and full-breasted women, Krishna and Radha in all the combinations and permutations man and woman have ever devised. The cluttered screen had something of the same feverish intensity, although I admit the streamlined stick figures lacked the *volupté,* the three-dimensional fleshiness of those shining stone images under the Indian sun. I brooded over the extensive choice and selected one that struck my fancy.

Lastly came the most delicate matter of all: the computer wished to know my name and ID number.

Some say that that regulation was tacked on by vindictive legislative prudes, fighting a desperate rearguard battle to scuttle the entire program of legalized prostitution. The reasoning was that no one would use the place in the knowledge that his identity was being recorded on the master computer's memory film, perhaps to be spewed forth later as part of a potentially destructive dossier. The officials in charge of the enterprise, doing their best to cope with this troublesome requirement, announced vociferously that all data would remain forever confidential; yet I suppose there are some who fear to enter the house of automated assignations simply because they must register their presence. Well, what had I to fear? My academic tenure is interruptible only for reasons of moral turpitude, and there can be nothing turpid about making use of a government-operated facility such as this. I gave my name and identifying number. Briefly I wondered how Vornan, who lacked an identifying number, would make out; evidently the computer had been forewarned of his presence, though, for he was passed through to the next stage of our processing without difficulty.

A slot opened in the base of the computer output. It contained a privacy mask, I was told, which I was to slip over my head. I withdrew the mask, distended it, and pulled it into place. The thermoplastic compound fit itself to my features as though it were a second skin, and I wondered how anything so snug could be concealing; but I caught sight of myself in the momentarily blank face of the screen, and the reflection was not that of any face I would have recognized. Mysteriously, the mask had rendered me anonymous.

The screen now told me to step forward as the door opened. I obeyed. The front of my cubicle lifted; I passed through to a helical ramp leading to some upper level of the huge building. I caught sight of other men ascending on ramps to my left and right; like spirits going to salvation they rose, borne upward by silent glidewalks, their faces hidden, their bodies tensed. From above streamed the cool radiance of a gigantic light tank, bathing us all in brilliance. A figure waved to me from an adjoining ramp. Unmistakably it was Vornan; masked though he was, I detected him by the slimness of his figure, the jauntiness of his stance, and by a certain aura of strangeness that seemed to enfold him even with his features hidden. He soared past me and disappeared, swallowed up by the pearly radiance above. A moment later I was in that zone of radiance too, and swiftly and easily I passed through another portal that admitted me to a cubicle not much larger than the one in which the computer had interviewed me.

Another screen occupied the left-hand wall. To the far side was a washstand and a molecular cleanser; the center of the cubicle was occupied by a chaste double bed, freshly made. The entire environment was grotesquely antiseptic. If this is legalized prostitution, I thought, I prefer streetwalkers . . . if there are any. I stood beside the bed, eyeing the screen. I was alone in the room. Had the mighty machine faltered? Where was my paramour?

But they were not finished scrutinizing me. The screen glowed and words streamed across it: *Please remove your clothing for medical examination.*

Obediently, I stripped and placed my garments in a hopper that debouched from the wall in response to some silent signal. The hopper closed again; I suspected that my clothes would be fumigated and purified while they were in there, and I was correct. I stood naked but for my mask, Everyman reduced to his final prop, as scanners and sensors played a subtle greenish light over my body, searching for the chancres of venereal disease, most likely. The examination lasted some sixty seconds. Then the screen invited me to extend my arm, and I did so, whereupon a needle descended and speedily removed a small sample of my blood. Unseen monitors searched that fragment of mortality for the tokens of corruption, and evidently found nothing that threatened the health of the personnel of this establishment, for in another moment the screen flashed some sort of light pattern that signified I had passed my tests. The wall near the washstand opened and a girl came through.

"Hello," she said. "I'm Esther, and I'm *so* glad to know you. I'm sure we're going to be great friends."

She was wearing a gauzy smock through which I could see the outlines of her slender body. Her hair was red, her eyes were green, her face bore the look of intelligence, and she smiled with a fervor that was not altogether mechanical, I thought. In my innocence I had imagined that all prostitutes were coarse, sagging creatures with gaping pores and sullen, embittered faces, but Esther did not fit my preconceived image. I had seen girls much like her on the campus at Irvine; it was quite possible that I had seen Esther herself there. I would not ask her that time-hoared question: What's a nice girl like you doing in a place like this? But I wondered. I wondered.

Esther eyed my body appraisingly, perhaps not so much to judge my masculinity as perhaps to hunt out any medical shortcomings that the sensor system might have overlooked. Yet she managed to transform her glance into something more than a merely clinical one; it was provocative as well. I felt curiously exposed, probably because I am not accustomed to meeting young ladies for the first time under such circumstances. After her quick survey Esther crossed the room and touched her hand to a control at the base of the screen. "We don't want them peeping at us, do we?" she asked brightly, and the screen darkened. I hazarded a private guess that this was part of the regular routine, by way of convincing the customer that the great staring eye of the computer would not spy on his amours; and I guessed also that despite the conspicuous gesture of turning off the screen, the room was still being monitored and would continue to be under surveillance while I was in it. Surely the designers of this place would not leave the girls wholly at the mercies of any customer with whom they might be sharing a cubicle. I felt queasy about going to bed with someone knowing that my performance was being observed and very likely taped and coded and filed, but I overcame my hesitation, telling myself that I was here purely on a lark. This bordello was clearly no place for an educated man. It invited too much suspicion. But no doubt it suited the needs of those who had such needs.

As the glow of the screen darkened, Esther said, "Shall I turn the room light off?"

"It doesn't matter to me."

"I'll turn it down, then." She did something to the knob and the room dimmed. In a quick lithe gesture she slipped off her smock. Her body was smooth and pale, with narrow hips and small, girlish breasts whose translucent skin revealed a network of fine blue veins. She reminded me very much of Aster Mikkelsen as Aster had looked on that spy pickup the week before. Aster ... Esther ... for one moment of dreamy confusion I confounded the two and wondered why a world-famous biochemist would be doubling as a tart. Smiling amiably, Esther stretched out on the bed, lying on her side with her knees drawn up; it was a friendly, conversational posture, nothing blatant about it. I was grateful for that. I had expected a girl in such a place to lie back, part her legs, and say, "Come on, buddy, get aboard," and I was relieved that Esther did no such thing. It occurred to me that in my interview below, the computer had sized up my personality, marked me as a member of the inhibited academic class, and had passed along to Esther, preparing herself for work, a memorandum to the effect that I was to be treated in a dignified manner.

I sat down alongside her.

"Would you like to talk awhile?" she asked. "We have plenty of time."

"All right. You know, I've never been here before."

"I do know."

"How?"

"The computer told me. The computer tells us everything."

"*Everything?* My nàme?"

"Oh, no, not your name! I mean, all the *personal* things."

I said, "So what do you know about me, Esther?"

"You'll see in a little while." Her eyes sparkled mischievously. Then she said, "Did you see the man from the future when you came in?"

"The one called Vornan-19?"

"Yes. He's supposed to be here today. Just about this time. We got a special notice over the master line. They say he's awfully handsome. I've seen him on the screen. I wish I'd get a chance to meet him."

"How do you know you aren't with him right now?"

She laughed. "Oh, no! I know I'm not!"

"But I'm masked. I could be——"

"You aren't. You're just teasing me. If I was getting him, they would have notified me."

"Maybe not. Maybe he prefers secrecy."

"Well, maybe so, but anyway I know you're not the man from the future. Mask or no mask, you aren't fooling me."

I let my hand roam along the smoothness of her thigh. "What do you think of him, Esther? Do you believe he's really from the year 2999?"

"Don't you think so?"

"I'm asking you what you think."

She shrugged. Taking my hand, she drew it slowly up over her taut belly until it was cupping the small cool mound of her left breast, as though she hoped to deflect my troublesome questions by leading me into the act of passion. Pouting a little, she said, "Well, they all say he's real. The President and everyone. And they say he's got special powers. That he can give you a kind of electric shock if he wants." Esther giggled suddenly. "I wonder if—if he can shock a girl while he's—you know, while he's with her."

"Quite likely. If he's really what he says he is."

"Why don't you believe in him?"

I said, "It all seems phony to me. That a man should drop out of the sky—literally—and claim to come from a thousand years in the future. Where's the proof? How am I supposed to know he's telling the truth?"

"Well," Esther said, "there's that look in his eyes. And his smile. There's something strange about him, everyone says. He talks strange too, not with an accent, exactly, but yet his voice comes out peculiar. I believe in him, yes. I'd like to make love with him. I'd do it for free."

"Perhaps you'll have the chance," I said.

She grinned. But she was growing restless, as though this conversation exceeded the boundaries of the usual sort of small talk she was in the habit of making with dilatory clients. I pondered the impact that Vornan-19 had had even on this crib-girl, and I wondered what Vornan might be doing elsewhere in this building at this very moment. I hoped someone in Kralick's outfit was monitoring him. Ostensibly I was in here to keep an eye on him, but, as they must have known, there was no way for me to make contact with Vornan once we were past the lobby, and I feared an outbreak of our guest's by-now-familiar capacity for creating chaos. It was beyond my control, though. I slid my hands across Esther's accessible sleekness. She lay there, lost in dreams of embracing the man from the future, while her body undulated in the passionate rhythms she knew so well. The computer had prepared her adequately for her task; as our bodies joined, she slid into the position I had chosen, and she discharged her duties with energy and a reasonable counterfeit of desire.

Afterward we rolled apart. She looked satisfactorily satisfied; part of the act, I assumed. She indicated the washstand and snapped on the molecular cleanser so that I could be purified of the stains of lust. We still had time left, and she said, "Just for the record: wouldn't *you* like to meet Vornan-19? Just to convince yourself that he's the real thing?"

I debated. Then I said gravely, "Why, yes, I think I would. But I suppose I never shall."

"It's exciting to think that he's right here in this building, isn't it? Why, he might be right next door! He might be coming here next . . . if he wants another round." She crossed the room to me and slipped her arms about me. Large, glossy eyes fastened on my own. "I shouldn't be talking about him so much. I don't know how I started. We aren't supposed to mention other men when—when— listen, did I make you happy?"

"Very much, Esther. I wish I could show—"

"Tipping isn't allowed," she said hastily as I fumbled for

my credit plate. "But on the way out the computer may ask you for a report on me. They pick one out of ten customers for a sampling. I hope you'll have a good word for me."

"You know I will."

She leaned up and kissed me lightly, passionlessly, on the lips. "I like you," she said. "Honestly. That isn't just a standard line. If you ever come back here, I hope you'll ask for me."

"If I ever do, I certainly will," I said, meaning it. "That's a solemn promise."

She helped me dress. Then she vanished through her door, disappearing into the depths of the building to perform some rite of purification before taking on her next assignment. The screen came to life again, notifying me that my credit account would be billed at the standard rate, and requesting me to leave by the rear door of my cubicle. I stepped out onto the glidewalk and found myself drawn through a region of misty perfumed loveliness, a vaulted gallery whose high ceiling was festooned with strips of shimmertape; so magical was this realm that I scarcely noticed anything until I discovered that I was descending once more, gliding into a vestibule as large as the one through which I had entered, but at the opposite side of the building.

Vornan? Where was Vornan?

I emerged into the feeble light of a winter afternoon, feeling faintly foolish. The visit had been educational and recreational for me, but it had hardly served the purpose of keeping watch over our unpredictable charge. I paused on the wide plaza, wondering if I should go back inside and search out Vornan. Was it possible to ask the computer for information on a customer? While I hesitated, a voice from behind said, "Leo?"

It was Kralick, sitting in a gray-green limousine from whose hood projected the blunt snouts of a communications rig's antennae. I walked toward the car.

"Vornan's still inside," I said. "I don't know what—"

"It's all right. Get in."

I slipped through the door that the Government man held open for me. To my discomfort I found Aster Mikkelsen in the rear of the car, her head bent low over some sort of data sheets. She smiled briefly at me and went back to what she was analyzing. It troubled me to step directly from the brothel into the company of the pure Aster.

Kralick said, "I've got a full pickup running on our friend. It might interest you to know that he's on his fourth woman now, and shows no sign of running out of pep. Would you like to look?"

"No, thanks," I told him as he started to activate the screen. "That's not my kick. Is he making any trouble in there?"

"Not in his usual fashion. He's just using up a lot of girls. Going down the roster, trying out positions, capering like a goat." Muscles clenched suddenly in Kralick's cheeks. He swung about to face me and said, "Leo, you've been with this guy for nearly two weeks, now. What's your opinion? Real or fake?"

"I honestly don't know, Sandy. There are times when I'm convinced that he's absolutely authentic. Then I stop and pinch myself and say that nobody can come back in time, that it's a scientific impossibility, and that in any case Vornan's just a charlatan."

"A scientist," said Kralick heavily, "ought to begin with the evidence and construct a hypothesis around it, leading to a conclusion, right? Not start with a hypothesis and judge the evidence in terms of it."

"True," I conceded. "But what do you regard as evidence? I have experimental knowledge of time-reversal phenomena, and I know that you can't send a particle of matter back half a second without reversing its charge. I have to judge Vornan against that."

"All right. And the man of A.D. 999 also knew that it

146

was impossible to fly to Mars. We can't venture to say what's possible a thousand years on and what isn't. And it happens that we've acquired some new evidence today."

"Which is?"

Kralick said, "Vornan consented to undergo the standard medical examination in there. The computer got a blood sample from him and a lot of other stuff, and relayed it all to us out here, and Aster's been going over it. She says he's got blood of a type she's never seen before, and that it's full of weird antibodies unknown to modern science—and that there are fifty other physical anomalies in Vornan's medical checkout. The computer also picked up traces of unusual electrical activity in his nervous system, the gimmick that he uses to shock people he doesn't like. He's built like an electric eel. I don't think he comes from this century at all, Leo. And I can't tell you how much it costs me to say a thing like that."

From the back seat Aster said in her lovely flutelike voice, "It seems strange that we should be doing fundamental research by sending him into a whorehouse, doesn't it, Leo? But these findings are very odd. Would you like to see the tapes?"

"I wouldn't be able to interpret them, thanks."

Kralick swiveled around. "Vornan's finished with Number Four. He's requesting a fifth."

"Can you do me a favor? There's a girl in there named Esther, a slim pretty little redhead. I'd like you to arrange things with your friend the computer, Sandy. See to it that Esther is his next sweetheart."

Kralick arranged it. Vornan had requested a tall, curvy brunette for his next romance, but the computer slipped Esther in on him instead, and he accepted the substitution, I suppose, as a forgivable defect in our medieval computer technology. I asked to watch the video pickup, and Kralick switched it on. There was Esther, wide-eyed, timid, her professional poise ragged as she found herself in the presence of the man of her dreams. Vornan spoke to her elegantly, soothing her, calming her. She removed her smock and they moved toward the bed, and I had Kralick cut off the video.

Vornan was with her a long while. His insatiable virility seemed to underline his alien origin. I sat brooding, looking into nowhere, trying to let myself accept the data Kralick had collected today. My mind refused to make the jump. I could not believe, even now, that Vornan-19 was genuine, despite the chill I had felt in Vornan's presence and all the rest.

"He's had enough," Kralick said finally. "He's coming out. Aster, clean up all the equipment, fast."

While Aster concealed the monitoring pickups, Kralick sprinted from the car, got Vornan, and led him swiftly across the plaza. In the brutal winter weather there were no disciples about to throw themselves before him, nor any rampaging Apocalyptists, so for once we were able to make a clean, quick exit.

Vornan was beaming. "Your sexual customs are fascinating," he said, as we drove away. "Fascinating! So wonderfully primitive! So full of vigor and mystery!" He clapped his hands in delight. I felt the odd chill again creeping through my limbs, and it had nothing to do with the weather outside the car. I hope Esther is happy now, I thought. She'll have something to tell her grandchildren. It was the least I could have done for her.

## * ELEVEN *

WE DINED THAT evening at a very special restaurant in Chicago, a place whose distinction is that it serves meats almost impossible to obtain elsewhere: buffalo steak, filet of bear, moose, elk, such birds as pheasant, partridge, grouse. Vornan had heard about it somehow and wanted to sample its mysterious delights. It was the first time we had gone to a public restaurant with him, a point that troubled us; already an ominous tendency was developing for uncontrollable crowds to gather about him everywhere, and we feared what might happen in a restaurant. Kralick had asked the restaurant management to serve its specialties at our hotel, and the restaurant was willing—for a price. But Vornan would have none of that. He wished to dine out, and dine out we did.

Our escort of Government people took precautions. They were learning fast how to cope with Vornan's unpredictable ways. It turned out that the restaurant had both a side entrance and a private dining room upstairs, so we were able to sweep our guest into the place and past the regular diners without problems. Vornan seemed displeased to find himself in an isolated room, but we pretended that in our society it was the acme of luxury to eat away from the vulgar throng, and Vornan took the story for what it was worth.

Some of us did not know the nature of the restaurant. Heyman thumbed the menu cube, peered at it for a long moment, and delivered a thick Teutonic hiss. He was sizzling in wrath over the bill of fare. "Buffalo!" he cried. "Moose! These are rare animals! We are to eat valuable scientific specimens? Mr. Kralick, I protest! This is an outrage!"

Kralick had suffered much on this jaunt, and Heyman's testiness had been nearly as much of a bother to him as Vornan's flamboyance. He said, "I beg your pardon, Professor Heyman. Everything on the menu is approved by the Department of the Interior. You know, even the herds of rare animals need to be thinned occasionally, for the good of the species. And—"

"They could be sent to other conservation preserves," Heyman rumbled, "not slaughtered for their meat! My God, what will history say of us? We who live in the last century when wild animals are found on the earth, killing and eating the priceless few survivors of a time when—"

"You want the verdict of history?" Kolff asked. "There sits history, Heyman! Ask its opinion!" He waved a beefy hand at Vornan-19, in whose authenticity he was not a believer, and guffawed until the table shook.

Serenely Vornan said, "I find it quite delightful that you should be eating these animals. I await my chance to share in the pleasure of doing so."

"But it isn't right!" Heyman spluttered. "These creatures—do any of them exist in your time? Or are they all gone—all eaten?"

"I am not certain. The names are unfamiliar. This buffalo, for example: What is it?"

"A large bovine mammal covered with shaggy brown fur," said Aster Mikkelsen. "Related to the cow. Formerly found in herds of many thousands on the western prairies."

"Extinct," said Vornan. "We have some cows, but no relatives of cows. And moose?"

"A large-horned animal of the northern forests. That's a moose head mounted on the wall, the one with the huge antlers and the long, drooping snout," said Aster.

"Absolutely extinct. Bear? Grouse? Partridge?"

Aster described each. Vornan replied gleefully that no such animals were known to exist in his era. Heyman's face turned a mottled purple. I had not known he harbored conservationist leanings. He delivered a choppy sermon on the extinction of wildlife as a symbol of a decadent civilization, pointing out that it is not barbarians who eliminate species but rather the fastidious and cultured, who seek the amusements of the hunt and of the table, or who thrust the outposts of civilization into the nesting grounds of strange and obscure creatures. He spoke with passion and even some wisdom; it was the first time I had heard the obstreperous historian say anything of the faintest value to an intelligent person. Vornan watched him with keen interest as he spoke. Gradually a look of pleasure spread across our visitor's face, and I thought I knew why: Heyman was arguing that extinction of species comes with the spread of civilization, and Vornan, who privately regarded us as little more than savages, doubtless thought that line of reasoning extremely funny.

When Heyman finished, we were eyeing one another and our menu cubes in shamefaced fashion, but Vornan broke the spell. "Surely," he said, "you will not deny me the pleasure of cooperating in the great extinction that makes my own time so barren of wildlife? After all, the animals we are about to eat tonight are already dead, are they not? Let me take back to my era the sensation of having dined on buffalo and grouse and moose, please."

Of course there was no question of dining somewhere else that night. We would eat here feeling guilty or we would eat here without guilt. As Kralick had observed, the restaurant used only licensed meat obtained through Government channels, and so was not directly causing the disappearance of any endangered species. The meat it served came from rare animals, and the prices showed it, but it was idle to blame a place like this for the hardships of twentieth-century wildlife. Still, Heyman had a point: the animals *were* going. I had seen somewhere a prediction that in another century there would be no wild animals at all except those in protected preserves. If we could credit Vornan as a genuine ambassador from posterity, that prediction had come to pass.

We ordered. Heyman chose roast chicken; the rest of us dipped into the rarities. Vornan requested and succeeded in getting a kind of smorgasbord of house specialties: a miniature filet of buffalo, a strip of moose steak, breast of pheasant, and one or two of the other unusual items.

Kolff said, "What animals *do* you have in your—ah— epoch?"

"Dogs. Cats. Cows. Mice." Vornan hesitated. "And several others."

"Nothing but domestic creatures?" asked Heyman, aghast.

"No," said Vornan, and propelled a juicy slab of meat to his mouth. He smiled pleasantly. "Delicious! What a loss we have suffered!"

"You see?" Heyman cried. "If only people had——"

"Of course," said Vornan sweetly, "we have many interesting foods of our own. I must admit there's a pleasure in putting a bit of meat from a living creature into one's mouth, but it's a pleasure that only the very few might enjoy. Most of us are rather fastidious. It takes a strong stomach to be a time traveler."

"Because we are filthy, depraved, hideous barbarians?" Heyman asked loudly. "Is that your opinion of us?"

Not at all discomfited, Vornan replied, "Your way of life is quite different from my own. Obviously. Why else would I have taken the trouble to come here?"

"Yet one way of life is not inherently superior or inferior to the other," Helen McIlwain put in, looking up fiercely from a huge slab of what I recall as elk steak. "Life may be more comfortable in one era than in another, it may be healthier, it may be more tranquil, but we may not use the terms *superior* or *inferior*. From the viewpoint of cultural relativism——"

"Do you know," said Vornan, "that in my time such a thing as a restaurant is unknown? To eat food in public, among strangers—we find it inelegant. In the Centrality, you know, one comes in contact with strangers quite often. This is not true in the outlying regions. One is never hostile to a stranger, but one would not eat in his presence, unless one is planning to establish sexual intimacy. Customarily we reserve eating for intimate companions alone." He chuckled. "It's quite wicked of me to want to visit a restaurant. I regard you all as intimate companions, you must realize——" His hand swept the whole table, as though he would be willing to go to bed even with Lloyd Kolff if Kolff were available. "But I hope that you will

152

grant me the pleasure of dining in public one of these days. Perhaps you were trying to spare my sensibilities by arranging for us to eat in this private room. But I ask you to let me indulge my shamelessness a bit the next time."

"Wonderful," Helen McIlwain said, mainly to herself. "A taboo on public eating! Vornan, if you'd only give us more insight into your own era. We're so eager to know anything you tell us!"

"Yes," Heyman said. "This period known as the Time of Sweeping, for instance—"

"—some information on biological research in—"

"—problems of mental therapy. The major psychoses, for example, are of great concern to —"

"—a chance to confer with you on linguistic evolution in—"

"—time-reversal phenomena. And also some information on the energy systems that—" It was my own voice, weaving through the thickened texture of our table talk. Naturally Vornan replied to none of us, since we were all babbling at once. When we realized what we were doing, we fell into embarrassed silence, awkwardly letting bits of words tumble over the brink of our discomfort to shatter in the abyss of self-consciousness. For an instant, there, our frustrations had broken through. In our days and nights of merry-go-round with Vornan-19, he had been infuriatingly elliptical about his own alleged era, dropping a hint here, a clue there, never delivering anything approaching a formal discourse on the shape of that future society from which he claimed to be an emissary. Each of us overflowed with unanswered questions.

They were not answered that night. That night we dined on the delicacies of a waning era, breast of phoenix and *entrecôte* of unicorn, and listened closely as Vornan, more conversationally inclined than usual, dropped occasional nuggets about the feeding habits of the thirtieth century. We were grateful for what we could learn. Even Heyman grew so involved in the situation that he ceased to

153

bewail the fate of the rarities that had graced our plates.

When the time came to leave the restaurant, we found ourselves in an unhappily familiar kind of crisis. Word had circulated that the celebrated man from the future was here, and a crowd had gathered. Kralick had to order guards armed with neural whips to clear a path through the restaurant, and for a while it looked as though the whips might have to be used. At least a hundred diners left their tables and shuffled toward us as we came down from the private room. They were eager to see, to touch, to experience Vornan-19 at close range. I eyed their faces in dismay and alarm. Some had the scowls of skeptics, some the glassy remoteness of the idle curiosity-seeker; but on many was that eerie look of reverence that we had seen so often in the past week. It was more than mere awe. It was an acknowledgment of an inner messianic hunger. These people wanted to drop on their knees before Vornan. They knew nothing of him but what they had seen on their screens, and yet they were drawn to him and looked toward him to fill some void in their own lives. What was he offering? Charm, good looks, a magnetic smile, an attractive voice? Yes, and alienness, for in word and deed he was stamped with strangeness. I could almost feel that pull myself. I had been too close to Vornan to worship him; I had seen his colossal esurience, his imperial self-indulgence, his gargantuan appetite for sensual pleasure of all sorts, and once one has seen a messiah coveting food and impaling legions of willing women, it is hard to feel truly reverent toward him. Nevertheless, I sensed his power. It had begun to transform my own evaluation of him. I had started as a skeptic, hostile and almost belligerent about it; that mood had softened, until I had virtually ceased to add the inevitable qualifier, "*if* he is genuine," to everything I thought about Vornan-19. It was not merely the evidence of the blood sample that swayed me, but every aspect of Vornan's conduct. I found

154

it now harder to believe he might be a fraud than that he had actually come to us out of time, and this of course left me in an untenable position vis-à-vis my own scientific specialty. I was forced to embrace a conclusion that I still regarded as physically impossible: doublethink in the Orwellian sense. That I could be trapped like this was a tribute to Vornan's power; and I believed I understood something of what these people desired as they pressed close, straining to lay hands on the visitor as he passed before them.

Somehow we got out of the restaurant without any unpleasant incident. The weather was so frigid that there were only a few stragglers in the street. We sped past them and into the waiting cars. Blank-faced chauffeurs convoyed us to our hotel. Here, as in New York, we had a string of connected rooms in the most secluded part of the building. Vornan excused himself at once when we came to our floor. He had been sleeping with Helen McIlwain for the past few nights, but it seemed that our trip to the brothel had left him temporarily without interest in women, not too surprisingly. He disappeared into his room. The guards sealed it at once. Kralick, looking drained and pale, went off to file his nightly report to Washington. The rest of us assembled in one of the suites to unwind a bit before going to bed.

The committee of six had been together long enough now for a variety of patterns to manifest themselves. We were still divided on the question of Vornan's authenticity, but not as sharply as before. Kolff, an original skeptic, was still positive of Vornan's phoniness, though he admired Vornan's technique as a confidence man. Heyman, who had also come out against Vornan at the outset, was not so sure now; it clearly went against his nature to say so, but he was wavering in Vornan's direction, mainly on the basis of a few tantalizing hints Vornan had dropped on the course of future history. Helen McIlwain continued to accept Vornan as authentic. Morton Fields, on the other hand, was growing disgruntled and backing away from his original positive appraisal. I think he was jealous of Vornan's sexual prowess and was trying to get revenge by disavowing his legitimacy.

The original neutral, Aster, had chosen to wait until more evidence was in. Evidence had come in. Aster now was wholly of the opinion that Vornan came from further along the human evolutionary track, and she had biochemical proof that satisfied her of that. As I have noted, I too had been swayed toward Vornan, though purely on emotional grounds; scientifically he remained an impossibility for me. Thus we now had two True Believers, two vacillating ex-skeptics inclined to take Vornan's story at face value, one former believer moving to the opposite pole, and one remaining diehard apostate. Certainly the movement had been to Vornan's benefit. He was winning us.

So far as the emotional crosscurrents within our group went, they were strong and violent. We agreed on just one thing: that we were all heartily sick of F. Richard Heyman. The very sight of the historian's coarse reddish beard had become odious to me. We were weary of his pontificating, his dogmatism, and his habit of treating the rest of us as not-too-bright undergraduates. Morton Fields, too, was outlasting his welcome in our midst. Behind his ascetic façade he had revealed himself as a mere lecher, which I did not really mind, and as a conspicuously unsuccessful one, which I found objectionable. He had lusted after Helen and had been turned away; he had lusted after Aster and had failed utterly. Since Helen practiced a kind of professional nymphomania, operating under the assumption that a lady anthropologist had a duty to study *all* of mankind at the closest possible range, her rejection of Fields was the most cutting kind of rebuff. Before our tour was a week old, Helen had bedded down with all of us at least once, except for Sandy Kralick, who was too much in awe of her to think of her in sexual terms, and for poor Fields. Small wonder that his soul was souring. I suppose Helen had some private scholarly disagreement with him, dating back prior to the Vornan assignment, that motivated her unsubtle psychological castration of him. Fields' next move had been toward Aster; but Aster was as unworldly as an angel, and blithely fended him off without seeming even to comprehend what he wanted from her. (Even though Aster had taken that shower with Vornan, none of us could believe that anything carnal had taken place between them. Aster's crystalline innocence seemed proof even against Vornan's irresistible masculine charm, we felt.)

Thus Fields had the sexual problems of a pimply adolescent, and as you might imagine, those problems erupted in many ways during ordinary social discussions. He expressed his frustrations by erecting opaque façades of terminology behind which he glowered and raged and spat. This drew the disapproval of Lloyd Kolff, who in his Falstaffian heartiness could see Fields only as something to be deplored; when Fields got annoying enough, Kolff tended to slap him down with a jovial growl that only made matters worse. With Kolff I had no quarrel; he swilled his way pleasantly from night to night and made a cheerfully ursine companion on what might otherwise have been a more dreary assignment. I was grateful, too, for Helen McIlwain's company, and not only in bed. Monomaniac though she might be on the subject of cultural relativism, she was lively, well-informed, and enormously entertaining; she could always be depended on to puncture some immense procedural debate with a few choice words on the amputation of the clitoris among North African tribeswomen or on ceremonial scarification in New Guinea puberty rites. As for Aster the unfathomable, Aster the impenetrable, Aster the inscrutable, I could not honestly say that I liked her, but I found her an agreeable quasi-feminine enigma. It troubled me that

157

I had seen her bareness via that spy pickup; enigmas should remain total enigmas, and now that I had looked upon Aster bare, I felt that her mystery had in part been breached. She seemed deliciously chaste, a Diana of biochemistry, magically sustained at the age of sixteen forever. In our frequent debates over ways and means of dealing with Vornan, Aster seldom spoke, but what she did have to say was invariably reasonable and just.

Our traveling circus moved along, forging westward from Chicago as January ebbed. Vornan was as indefatigable a sightseer as he was a lover. We took him to factories, power plants, museums, highway interchanges, weather-control stations, transportation monitor posts, fancy restaurants, and a good deal more, some of it at official request, some of it at Vornan's insistence. He managed to stir up a good deal of trouble for us nearly everywhere. Perhaps by way of establishing that he was beyond "medieval" morality, he abused the hospitality of his hosts in a variety of delicately outrageous ways: seducing victims of all available sexes, flagrantly insulting sacred cows, and indicating unmistakably that he regarded the gadgety, formidably scientific world in which we lived as quaintly primitive. I found his thumb-to-nose insolence cheerfully refreshing; he fascinated as well as repelled. But others, both in and out of our group, did not think so. Nevertheless, the very outrageousness of his behavior seemed to guarantee the authenticity of his claim, and there were surprisingly few protests at his antics. He was immune, the guest of the world, the wanderer out of time; and the world, though baffled and uncertain, received him cordially.

We did our best to head off calamities. We learned how to shield Vornan from pompous, easily vulnerable individuals who would surely call forth some mischief from him. We had seen him stare in playful awe at the immense bosom of a matronly patron of the arts who was guiding us through the splendid museum in Cleveland; he regarded the deep valley between the two upthrust white peaks with such keen concentration that we should have anticipated trouble, but we failed to intervene when Vornan abruptly reached out a finger, gaily plunged it into that cosmic cleavage, and produced the mildest of his puzzling repertoire of electric shocks. After that we kept busty middle-aged women in low-cut dresses away from him. We learned to shunt him away from other such targets for the puncturing of vanity, and if we had one success for each dozen failures, that was sufficient.

Where we did not do so well was in extracting information from him about the epoch from which he said he came or about anything that had taken place between then and now. He let us have a morsel occasionally, such as his vague reference to an undescribed political upheaval that he referred to as the Time of Sweeping. He mentioned visitors from other stars, and talked a bit about the political structure of the ambiguous national entity he called the Centrality, but in essence he told us nothing. There was no substance to his words; he gave us only sketchy outlines.

Each of us had ample opportunity to question him. He submitted in obvious boredom to our interrogations, but slid away from any real grilling. I spoke to him for several hours one afternoon in St. Louis, trying to pump him on the subjects of most immediate interest to me. I drew blanks.

"Won't you tell me a little about how you reached our time, Vornan? The actual transport mechanism?"

"You want to know about my time machine?"

"Yes. Yes. Your time machine."

"It's not really a machine, Leo. That is, you mustn't think of it as having levers and dials and such."

"Will you describe it for me?"

He shrugged. "That isn't easy. It's—well, more of an abstraction than anything else. I didn't see much of it. You step into a room, and a field begins to operate, and—" His voice trailed off. "I'm sorry. I'm not a scientist. I just saw the room, really."

"Others operated the machine?"

"Yes, yes, of course. I was only the passenger."

"And the force that moves you through time—"

"Honestly, love, I can't imagine what it's like."

"Neither can I, Vornan. That's the whole trouble. Everything I know about physics shrieks out that you can't send a living man back through time."

"But I'm here, Leo. I'm the proof."

"Assuming that you ever traveled through time."

He looked crestfallen. His hand caught mine; his fingers were cool and oddly smooth. "Leo," he said, wounded, "are you expressing suspicion?"

"I'm simply trying to find out how your time machine works."

"I'd tell you if I knew. Believe me, Leo. I have nothing but the warmest feelings for you personally, and for all the earnest, struggling, sincere individuals I've found here in your time. But I just don't know. Look, if you got into your car and drove back into the year 800, and someone asked you to explain how that car works, would you be able to do it?"

"I'd be able to explain some fundamental principles. I couldn't build an automobile myself, Vornan, but I know what makes it move. You aren't even telling me that."

"It's infinitely more complex."

"Perhaps I could *see* the machine."

"Oh, no," said Vornan lightly. "It's a thousand years up the line. It tossed me here, and it will bring me back when I choose to leave, but the machine itself, which I tell you is not exactly a machine, stays up there."

"How," I asked, "will you give the signal to be taken back?"

He pretended not to have heard. Instead he began questioning me about my university responsibilities; his trick was standard, to meet an awkward question with his own line of interrogation. I could not wring a drop of information from him. I left the session with my basic skepticism reborn. He could not tell me about the mechanics of travel in time because he had not traveled in time. Q.E.D.: phony. He was just as evasive on the subject of energy conversion. He would not tell me when it had come into use, how it worked, who was credited with its invention.

The others, though, occasionally had better luck with Vornan. Most notably Lloyd Kolff, who, probably because he had voiced doubts of Vornan's genuineness to Vornan himself, was treated to a remarkable disquisition. Kolff had not troubled much to interrogate Vornan in the early weeks of our tour, possibly because he regarded Vornan as a synthetic artifact, possibly because he was too lazy to bother. The old philologist had revealed an awesomely broad streak of indolence; he was quite clearly coasting on professional laurels earned twenty or thirty years before, and now preferred to spend his time wenching and feasting and accepting the sincere homage of younger men in his discipline. I had discovered that old Lloyd had not published a meaningful paper since 1980. It began to seem as if he regarded our current assignment as a mere joyride, a relaxing way to pass a winter that might otherwise have to be endured in the grayness of Morningside Heights. But in Denver one snowbound February night Kolff finally decided to tackle Vornan from the linguistic angle. I don't know why.

They were closeted a long time. Through the thin walls of the hotel we could hear Kolff's booming voice chanting rhythmically in a language none of us understood: reciting Sanskrit erotic verse for Vornan, maybe. Then he translated, and we could catch an occasional salacious word, even a wanton line or two about the pleasures of love. We lost interest after a while; we had heard Kolff's recitals before. When I bothered to eavesdrop again, I caught Vornan's light laughter cutting like a silver scalpel through

Kolff's earthy boomings, and then I dimly detected Vornan speaking in an unknown tongue. Matters seemed serious in there. Kolff halted him, asked a question, recited something of his own, and Vornan spoke again. At that point Kralick came into our room to give us copies of the morning's itinerary—we were taking Vornan to a gold mine, no less—and we ceased to pay attention to Kolff's interrogation.

An hour later Kolff came into the room where the rest of us sat. He looked flushed and shaken. He tugged heavily at a meaty earlobe, clutched the rolls of flesh on the back of his neck, cracked his knuckles with a sound like that of ricocheting bullets. "Damn," he muttered. "By everlasting eternal damn!" Striding across the room, he stood for a while at the window, peering out at snow-capped skyscrapers, and then he said, "Is there what to drink?"

"Rum, Bourbon, Scotch," Helen said. "Help yourself."

Kolff barreled over to the table where the half-empty bottles stood, picked up the Bourbon, and poured himself a slug that would paralyze a hippo. He downed it straight, in three or four greedy gulps, and let the glass drop to the spongy floor. He stood with feet firmly planted, worrying his earlobe. I heard him cursing in what might have been Middle English.

At length Aster said, "Did you learn anything from him?"

"Yah. Very much." Kolff sank into an armchair and switched the vibrator on. "I learned from him that he is no phony!"

Heyman gasped. Helen looked astonished, and I had never seen her poise shaken before. Fields blurted, "What the hell do you mean, Lloyd?"

"He talked to me . . . in his own language," Kolff said thickly. "For half an hour. I have taped it all. I'll give it to the computer tomorrow for analysis. But I can tell it was

162

not faked. Only a genius of linguistics could have invented a language like that, and he would not have done it so well." Kolff smacked his forehead. "My God! My God! A man out of time! How can it be?"

"You understood him?" Heyman asked.

"Give me more to drink," said Kolff. He accepted the Bourbon bottle from Aster and put it to his lips. He scratched his hairy belly. He passed his hand before his eyes as though trying to sweep away cobwebs. Eventually he said, "No, I did not understand him. I detected only patterns. He speaks the child of English ... but it is an English as far from our time as the language of the Anglo-Saxon Chronicle. It is full of Asian roots. Bits of Mandarin, bits of Bengali, bits of Japanese. There is Arabic in it, I am sure. And Malay. It is a chop suey of language." Kolff belched. "You know, our English, it is already a big stew. It has Danish, Norman French, Saxon, a mess of things, two streams, a Latin and a Teutonic. So we have duplicate words, we have *preface* and *foreword,* we have *perceive* and *know, power* and *might.* Both streams, though, they flow from the same source, the old Indo-European *mutter*-tongue. Already in Vornan's time they have changed that. They have taken in words from other ancestral groups. Stirred everything all around. Such a language! You can say anything in a language like that. Anything! But the roots only are there. The words are polished like pebbles in a stream, all roughness smoothed away, the inflections gone. He makes ten sounds and he conveys twenty sentences. The grammar—it would take me fifty years more to *find* the grammar. And five hundred to understand it. The withering away of grammar—a bouillabaisse of sounds, a pot-au-feu of language— incredible, incredible! There has been another vowel shift, far more radical than the last one. He speaks ... like poetry. Dream poetry no one can understand. I caught bits, only pieces ..." Kolff fell silent. He massaged the huge bowl of his belly. I had never seen him serious before. It was a profoundly moving moment.

Fields shattered it. "Lloyd, how can you be sure you aren't imagining all this? A language you can't understand, how can you interpret it? If you can't detect a grammar, how do you know it isn't just gibberish he was drooling?"

"You are a fool," Kolff replied easily. "You should take your head and have the poison pumped out of it. But then your skull would collapse."

Fields sputtered. Heyman stood up and walked back and forth in quick penguinlike strides; he seemed to be going through a new internal crisis. I felt great uneasiness myself. If Kolff had been converted, what hope remained that Vornan might not be what he claimed to be? The evidence was mounting. Perhaps all this was a boozy figment of Kolff's decaying brain. Perhaps Aster had misread the data of Vornan's medical examination. Perhaps. Perhaps. God help me, I did not *want* to believe Vornan was real, for where would that leave my own scientific accomplishments, and it pained me to know that I was violating that fuzzy abstraction, the code of science, by setting up an *a priori* structure for my own emotional convenience. Like it or not, that structure was toppling. Maybe. How long, I wondered, would I try to prop it up? When would I accept, as Aster had accepted, as Kolff had now accepted? When Vornan made a trip in time before my eyes?

Helen said sweetly, "Why don't you play us the tape, Lloyd?"

"Yes. Yes. The tape." He produced a small recording cube, and fumbling a bit, managed to press it into the pickup slot of a playback unit. He thumbed for sonic and suddenly there flowed through the room a stream of soft, eroded sounds. I strained to hear. Vornan spoke liltingly, playfully, artfully, varying pitch and timbre, so that his speech was close to song, and now and then a tantalizing

164

fragment of a comprehensible word seemed to whirl past my ears. But I understood nothing. Kolff made steeples of his thick fingers, nodded and smiled, waved his shoe at some particularly critical moment, murmured now and then, "Yes? You see? You *see?*" but I saw not, neither did I hear; it was pure sound, now pearly, now azure, now deep turquoise, all of it mysterious, none of it intelligible. The cube whirled to its finish, and when it was over we sat silently, as if the melody of Vornan's words still lingered, and I knew that nothing had been proven, not to me, though Lloyd might choose to accept these sounds as the child of English. Solemnly Kolff rose and pocketed the cube. He turned to Helen McIlwain, whose features were transfigured as though she had attended some incredibly sacred rite. "Come," he said, and touched her bony wrist. "It is the time for sleeping, and not a night for sleeping alone. Come." They went out together. I still heard Vornan's voice, gravely declaiming some lengthy passage in a language centuries unborn, or possibly rattling off a skein of nonsense, and I felt lulled to dreaminess by the sound of the future or the sound of ingenious fraud.

* TWELVE *

OUR CARAVAN MOVED westward from snowy Denver to a sunny welcome in California, but I did not remain with the others. A great restlessness had come over me, an impatience to get away from Vornan and Heyman and Kolff and the rest at least for a little while. I had been on this tour for over a month, now, and it was telling on me. So I asked Kralick for permission to take a brief leave of absence; he granted it and I headed south into Arizona, to the desert home of Jack and Shirley Bryant, with the understanding that I would rejoin the group a week later in Los Angeles.

It had been early January when I had last seen Jack and Shirley; now it was mid-February, so hardly any time had really passed. Yet inwardly a great deal of time must have elapsed, for them and for me. I saw changes in them. Jack looked drawn and frayed, as though he had been sleeping poorly lately; his motions were nervous and jerky, and I was reminded of the old Jack, the pallid eastern boy who had come to my laboratory so many years ago. He had retrogressed. The calm of the desert had fled from him. Shirley too seemed to be under some kind of strain. The sheen of her golden hair was dulled, and her postures now were rigid ones; I saw trusses of taut muscles form again and again in her throat. Her response to tension was an overcompensating gaiety. She laughed too often and too loudly; her voice often rose unnaturally in pitch, becoming shrill, harsh, and vibrant. She seemed much older; if she had looked twenty-five in December instead of her proper thirty-odd, now she seemed at the brink of her forties. All this I noticed in the first few minutes of my arrival, when such alterations are the most conspicuous. But I said nothing of what I saw, and just as well, for the first words were Jack's:

"You look tired, Leo. This business must have taken a lot out of you."

And Shirley:

"Yes, poor Leo. All that silly traveling around. You need a good rest. Can't you contrive to stay here longer than a week?"

"Am I that much of a wreck?" I asked. "Is it so obvious?"

"A little Arizona sunshine will work wonders," Shirley said, and laughed in that dreadful new way of hers.

That first day we did little but soak up Arizona sunshine. We lay, the three of us, on their sun deck, and after these weeks of soggy eastern winter it was pure delight to feel the warmth on my bare skin. Tactful as always, neither of them brought up the subject of my recent activities that day; we sunned and dozed, chatted a little, and in the evening feasted on grilled steak and a fine bottle of Chambertin '88. As the chill of night swept down on the desert, we sprawled on the thick rug to listen to Mozart's dancing melodies, and all that I had done and seen in the last weeks sloughed away and became unreal to me.

In the morning I woke early, for my inner clock was confused by the crossing of time zones, and walked for a while in the desert. Jack was up when I returned. He sat at the edge of the dry wash, carving something from a bit of gnarled, greasy-looking wood. As I drew near, he blurted, "Leo, did you find out anything about—"

"No."

"—energy conversion.".

I shook my head. "I've tried, Jack. But there's no way to learn anything from Vornan that he doesn't want to tell you. And he won't give hard data on anything. He's devilish about answering questions."

"I'm in knots, Leo. The possibility that something I've devised will wreck society—"

"Drop it, will you? You've penetrated a frontier, Jack. Publish your work and accept your Nobel, and to hell with any misuse that posterity hands out. You've done pure research. Why crucify yourself over possible applications?"

"The men who developed the bomb must have said the same things," Jack murmured.

"Have any bombs been dropping lately? Meanwhile your house runs on a pocket reactor. You might be lighting wood fires if those old boys hadn't found out about nuclear fission."

"But their souls—their *souls*—"

I lost patience. "We revere their damned souls! They were scientists; they did their best, and they got somewhere. And changed the world, sure, but they had to. There was a war then, you know? Civilization was endangered. They invented something that caused a lot of trouble, yeah, but it did a lot of good, too. You haven't even invented anything. Equations. Basic principles. And here you sit pitying yourself because you think you've betrayed mankind! All you've done has been to use your *brain,* Jack, and if that's a betrayal of mankind in your philosophy, then you'd better——"

"All right, Leo," he said quietly. "I plead guilty to a charge of self-pity and voluntarily solicited martyrdom. Sentence me to death and then let's change the subject. What's your considered opinion of this man Vornan? Real? Fake? You've seen him at close range."

"I don't know."

"Good old Leo," he said savagely. "Always incisive! Always ready with the firm answer!"

"It isn't that simple, Jack. Have you been watching Vornan on the screens?"

"Yes."

"Then you know he's complex. A tricky bastard, the trickiest I've ever seen."

"But don't you have some intuitive feel, Leo, some immediate response, a yes or a no, true or false?"

"I have," I said.

"Keeping it a secret?"

I moistened my lips and scuffed at the sandy ground. "What I intuit is that Vornan-19 is what he says he is."

"A man from 2999?"

"A traveler out of the future," I said.

Behind me, Shirley laughed in a sharp crescendo. "That's wonderful, Leo! You've finally learned how to embrace the irrational!"

She had come up behind us, nude, a goddess of the morning, heart-stoppingly beautiful, her hair like a flag in the breeze. But her eyes were too brilliant, shining with that new fixed glitter.

"The irrational is a thorny mistress," I said. "I'm not happy to share my bed with her."

168

"Why do you think he's real?" Jack pressed.

I told him about the blood sample and about Lloyd Kolff's experience with Vornan's spoken language. I added some purely intuitive impressions I had gathered. Shirley seemed delighted, Jack pensive. He said finally, "You don't know a thing about the scientific background of his supposed means of time transport?"

"Zero. He isn't saying."

"Small wonder. He wouldn't want 2999 invaded by a bunch of hairy barbarians who've whipped up a time machine out of his description."

"Maybe that's it—a security matter," I said.

Jack closed his eyes. He rocked back and forth on his haunches. "If he's real, then the energy thing is real, and the possibility still exists that—"

"Cut it, Jack," I said fiercely. "Snap out!"

With an effort he interrupted his lamentations. Shirley tugged him to his feet. I said, "What's for breakfast?"

"What about brook trout, straight out of the freeze?"

"Good enough." I slapped her amiably on her firm rump to send her scampering into the house. Jack and I strolled after her. He was calmer now.

"I'd like to sit down myself and talk with this Vornan," Jack said. "Ten minutes, maybe. Could you arrange that?"

"I doubt it. Very few private interviews are being granted. The Government's keeping him on a tight rein—or trying to. And I'm afraid if you aren't a bishop or a holding-company president or a famous poet, you won't stand a chance. But it doesn't matter, Jack. He won't tell you what you want to know. I'm sure of it."

"Still, I'd like to try to get it out of him. Keep it in mind."

I promised that I would, but I saw little chance of it. We managed to get into less problematical topics at breakfast. Afterward, Jack disappeared to finish something he was writing, and Shirley and I went to the sun deck. She

169

was worried about Jack, she said; he was so totally obsessed with what the future might think of him. She did not know how to get him unwound. "It's nothing new, you understand. It's been going on ever since I've known him, since he was with you at the University. But since Vornan showed up, it's become fifty times as bad. He genuinely thinks now that his manuscript is going to reshuffle all of future history. He said last week that he wished the Apocalyptists were right: He wants the world to be blown up next January. He's sick, Leo."

"I see. But it's a sickness that he won't try to cure."

In a low voice, leaning close to me so that I could have put my lips to hers, she said, "Were you holding anything back from him? Tell me the truth. What did Vornan say about energy?"

"Nothing. I swear."

"And do you really believe he's—"

"Most of the time. I'm not convinced. You know, I've got scientific reservations."

"Aside from them?"

"I believe," I said.

We were silent. I let my eyes roam down the ridge of her spine to the blossoming of her hips. Beads of perspiration glittered on her upturned tawny buttocks. Her toes were outstretched and pressed close in a little gesture of tension.

She said, "Jack wants to meet Vornan."

"I know."

"So do I. Let me confess it, Leo. I'm hungry for him."

"Most women are."

"I've never been unfaithful to Jack. But I would be, with Vornan. I'd tell Jack first, of course. But I'm drawn to him. Just seeing him on television, I want to touch him, to have him against me, in me. Am I shocking you, Leo?"

"Don't be silly."

"The comforting thing is that I know I'll never get the

170

chance. There must be a million women ahead of me in line. Have you noticed, Leo, the hysteria that's building up over this man? It's almost a cult. It's killing off Apocalyptism practically overnight. Last fall everyone thought the world was about to end, and now everyone thinks we're going to fill up with tourists from the future. I watch the faces of the people on the screens, the ones who follow Vornan around, cheering, kneeling. He's like a messiah. Does any of this sound sensible to you?"

"All of it does. I'm not blind, Shirley. I've seen it up close."

"It frightens me."

"Me also."

"And when you say you think he's real—you, hardheaded old Leo Garfield—that's even more scary." Shirley gave me the shrill giggle again. "Living out here on the edge of nowhere, I sometimes think the whole world's crazy except Jack and me."

"And lately you've had your doubts about Jack."

"Well, yes." Her hand covered mine. "Why should people be responding to Vornan like this?"

"Because there's never been anyone like him before."

"He's not the first charismatic figure to come along."

"He's the first one peddling this particular tale," I said. "And the first in the era of modern communications. The whole world can see him in three dimensions and natural color all the time. He gets to them. His eyes—his smile—the man's got a power, Shirley. You feel it through the screen. I feel it close up."

"What will happen, eventually?"

"Eventually he'll go back to 2999," I said lightly, "and write a best-seller about his primitive ancestors."

Shirley laughed hollowly and we let the conversation trickle to nothingness. Her words troubled me. Not that I was surprised to find she was drawn to Vornan, for she was far from alone in that; what upset me was her willingness to admit it to me. I resented becoming the confidant of her passions. A woman admits her illicit desires to a harem eunuch, perhaps, or to another woman, but not to a man whom she realizes has suppressed designs of his own on her. Surely she knew that but for my respect for their marriage, I would have reached out for her long ago and would have been received willingly. So why tell me such things, knowing that they must hurt me? Did she think I would use my supposed influence to lure Vornan into her bed? That out of love for her I would play the panderer?

We lazed away the day. Toward late afternoon Jack came to me and said, "Maybe you aren't interested, but Vornan's on the screen. He's being interviewed in San Diego by a panel of theologians and philosophers and stuff. Do you want to watch?"

Not really, I thought. I had come here to escape from Vornan, and somehow no moment passed without mention of him. But I failed to answer, and Shirley said yes. Jack activated the screen nearest us, and there was Vornan, big as life, radiating charm in three dimensions. The camera gave us a view of the panel: five distinguished experts in eschatology, some of whom I recognized. I spied the long nose and drooping brows of Milton Clayhorn, one of the pundits of our San Diego campus, the man who, they say, has been devoting his career to getting Christ out of Christianity. I saw the blunt features and time-freckled skin of Dr. Naomi Gersten, behind whose hooded eyes lurked six thousand years of Semitic anguish. The other three seemed familiar; I suspected they had been neatly chosen to represent each creed. We had come in late in the discussion, but as it turned out, just in time for the detonation of Vornan's megaton bomb.

"—no organized religious movement in your era whatever?" Clayhorn was saying. "A withering away of the church, so to speak?"

Vornan nodded curtly.

"But the religious idea itself," Clayhorn vociferated.

172

"That can't be gone! There are certain eternal verities! Man must establish a relationship delineating the boundaries of the universe and the boundaries of his own soul. He——"

"Perhaps," Dr. Gersten said to Vornan in her small cracked voice, "you could tell us if you understand at all what we mean by religion, eh?"

"Certainly. A statement of human dependence on a more powerful external force," said Vornan, looking pleased with himself.

A furry-voiced moderator said, "I think that's an excellent formulation, don't you, Monsignor?"

I recognized now the long-chinned man in the turned-about collar: Meehan, a television priest, a figure of fair charisma himself, who spent a moment summoning resonance and said, "Yes, that's excellently put, in its fashion. It's refreshing to know that our guest comprehends the concept of religion, even if"——the Monsignor showed a momentary crack in his façade——"as he says, our present-day religions have ceased to play a meaningful role in the life of his times. I venture to say that perhaps Mr. Vornan is underestimating the strength of religion in his day, and possibly is, as so many individuals do today, projecting his personal lack of belief onto society as a whole. Might I have a comment on that?"

Vornan smiled. Something ominous sparkled in his eyes. I felt the clutch of fear. Using the eyes and the lips at once! He was cranking up the catapult for a blow that would smash the enemy walls. The panel members saw it too. Clayhorn cringed. Dr. Gersten seemed to vanish like a wary tortoise into the folds of her own neck. The famed Monsignor braced himself as if for the blade of the guillotine.

Vornan said mildly, "Shall I tell you what we have learned of man's relationship to the universe? We have discovered, you see, the manner by which life came into being on the earth, and our knowledge of the Creation has had its effect on our religious beliefs. I am not an archaeologist, please understand, and I can give no details beyond what I say here. But this is what we now know: Once, in the distant past, our planet was wholly lifeless. There was a sea covering nearly everything, with rocks here and there, and both sea and land were lacking even in the merest microbe. Then our planet was visited by explorers from another star. They did not land. They merely orbited our world and saw that it was without life, and thus of no interest to them. They paused only long enough to jettison certain garbage that had accumulated aboard their ship, and then journeyed elsewhere, while the garbage they had dumped descended through the atmosphere of the earth and found its way into the sea, introducing certain factors that created a chemical disturbance which set in motion the beginning of the process that resulted in the phenomenon known as"—the panel was in turmoil; the camera swung in mercilessly to reveal the grimaces, the scowls, the wild eyes, the stony jaws, the gaping lips—"life on earth."

## * THIRTEEN *

AT THE END of my week of reprieve I kissed Shirley good-bye, told Jack to go easy on himself, and sped off to Tucson to be podded to Los Angeles. I arrived there only hours after the rest of the team had come up the coast from San Diego. The impact of that interview with Vornan still reverberated through the land. Perhaps never before in human history had a major theological dogma been enunciated over television on a global hookup; certainly this one spread through the world even as the contamination of the primordial garbage had infected the sterile seas. Quietly, amiably, with great delicacy and restraint, Vornan had undermined the religious faith of four billion human beings. One had to admire his skill, surely.

Jack and Shirley and I had watched the unfolding of the reaction in cool fascination. Vornan had presented his belief as received fact, the result of careful investigation and of corroborative detail obtained from beings who had visited the world of his time. As usual, he offered no substructure of data, merely the bald, elliptical statement. But anyone who had swallowed the news that a man had come to us from 2999 would not have much difficulty swallowing that man's story of the Creation; all it took was flexible jaws. WORLD STARTED FROM GARBAGE, said the tapes the next day, and swiftly the concept moved into the public domain.

The Apocalyptists, who had been quiescent for a few weeks, came back to life. They led vigorous protest rallies through the cities of the world. The screen showed us their fixed faces, their gleaming eyes, their defiant banners. I learned something I had not suspected previously about this mushroom cult: it was a patchwork of disparate components, made up of the alienated, the rootless, the youthfully rebellious, and—amazingly—the devout. In the midst of the orgies of the Apocalyptists, among all the scatological rites and exhibitionist fervor, were the shabby, slab-jawed Fundamentalists, the quintessence of American Gothic, deeply persuaded that the world would indeed shortly come to its finish. We saw these people now for the first time dominant in the Apocalyptist riots. They did not commit bestialities themselves, but they paraded among the fornicators, benevolently accepting the shamelessness as a sign of the approaching end. To these people Vornan was Antichrist and his creation-from-garbage dogma was thunderous blasphemy.

To others it was The Word. The inchoate band of Vornan-worshipers that had been taking form in every city now had not only a prophet but a creed. We are trash and the descendants of trash, and we must put aside all mystical self-exaltation and accept reality, these people said. There is no God, and 'Vornan is His prophet! When I came to Los Angeles I found both these conflicting groups in full panoply, and Vornan under heavy guard. Only with great difficulty did I manage to get back to our group. They had to fly me in by helicopter, putting me down on the roof of a hotel in downtown Los Angeles, while far below me the Apocalyptists capered and the worshipers of Vornan sought to abase themselves before their idol. Kralick led me to the edge of the roof and had me look down. at the swirling, writhing mass in the streets.

"How long has this been going on?" I asked.

"Since nine this morning. We arrived at eleven. We could call in troops, but for the moment we'll just sit tight. The mob stretches from here to Pasadena, they say."

"That's impossible! We—"

"Look out there."

It was true. A ribbon of brightness wound through the streets, coiling past the sparkling towers of the city's reconstructed nucleus, weaving toward the distant stack of freeways and vanishing somewhere to the east. I could hear cries, shouts, gurgles. I did not want to look any longer. It was a siege.

Vornan was greatly amused at the forces he had unleashed. I found him holding court in the customary suite on the hotel's eighty-fifth floor; about him were Kolff, Heyman, Helen, and Aster, a few media people, and a great deal of equipment. Fields was not there. I learned later that he was sulking, having made another pass at Aster the night before in San Diego. Vornan was speaking about California weather, I think, when I came in. He rose at once and glided to me, seizing my elbows and locking his eyes to mine.

"Leo, old man! How we've missed you!"

I was taken off stride by his chummy approach. But I

managed to say, "I've been following your progress by screen, Vornan."

"You heard the San Diego interview?" Helen asked.

I nodded. Vornan seemed very pleased with himself. He waved vaguely toward the window and said, "There's a big mob out there. What do you think they want?"

"They're waiting for your next revelation," I told him.

"The gospel according to St. Vornan," Heyman muttered darkly.

From Kolff, later, I got confusing news. He had run Vornan's speech samples through the departmental computer at Columbia, with uncertain results. The computer was baffled by the structure of the language, and had sorted everything out into phonemes without coming to conclusions. Its analysis indicated the possibility that Kolff was right in thinking of the words as an evolved language, and also the possibility that Vornan had simply been mouthing noises at random, occasionally hitting on some combination of sounds that seemed to represent a futuristic version of a contemporary word. Kolff looked despondent. In his first flush of enthusiasm he had released his evaluation of Vornan's talk to the media, and that had helped to fan the global hysteria; but now he was not at all sure that he had made the correct interpretation. "If I am wrong," he said, "I have destroyed myself, Leo. I have lent all my prestige to nonsense, and if that is so, I have no more prestige." He was shaking. He seemed to have lost twenty pounds in the few days since I had last seen him; pockets of loose skin dangled on his face.

"Why not run a recheck?" I asked. "Get Vornan to repeat what he taped for you before. Then feed both tapes to the computer and check the correlation function. If he was improvising gibberish the last time, he won't be able to duplicate it."

"My friend, that was my first thought."

"And?"

"He will not speak to me in his language again. He has lost interest in my researches. He refuses to utter a syllable."

"That sounds suspicious to me."

"Yes," said Kolff sadly. "Of course it is suspicious. I tell him that by doing this simple thing, he can destroy forever all doubts about his origin, and he says no. I tell him that by refusing, he is inviting us to regard him as an impostor, and he says he does not care. Is he bluffing? Is he a liar? Or does he genuinely not care? Leo, I am destroyed."

"You heard a linguistic pattern, didn't you, Lloyd?"

"Certainly I did. But it may have been only an illusion— a coincidental striking of sound values." He shook his head like a wounded walrus, muttered something in Persian or Pushtu, and went shuffling away, bowed, sagging. And I realized that Vornan had diabolically canceled out one of the major arguments for accepting him as genuine. Deliberately. Wantonly. He was toying with us ... with all of us.

Dinner was served to us at the hotel that night. There was no question of our going outside, not with thousands of people in the streets about us. One of the networks screened a documentary on Vornan's progress through the land, and we watched it. Vornan watched with us, although in the past he had not shown much interest in what the media had to say about him. In a way I wished he had not seen it. The documentary concentrated on the impact he had had on mass emotions, and showed things I had not suspected: Adolescent girls in Illinois writhing in drug-induced ecstasy before a tridim photo of our visitor. Africans lighting immense ceremonial bonfires in whose greasy blue smoke the image of Vornan was said to take form. A woman in Indiana who had collected tapes of every telecast dealing with the man from the future, and who was selling replicas of them mounted in special reli-quaries. We saw a massive westward movement under

178

way; hordes of curiosity-seekers were spilling across the continent, hoping to catch up with Vornan as he moved about. The camera's eye descended into the swirling mobs we had been seeing so often, showing us the fixed faces of fanatics. These people wanted revelation from Vornan; they wanted prophecies; they wanted divine guidance. Excitement flickered like heat-lightning wherever he went. If Kolff ever let that cube of Vornan's speech get into public circulation, it would provoke a new manifestation of glossolalia, I realized—a wild outburst of speaking in tongues as holy babbling became the way to salvation once more. I was frightened. In the slower moments of the documentary I stole glances at Vornan and saw him nodding in satisfaction, eminently pleased with the stir he was causing. He seemed to revel in the power that publicity and curiosity had placed in his hands. Anything he might choose to say would be received with high interest, discussed and discussed again, and swiftly would harden into an article of faith accepted by millions. It has been given only to a very few men in history to have such power, and none of Vornan's charismatic predecessors had had his access to communications channels.

It terrified me. Up to now he had seemed wholly unconcerned by the world's response to him, as aloof as he had been the day he strolled naked up the Spanish Stairs while a Roman policeman shouted at him to halt. Now, though, a feedback was appearing. He watched his own documentaries. Was he enjoying the confusion he engendered? Was he consciously planning new upheavals? Vornan acting in lighthearted innocence created chaos enough; Vornan motivated by deliberate malice could smash civilization. I had been scornful of him at first, and then amused by him. Now I was afraid of him.

Our gathering broke up early. I saw Fields speaking urgently to Aster; she shook her head, shrugged, and walked away from him, leaving him scowling. Vornan went up to him and touched him lightly on the shoulder. I have no idea what Vornan said to him, but Fields' expression was even darker afterward. He went out, trying to slam a slamproof door. Kolff and Helen left together. I lingered awhile for no particular reason. My room was next to Aster's, and we walked down the hall together. We stood awhile talking in front of her door. I had the odd impression that she was going to invite me in to spend the night; she seemed more animated than usual, eyelashes fluttering, delicate nostrils flaring. "Do you know how much longer we'll be on this tour?" she asked me. I told her that I didn't know. She was thinking of getting back to her laboratory, she said, but then she confessed wryly, "I'd leave right now except that I'm getting interested in this despite myself. Interested in Vornan. Leo, do you notice that he's changing?"

"How?"

"Becoming more aware of what's happening around him. He was so divorced from it at first, so alien. Do you remember the time he asked me to take a shower with him?"

"I can't forget it."

"If it had been another man, I would have refused, of course. But Vornan was so blunt about it—the way a child would be. I knew he meant no harm. But now—now he seems to want to *use* people. He isn't just sightseeing any more. He's manipulating everyone. Very subtly."

I told her that I had thought all these thoughts too, during the television program a little earlier. Her eyes glowed; points of rosiness sprouted in her cheeks. She moistened her lips, and I waited for her to tell me that she and I had much in common and ought to know one another better; but all she said was, "I'm afraid, Leo. I wish he'd go back where he came from. He's going to make real trouble."

"Kralick and Company will prevent that."

"I wonder." She flashed a nervous smile. "Well, good night, Leo. Sleep well."

180

She was gone. I stared for a long moment at her closed door, and the stolen image of her slim body drifted up out of my memory bank. Aster had not had much physical appeal for me up till now; she hardly seemed a woman at all. Suddenly I understood what Morton Fields saw in her. I desired her fiercely. Was this, too, some of Vornan's mischief? I smiled. I was blaming him for everything now. My hand rested on the plate of Aster's door, and I debated asking her to admit me, but I entered my own room instead. I sealed the door, undressed, prepared myself for sleep. Sleep did not come. I went to the window to stare at the mobs, but the mobs had dissipated. It was past midnight. A slice of moon dangled over the sprawling city. I drew out a blank notepad and began to sketch some theorems that had drifted into my mind during dinner: a way of accounting for a double reversal of charge during time travel. Problem: assuming that time-reversal is possible, create a mathematical justification for conversion from matter to anti-matter to matter again before the completion of a journey. I worked quickly and for a while even convincingly. I came to the verge of picking up the phone and getting a data hookup with my computer so I could run some verifying mockups of the system. Then I saw the flaw near the beginning of my work, the stupid algebraic error, the failure to keep my signs straight. I crumpled the sheets and threw them away in disgust.

I heard a tapping at my door. A voice: "Leo? Leo, are you awake?"

I nudged the scanner beside my bed and got a dim image of my visitor. Vornan! Instantly I sprang up and unsealed the door. He was dressed in a thin green tunic as though to go out. His presence astonished me, for I knew that Kralick sealed him in his room each night, and at least in theory there was no way for Vornan to break that seal, which was supposed to protect him but which also imprisoned him. Yet he was here.

"Come in," I said. "Is anything wrong?"

"Not at all. Were you sleeping?"

"Working. Trying to calculate how your blasted time machine works, in fact."

He laughed lightly. "Poor Leo. You'll wear out your brain with all that thinking."

"If you really felt sorry for me, you'd give me a hint or two about it."

"I would if I could," he said. "But it's impossible. I'll explain why downstairs."

"Downstairs?"

"Yes. We're going out for a little walk. You'll accompany me, won't you, Leo?"

I gaped. "There's a riot going on outside. We'll be killed by the hysterical mob!"

"I think the mob has gone away," said Vornan. "Besides, I have *these*." He extended his hand. In his palm lay two limp plastic masks of the sort we had worn at the Chicago brothel. "No one will recognize us. We'll stroll the streets of this wonderful city in disguise. I want to go out, Leo. I'm tired of official promenades. I feel like exploring again."

I wondered what to do. Call Kralick and have Vornan locked into his room again? That was the sensible response. Masks or not, it was rash to leave the hotel without a guard. But it would be a betrayal to turn Vornan in like that. Obviously he trusted me more than any of the others; perhaps there was even something he wished to tell me in confidence, beyond the range of Kralick's spy-pickups. I would have to take the risks in the hope of winning from him some nugget of valuable information.

"All right. I'll go with you."

"Quickly, then. If someone monitors your room——"

"What about *your* room?"

He laughed smugly. "My room has been adjusted. Those who pry will think I am still in it. But if I am seen in here as well—get dressed, Leo."

182

I threw on some clothing and we left the room. I sealed it from the outside. In the hall lay three of Kralick's men, sound asleep; the green globe of an anesthetic balloon drifted in the air, and as its temperature-sensitive scanning plate picked up my thermals it homed in on me. Vornan lazily reached up for it, caught its trailing strand of plastic tape, and tugged it down to turn it off. He grinned conspiratorially at me. Then, like a boy running away from home, he darted across the hall, motioning to me to follow him. At a nudge a service door in the corridor opened, revealing a tumbletube for linens. Vornan beckoned me to enter.

"We'll land in the laundry room!" I protested.

"Don't be foolish, Leo. We'll get off before the last stop."

Mine not to reason why. I entered the tumbletube with him and down we caromed, flushed like debris to the depths of the building. A catchnet erupted across the tube unexpectedly and we bounced into it. I thought it was some kind of trap, but Vornan said simply, "It's a safety device to keep hotel employees from falling into the linen conveyor. I've been talking to the chambermaids, you see. Come on!" He stepped out of the net, which I suppose had been activated by mass-detectors along the sides of the tube, and we perched on a ledge of the chute while he opened a door. For a man who scarcely understood what a stock exchange was, he had a remarkably complete knowledge of the inner workings of this hotel. The catchnet withdrew into the tube wall the moment I was out of it; an instant later some soiled linens zoomed past us from above and vanished into the maw of the laundry pit somewhere far below. Vornan beckoned again. We went scrambling down a narrow passageway lit from above by strips of cold light, and emerged finally in one of the hallways of the hotel. By a prosaic staircase we took ourselves to a sublobby and out unnoticed into the street.

All was quiet. We could see where the rioters had been. Stenciled slogans gleamed up from the sidewalk and glistened on the sides of buildings: THE END IS NEAR, PREPARE TO MEET YOUR MAKER, stuff like that, the classic billboard ruminations. Bits of clothing were scattered everywhere. Mounds of foam told me that the riot had not been dispersed without effort. Here and there a few sleepers lay, stunned or drunk or simply resting; they must have crept out of the shadows after the police had cleared the area.

We donned our masks and moved silently through the mildness of the Los Angeles night. Here in the early hours of morning little was taking place in the downtown district; the towers all about us were hotels and office buildings, and the nightlife went elsewhere. We strolled at random. Occasionally an advert balloon dawdled through the sky a few hundred feet above us, flashing its gaudy incitements. Two blocks from our hotel we paused to examine the window of a shop selling spy devices. Vornan seemed wholly absorbed. The shop was closed, of course, and yet as we lingered on a sensor plate embedded in the pavement a mellifluous voice told us the store hours and invited us to return in daytime. Two doors down we came to a sportsman's shop specializing in fishing equipment. Our presence tripped another sidewalk trigger that yielded a sales talk aimed at deep-sea fishermen. "You've come to the right place," a mechanical voice proclaimed. "We carry a full line. Hydrophotometers, plankton samplers, mud penetrometers, light-scattering meters, tide recorders, hydrostatic actuators, radar buoys, clinometers, sludge detectors, liquid-level indicators—"

We moved on.

Vornan said, "I love your cities. The buildings are so tall—the merchants are so aggressive. We have no merchants, Leo."

"What do you do if you need a sludge detector or a plankton sampler?"

"They are available," he said simply. "I rarely need such things."

"Why have you told us so little about your time, Vornan?"

"Because I have come here to learn, not to teach."

"But you're not rushed for time. You could reciprocate. We're morbidly curious about the shape of things to come. And you've said so little. I have only the vaguest picture of your world."

"Tell me how it seems to you."

"Fewer people than we have today," I said. "Very sleek, very orderly. Gadgets kept in the background, yet anything at all available when needed. No wars. No nations. A simple, pleasant, happy world. It's hard for me to believe in it."

"You've described it well."

"But how did it come to get that way, Vornan? That's what we want to know! Look at the world you've been visiting. A hundred suspicious nations. Superbombs. Tension. Hunger and frustration. Millions of hysterical people hunting for a receptacle for their faith. What happened? How did the world settle down?"

"A thousand years is a long time, Leo. Much can happen."

"What *did* happen, though? Where did the present nations go? Tell me about the crises, the wars, the upheavals."

We halted under a lamppost. Instantly its photosensors detected us and stepped up the output of light. Vornan said, "Suppose you tell me, Leo, about the organization, rise, and decline of the Holy Roman Empire."

"Where'd you hear about the Holy Roman Empire?"

"From Professor Heyman. Tell me what you know about the Empire, Leo."

"Why—next to nothing, I guess. It was some kind of European confederation seven or eight hundred years ago. And—and—"

"Exactly. You know nothing about it at all."

"I'm not claiming to be a practicing historian, Vornan."

"Neither am I," he said quietly. "Why do you think I should know anything more about the Time of Sweeping than you do about the Holy Roman Empire? It's ancient history to me. I never studied it. I had no interest in learning about it."

"But if you were planning to come back on a time trip, Vornan, you should have made it your business to study history the way you studied English."

"I needed English in order to communicate. I had no need of history. I am not here as a scholar, Leo. Only as a tourist."

"And you know nothing of the science of your era either, I suppose?"

"Nothing at all," he said cheerfully.

"What *do* you know? What do you do in 2999?"

"Nothing. Nothing."

"You have no profession?"

"I travel. I observe. I please myself."

"A member of the idle rich?"

"Yes, except we have no idle rich. I guess you'd call me idle, Leo. Idle and ignorant."

"And is everyone in 2999 idle and ignorant? Are work and scholarship and effort obsolete?"

"Oh, no, no, no," Vornan said. "We have many diligent souls. My somatic brother Lunn-31 is a collector of light impulses, a ranking authority. My good friend Mortel-91 is a connoisseur of gestures. Pol-13, whose beauty you would appreciate, dances in the psychodrome. We have our artists, our poets, our learned ones. The celebrated Ekki-89 has labored fifty years on his revivification of the Years of Flame. Sator-11 has assembled a complete set of crystal images of the Seekers, all of his own making. I am proud of them."

"And you, Vornan?"

"I am nothing. I do nothing. I am quite an ordinary man, Leo." There was a note in his voice I had not heard before, a throb that I took for sincerity. "I came here out of boredom, out of the lust for diversion. Others are possessed by their commitment to the endeavors of the spirit. I am an empty vessel, Leo. I can tell you no science, no history. My perceptions of beauty are rudimentary. I am ignorant. I am idle. I search the worlds for my pleasures, but they are shallow pleasures." Through the mask came the filtered gleam of his wondrous smile. "I am being quite honest with you, Leo. I hope this explains my failure to answer the questions of you and your friends. I am quite unsatisfactory, a man of many shortcomings. Does my honesty distress you?"

It did more than that. It appalled me. Unless Vornan's sudden burst of humility was merely a ploy, he was labeling himself a dilettante, a wastrel, an idler—a nobody out of time, diverting himself among the sweaty primitives because his own epoch had momentarily ceased to amuse him. His evasiveness, the voids in his knowledge, all seemed comprehensible now. But it was hardly flattering to know that this was our time traveler, that we had merited nothing better than Vornan. And I found it ominous that a self-proclaimed shallow floater had the power over our world that Vornan had effortlessly gained. Where would his quest for amusement lead him? And what, if any, restraints would he care to impose on himself?

I said as we walked on, "Why have no other visitors from your era come to us?"

Vornan chuckled. "What makes you think I am the first?"

"We've never—no one has—there hasn't been—" I paused, dithering, once more the victim of Vornan's gift for opening trapdoors in the fabric of the universe.

"I am no pioneer," he said gently. "There have been many here before me."

"Keeping their identity secret?"

"Of course. It pleased me to reveal myself. More serious-minded individuals go about things surreptitiously. They do their work in silence and depart."

"How many have there been?"

"I scarcely could guess."

"Visiting all eras?"

"Why not?"

"Living among us under assumed identities?"

"Yes, yes, of course," Vornan said lightly. "Often holding public office, I believe. Poor Leo! Did you think that I was blazing a trail, a miserable fool like me?"

I swayed, more sickened by this than anything. Our world honeycombed by strangers out of time? Our nations perhaps guided by these wanderers? A hundred, a thousand, fifty thousand travelers popping in and out of history? No. No. No. No. My mind rebelled at that. Vornan was playing with me now. There could be no alternative. I told him I did not believe him. He laughed. He said, "I give you my permission not to believe me. Do you hear that sound?"

I heard a sound, yes. It was a sound like that of a waterfall, coming from the direction of Pershing Square. There are no waterfalls in Pershing Square. Vornan sprinted forward. I hurried after him, my heart pounding, my skull throbbing. I could not keep up. He halted after a block and a half to wait for me. He pointed ahead, "Quite a number of them," he said. "I find this very exciting!"

The dispersed mob had regrouped, milling about Pershing Square and now beginning to overflow. A phalanx of capering humanity rolled toward us, filling the street from edge to edge. I could not tell for a moment which mob it was, the Apocalyptists or those who sought Vornan to worship him, but then I saw the crazily painted faces, the baleful banners, the zigging metal coils held high overhead as symbols of heavenly fire, and I knew that these were the prophets of doom bearing down on us.

I said, "We've got to get out of here. Back to the hotel!"

"I want to see this."

"We'll be trampled, Vornan!"

"Not if we're careful. Stay with me, Leo. Let the tide sweep over us."

I shook my head. The vanguard of the Apocalyptist mob was only a block from us. Wielding flares and sirens, the rioters were streaming in a wild rush toward us, screams and shrieks puncturing the air. Merely as bystanders, we might suffer at the hands of the mob; if we were recognized through our masks, we were dead. I caught Vornan's wrist and tugged in anguish, trying to drag him down a side street that led to the hotel. For the first time I felt his electrical powers. A low-voltage jolt made my hand leap back. I clamped it to him again, and this time he transmitted a burst of stunning energy that sent me reeling away, muscles twitching in a dislocated dance. I dropped to my knees and crouched half dazed while Vornan gaily raced toward the Apocalyptists, his arms spread wide.

The bosom of the mob enfolded him. I saw him slip between two of the front runners and vanish into the core of the surging, shouting mass. He was gone. I struggled dizzily to my feet, knowing that I had to find him, and took three or four uncertain steps forward. An instant later the Apocalyptists were upon me.

I managed to stay on my feet long enough to throw off the effects of the shock Vornan had given me. About me moved the cultists, faces thick with red and green paint; the acrid tang of sweat was in the air, and mysteriously, I spied one Apocalyptist to whose chest was strapped the hissing little globe of an ion-dispersal deodorant; this was strange territory for the fastidious. I was whirled around. A girl with bare jiggling breasts, whose nipples glowed with luminescence, hugged me. "The end is coming!" she shrilled. "Live while you can!" She clawed at my hands and pressed them to her breasts. I clutched warm flesh for a moment, before the current of the mob whirled her away from me; when I looked down at my palms I saw the luminescent imprints gleaming in them, like watchful eyes. Musical instruments of indeterminate ancestry honked and blared. Three high-stepping boys, arms locked, paraded before me, kicking at anyone who came close. A towering man in a goat's mask exposed his maleness jubilantly, and a heavy-thighed woman rushed toward him, offered herself, and clung tight. An arm snaked around my shoulders. I whirled and saw a gaunt, bony, grinning figure leaning toward me; a girl, I thought, from the costume and the long snarled silken hair, but then "her" blouse fell open and I saw the flat shining hairless chest with the two small dark circlets.

"Have a drink," the boy said, and thrust a squeezeflask at me. I could not refuse. The snout of the flask went between my lips and I tasted something bitter and thin. Turning away, I spat it out, but the flavor remained like a stain on my tongue.

We were marching fifteen or twenty abreast in several directions at once, though the prevailing movement was back toward the hotel. I fought my way against the tide, hunting for Vornan. Hands clutched at me again and again. I stumbled over a couple locked in lust on the sidewalk; they were inviting destruction and did not seem to mind. It was like a carnival, but there were no floats, and the costumes were wildly individualistic.

"Vornan!" I bellowed. And the mob took it up, magnifying the cry. "Vornan ... Vornan ... Vornan ... kill Vornan ... doom ... flame ... doom ... Vornan ..." It was the dance of death. A figure loomed before me, face marked with pustulent sores, dripping lesions, gaping cavities; a woman's hand rose to caress it and the makeup smeared so that I could see the handsome unmarred face beneath the artificial horrors. Here came a young man nearly seven feet high, waving a smoky torch and yelling

190

of the Apocalypse; there was a flat-nosed girl drenched in sweat, rending her garments; two pomaded young men tweaked her breasts, laughed, kissed one another, and catapulted on. I called out again, "Vornan!"

Then I caught sight of him. He was standing quite still, like a boulder in a flowing stream, and curiously the rampaging mob was passing on either side of him as it roared forward. Several feet of open space remained inviolate around him, as though he had carved a private pocket in the throng. He stood with arms folded, surveying the madness about him. His mask had been ripped, so that his cheek showed through it, and he was daubed with paint and glowing substances. I struggled toward him, was carried away by a sudden inner surge within the main flow, and fought my way back to him with elbows and knees, hammering a route through tons of flesh. When I was within a few feet of him I understood why the rioters were bypassing him. Vornan had created a little dike all around himself out of stacked human bodies, piling them two or three high on each side. They seemed dead, but as I watched, a girl who had been lying to Vornan's left stumbled to her feet and went reeling away. Vornan promptly reached toward the next Apocalyptist to come along, a cadaverous man whose bald skull was stained deep blue. A touch of Vornan's hand and the man collapsed, falling neatly into place to restore the rampart. Vornan had built a living wall with his electricity. I jumped over it and thrust my face close to his.

"For God's sake let's get out of here!" I yelled.

"We are in no danger, Leo. Keep calm."

"Your mask's ripped. What if you're recognized?"

"I have my defenses." He laughed. "What delight this is!"

I knew better than to try to seize him again. In his careless rapture he would stun me a second time and add me to his rampart, and I might not survive the experience. So I stood beside him, helpless. I watched a heavy foot descend on the hand of an unconscious girl who lay near me; when the foot moved on, the shattered fingers quivered convulsively, bending at the joints in a way that human hands do not normally bend. Vornan turned in a full circle, taking everything in.

He said to me, "What makes them believe the world is going to end?"

"How would I know? It's irrational. They're insane."

"Can so many people be insane at once?"

"Of course."

"And do they know the day the world ends?"

"January 1, 2000."

"Quite close. Why that day in particular?"

"It's the beginning of a new century," I said, "of a new millennium. Somehow people expect extraordinary things to happen then."

With lunatic pedantry Vornan said, "But the new century does not begin until 2001. Heyman has explained it to me. It is not correct to say that the century starts when—"

"I know all that. But no one pays attention to it. Damn you, Vornan, let's not stand here debating calendrics! I want to get away from here!"

"Then go."

"With you."

"I'm enjoying this. Look there, Leo!"

I looked. A nearly naked girl garbed as a witch rode on the shoulders of a man with horns sprouting from his forehead. Her breasts were painted glossy black, the nipples orange. But the sight of such grotesquerie did nothing to me now. I did not even trust Vornan's improvised barricade. If things got any wilder—

Police copters appeared abruptly. Long overdue, too. They hovered between the buildings, no more than a hundred feet up, and the whirr of their rotors sent a chilling draft upon us. I watched the dull gray nozzles extrude from the white globular bellies above us; then came the first spurts of the antiriot foam. The Apocalyptists seemed to welcome it. They rushed forward, trying to get into position under the nozzles; some of them stripped off what few garments they wore and bathed in it. The foam came bubbling down, expanding as it met the air, forming a thick viscous soapiness that filled the street and made movement almost impossible. Moving now in angular jerks like machines running down, the demonstrators lurched to and fro, fighting their way through the layers of foam. Its taste was oddly sweet. I saw a girl get a jolt of it in the face and stumble, blinded, mouth and nostrils engulfed in the stuff. She fell to the pavement and disappeared totally, for by now at least three feet of foam rose from the ground, cool, sticky, cutting all of us off at our thighs. Vornan knelt and drew the girl back into view, although she would not suffocate where she was. He cleared the foam tenderly from her face and ran his hands over her moist, slippery flesh. When he gripped her breasts, her eyes opened and he said quietly to her, "I am Vornan-19." His lips went to hers. When he released her, she scrambled away on her knees, burrowing through the foam. To my horror I saw that Vornan was without his mask.

We could scarcely move at all, now. Police robots were in the street, great shining domes of metal that buzzed easily through the foam, seizing the trapped demonstrators and hustling them into groups of ten or twelve. Sanitation mechs were already out to suck up the excess foam. Vornan and I stood near the outer border of the scene; slowly we sloshed through the foam and reached an open street. No one seemed to notice us. I said to Vornan, "Will you listen to reason now? Here's our chance to get back to the hotel without any more trouble."

"We have had little trouble so far."

"There'll be big trouble if Kralick finds out what you've been up to. He'll restrict your freedom, Vornan. He'll keep an army of guards outside your door and put a triple seal on it."

"Wait," he said. "I want something. Then we can go."

He darted back into the mob. By now the foam had hardened to a doughy consistency, and those in it were wallowing precariously. In a moment Vornan returned. He was dragging a girl of about seventeen who seemed dazed and terrified. Her costume was of transparent plastic, but flecks of foam were clinging to it, conveying a probably unwanted modesty. "Now we can go to the hotel," he said to me. And to the girl he whispered, "I am Vornan-19. The world does not end in January. Before dawn I will prove it to you."

*   FOURTEEN   *

WE DID NOT have to sneak back into the hotel. A cordon of searchers had spread out for blocks around it; within moments after we had escaped from the foam, Vornan tripped an identity-signal and some of Kralick's men picked us up. Kralick was in the hotel lobby, monitoring the detector screens and looking half berserk with anxiety. When Vornan strode up to him, still tugging the quivering Apocalyptist girl, I thought Kralick would have a fit. Blandly Vornan apologized for any trouble he might have caused, and asked to be conducted to his room. The girl accompanied him. I had an uncomfortable session with Kralick when they were out of sight.

"How did he get out?" he demanded.

"I don't know. He gimmicked the seal on his room, I suppose." I tried to persuade Kralick that I had meant to give an alarm when Vornan left the hotel, but had been prevented by circumstances beyond my control. I doubt that I convinced him, but at least I got across to him the fact that I had done my best to keep Vornan from becoming involved with the Apocalyptists, and that the entire exploit had been none of my doing.

There was a noticeable tightening of security in the weeks that followed. In effect, Vornan-19 became the prisoner and not merely the guest of the United States Government. Vornan had been more or less an honored prisoner all along, for Kralick had suspected it was unwise to let him move about freely; but aside from sealing his room at night and posting guards, no attempt had been made to exert physical restraint on him. Somehow he had coped with the seal and drugged his guards, but Kralick prevented a repetition by using better seals, self-tripping alarms, and more guards.

It worked, in the sense that Vornan did not go on any further unauthorized expeditions. But I think that that was more a matter of Vornan's own choice than of Kralick's added precautions. After his experience with the Apocalyptists, Vornan seemed to subside considerably; he became a more orthodox tourist, looking at this and that but holding back his more demoniacal comments. I feared this subdued version of our guest the way I would fear a quiescent volcano. But in fact he committed no new outrageous transgressions of propriety, stepped on no toes, was in many ways the model of tact. I wondered what he was storing up for us.

And so the weeks of the tour dragged on. We looked at Disneyland with Vornan, and although the place had been visibly refurbished, it plainly bored him. He was not interested in seeing synthetic reconstructions of other times and other places; he wanted to experience the United States of 1999 at first hand. At Disneyland he paid more attention to the other customers than to the amusements themselves. We swept him through the park unheralded, moving in a small close-knit group, and for once he attracted little attention. It was as if anyone who saw Vornan at Disneyland assumed that what he saw was part of the park, a clever plastic imitation of the man out of time, and passed by with no more than a nod and a smile.

We took him to Irvine and showed him the trillion-volt accelerator. That was my idea: I wanted a chance to get back to the campus for a few days, to visit my office and my house and be sure that all was still well. Letting Vornan near the accelerator was something of a calculated risk, I thought, remembering the havoc he had produced at Wesley Bruton's villa; but we saw to it that Vornan never came within reach of any of the control equipment. He stood beside me, gravely watching the screens, as I smashed atoms for him. He seemed interested, but it was the superficial interest a child might have shown: he liked the pretty patterns.

For a moment I forgot everything except the joy of manipulating the huge machine. I stood at the operating panel, with billions of dollars of equipment stretching above and before me, pulling switches and levers with the same glee Wesley Bruton had displayed while making his house work wonders. I pulverized atoms of iron and sent neutrons spraying madly about. I sent a stream of protons along the track and cut in the neutron injector so that the screen was spattered with the bright bursts of demolition lines. I conjured up quarks and antiquarks. I went through my entire repertoire, and Vornan nodded innocently, smiling, pointing. He could have deflated me as he had done the Stock Exchange man, simply by asking what the point of all this cumbersome apparatus might be, but he did not. I am not sure if his restraint was a matter of courtesy toward me—for I flattered myself that Vornan was closer to me than to any of the others who traveled with him—or if it was simply that for the moment his vein of impishness was played out, and he was content to stand and watch respectfully.

We took him next to the fusion plant on the coast. Again, this was my doing, though Kralick agreed it might be useful. I still had hopes, however flickering, of squeezing from Vornan some data on the energy sources of his era. Jack Bryant's too-sensitive conscience spurred me on. But the attempt was a failure. The manager of the plant explained to Vornan how we had captured the fury of the sun itself, setting up a proton-proton reaction within a magnetic pinch, and tapping power from the transmutation of hydrogen to helium. Vornan was permitted to enter the relay room where the plasma was regulated by sensors operating above the visible spectrum. What we were seeing was not the raging plasma itself—direct viewing of that was impossible—but a simulation, a re-creation, a curve following peak for peak every fluctuation of the soup of stripped-down nuclei within the pinch tank. It had been years since I had visited the plant myself, and I was awed. Vornan kept his own counsel. We waited for disparaging remarks; none came. He did not bother to compare our medieval scientific accomplishments with the technology of his own age. This new Vornan lacked bite.

Next we doubled back through New Mexico, where Pueblo Indians dwell in a living museum of anthropology. This was Helen McIlwain's big moment. She led us through the dusty mud village trailing anthropological data. Here in early spring the regular tourist season had not yet begun, and so we had the pueblo to ourselves; Kralick had arranged with the local authorities to close the reservation to outsiders for the day, so that no Vornan-seekers would come up from Albuquerque or down from Santa Fe to make trouble. The Indians themselves came shuffling out of their flat-roofed adobes to stare, but I doubt that many of them knew who Vornan was, and I doubt that any of them cared. They were pudgy people, round-faced, flat-nosed, not at all the hawk-featured Indians of legend. I felt sorry for them. They were Federal employees, in a sense, paid to stay here and live in squalor. Although they are permitted television and automobiles and electricity, they may not build houses in the modern styles, and must continue to grind corn meal, perform their ceremonial dances, and turn out pottery for sale to visitors. Thus we guard our past.

Helen introduced us to the leaders of the village: the governor, the chief, and the heads of two of the so-called secret societies. They seemed like sharp, sophisticated men, who could just as easily be running automobile agencies in Albuquerque. We were taken around, into a few of the houses, even down into the kiva, the town religious center, formerly sacrosanct. Some children did a ragged dance for us. In a shop at the edge of the plaza we were shown the pottery and turquoise-and-silver jewelry that the women of the village produced. One case held older pottery, made in the first half of the twentieth century, handsome stuff with a smooth finish and elegant semi-abstract patterns of birds and deer; but these pieces were priced at hundreds of dollars apiece, and from the look on the face of the salesgirl I gathered that they were not really for sale at all; they were tribal treasures, souvenirs of happier times. The real stock-in-trade consisted of cheap, flimsy little jugs. Helen said with scorn, "You see how they put the paint on *after* the pot's been fired, now? It's deplorable. Any child can do it. The University of New Mexico is trying to revive the old ways, but the people here argue that the tourists like the fake stuff better. It's brighter, livelier—and cheaper." Vornan drew a sour glare from Helen when he expressed his opinion that the so-called touristware was more attractive than the earlier pottery. I think he said it only to tease her, but I am not sure; Vornan's esthetic standards were always unfathomable, and probably to him the debased current work seemed as authentic a product of the remote past as the really fine pottery in the display case.

We had only one minor Vornan incident at the pueblo. The girl running the showroom was a slim adolescent beauty with long soft shining black hair and fine features that looked more Chinese than Indian; we were all quite taken by her, and Vornan seemed eager to add her to his collection of conquests. I don't know what would have happened if he had asked the girl to stage a command performance in his bed that night. Luckily, he never got that far. He was eyeing the girl in obvious lust as she moved about the showroom; I saw it, and so did Helen. When we left the building, Vornan turned as if to go back in and announce his desire. Helen blocked his way, looking more like a witch than ever, her eyes blazing against her flaming mop of red hair.

*"No,"* she said fiercely. "You *can't!"*

That was all. And Vornan obeyed. He smiled and bowed to Helen and walked away. I hadn't expected him to do that.

The new meek Vornan was a revelation to us all, but the public at large preferred the revelations of the Vornan it had come to know in January and February. Against all likelihood, interest in Vornan's deeds and words grew more passionate with each passing week; what might have been a nine-days' wonder was on its way toward becoming the sensation of the age. Some clever huckster assembled a quick, flimsy book about Vornan and called it *The New Revelation*. It contained transcripts of all of Vornan-19's press conferences and media appearances since his arrival at Christmastime, with some choppy commentary tying everything together. The book appeared in the middle of March, and some measure of its significance can be gathered from the fact that it came out not only in tape, cube, and facsim editions, but also in a printed text—a book, that is, in the old sense. A California publisher produced it as a slim paperbound volume with a bright red jacket and the title in incandescent ebony letters; an edition of a million copies sold out within a week. Very shortly, pirated editions were emerging from underground presses everywhere, despite the frantic attempts of the copyright owner to protect his property. Uncountable millions of *The New Revelation* flooded the land. I bought one myself, as a keepsake. I saw Vornan reading a copy. Both the genuine edition and the various ersatz ones had the same black-on-red color scheme, so that at a glance they were indistinguishable, and in the early weeks of spring those paperbound books covered the nation like a strange red snowfall.

The new creed had its prophet, and now it had its gospel too. I find it hard to see what sort of spiritual comfort could be derived from *The New Revelation,* and so I suppose the book was more of a talisman than a scripture; one did not take counsel from it, one merely carried it about, drawing sustenance from the feel of the shiny covers against the hands. Whenever we traveled with Vornan and a crowd assembled, copies of the book were held aloft like flashcards at a college football game, creating a solid red backdrop speckled with the dark letters of the title.

There were translations. The Germans, the Poles, the Swedes, the Portuguese, the French, the Russians, all had their own versions of *The New Revelation.* Someone on Kralick's staff was collecting the things and forwarding them to us wherever we went. Kralick usually turned them over to Kolff, who showed a weird bitter interest in each new edition. The book made its way into Asia, and reached us in Japanese, in several of the languages of India, in Mandarin, and in Korean. Appropriately, a Hebrew edition appeared, the right language for any holy book. Kolff liked to arrange the little red books in rows, shifting the patterns about. He spoke dreamily of making a translation of his own, into Sanskrit or perhaps Old Persian; I am not sure if he was serious.

Since the episode of his interview with Vornan, Kolff had been slipping into some kind of senile decay. He had been badly shocked by the computer's views on Vornan's speech sample; the ambiguity of that report had punctured his own buoyant conviction that he had heard the voice of the future, and now, chastened and humiliated, he had fallen back from his first enthusiastic verdict. He was not at all sure that Vornan was genuine or that he had really heard the ghosts of words in the liquid flow of Vornan's prattle. Kolff had lost faith in his own judgment, his own expertise, and we could see him crumbling now. This great Falstaff of a man was at least partly a humbug, as we had discovered during our tour; though his gifts were great and his learning was vast, he knew that his lofty reputation had been undeserved for decades, and abruptly he stood exposed as an uncertain maunderer. In pity for him I asked Vornan to grant Kolff a second interview and to repeat whatever it was he had recited the first time. Vornan would not do it.

"It is useless," he said, and refused to be prodded.

Kolff subdued seemed hardly to be Kolff at all. He ate little, said less, and by the beginning of April had lost so much weight that he seemed unrecognizable. His clothes and his skin itself hung slack on his shrunken frame. He moved along with us from place to place, but he was shambling blindly, hardly aware of what was happening about him. Kralick, concerned, wanted to relieve Kolff of his assignment and send him home. He discussed the matter with the rest of us, but Helen's opinion was decisive. "It'll kill him," she said. "He'll think he's being fired for incompetence."

"He's a sick man," said Kralick. "All this traveling—"

"It's a useful function."

"But he isn't being useful any more," Kralick pointed out. "He hasn't contributed anything in weeks. He just sits there playing with those copies of the book. Helen, I can't take the responsibility. He belongs in a hospital."

"He belongs with us."

"Even if it kills him?"

"Even if it kills him," Helen said vigorously. "Better to die in harness than to creep away thinking you're an old fool."

Kralick let her win the round, but we were fearful, for

we could see the inward rot spreading through old Lloyd day by day. Each morning I expected to be told that he had slipped away in his sleep; but each morning he was there, gaunt, gray-skinned, his nose now jutting like a pyramid in his diminished face. We journeyed to Michigan so that Vornan could see Aster's life-synthesis project; and as we walked the aisles of that eerie laboratory, Kolff clumped along behind us, a delegate from the walking dead witnessing the spawning of artificial life.

Aster said, "This was one of our earliest successes, if you can call it a success. We never could figure out what phylum to put it in, but there's no doubt that it's alive and that it breeds true, so in that sense the experiment was successful."

We peered into a huge tank in which a variety of underwater plants grew. Between the green fronds swam slender azure creatures, six to eight inches long; they were eyeless, propelled themselves by ripplings of a dorsal fin that ran their entire length, and were crowned by gaping mouths rimmed with agile translucent tentacles. At least a hundred of them were in the tank. A few appeared to be budding; smaller representatives of their kind protruded from their sides.

"We intended to manufacture coelenterates," Aster explained. "Basically, that's what we have here: a giant free-swimming anemone. But coelenterates don't have fins, and this one does, and knows how to use it. We didn't engineer that fin. It developed spontaneously. There's the phantom of a segmented body structure, too, which is an attribute belonging to a higher phylum. Metabolically, the thing is capable of adapting to its environment far more satisfactorily than most invertebrates; it lives in fresh or salt water, gets along in a temperature spectrum of about a hundred degrees, and handles any sort of food. So we've got a super-coelenterate. We'd like to test it in natural conditions, perhaps dump a few in a pond nearby, but frankly we're afraid to let the thing loose." Aster smiled self-consciously. "We've also been trying vertebrate synthesis lately, with rather less to show for it. Here . . ."

She indicated a tank in which a small brown creature lay limply on the bottom, moving in an occasional random twitch. It had two boneless-looking arms and a single leg; the missing leg did not seem ever to have been there. A whiplike tail drifted feebly about. To me it looked like a sad salamander. Aster seemed quite proud of it, though, for it had a well-developed skeletal structure, a decent nervous system, a surprisingly good set of eyes, and a full complement of internal organs. It did not, however, reproduce itself. They were still working on that. In the meantime, each of these synthetic vertebrates had to be built up cell by cell from the basic genetic material, which very much limited the scope of the experiment. But this was awesome enough.

Aster was in her element, now, and she led us on tirelessly, down one avenue of the long, brightly lit room and up the next, past giant frosted flasks and looming, sinister centrifuges, along alcoves occupied by fractionating columns, into annexes where mechanical agitators chuttered busily in reaction vats containing somber iridescent amber fluids. We peered through long fiber telescopes to spy on sealed rooms in which light, temperature, radiation, and pressure were meticulously controlled. We saw blowups of electron photomicrographs and garnet holograms that showed us the internal structures of mysterious cellular groups. Aster sprinkled her running commentary liberally with words laden with symbolic significance, a lab jargon that had its own mystic rhythm; we heard of photometric titrators, platinum crucibles, hydraulic plethysmographs, rotary microtomes, densitometers, electrophoresis cells, collodion bags, infrared microscopes, flowmeters, piston burettes, cardiotachometers: an incomprehensible and wonderful vocabulary. Painstakingly Aster revealed how the protein chains of life were put together and made to replicate themselves; she spelled

203

everything out simply and beautifully, and there were the wriggling mock-coelenterates and the flabby pseudo-salamanders to tell us of achievement. It was altogether marvelous.

As she drew us along, Aster fished for what concerned her most: Vornan's comments. She knew that some sort of not-quite-human life existed in Vornan's time, for he had spoken in ambiguous terms at one of our early meetings of "servitors," which did not have full human status because they were genetically unhuman, life-forms built out of "lesser life." From what he had said, these servitors did not seem to be synthetic creations, but rather some kind of composites constructed of humbler germ plasm drawn from living things: dog-people, cat-people, gnu-people. Naturally Aster wished to know more, and she had just as naturally learned not a shred more from Vornan-19. Now she probed again, getting nowhere. Vornan remained distantly polite. He asked a few questions: How soon, he wanted to know, would Aster be able to synthesize imitation humans? Aster looked hazy. "Five, ten, fifteen years," she said.

"If the world lasts that long," said Vornan slyly.

We all laughed, more an explosion of tensions than any real show of amusement. Even Aster, who had never displayed anything like a sense of humor, flashed a thin, mechanical smile. She turned away and indicated a tank mounted in a pressure capsule.

"This is our latest project," she said. "I'm not quite sure how it stands now, since as you all know I've been away from the laboratory since January. You see here an effort to synthesize a mammalian embryo. We have several embryos in various stages of development. If you'll come closer . . ."

I looked and saw a number of fishlike things coiled within small membrane-bounded cells. My stomach tightened in nervous response to the sight of these big-headed little creatures, born from a mess of amino acids, ripening toward who knew what kind of maturity. Even Vornan looked impressed.

Lloyd Kolff grunted something in a language I did not understand: three or four words, thick, harsh, guttural. His voice carried an undertone of anguish. I looked toward him and saw him standing rigid, one arm brought up at an acute angle across his chest, the other pointing straight out from his side. He seemed to be performing some extremely complex ballet step and had become frozen in mid-pirouette. His face was deep blue, the color of Ming porcelain; his red-rimmed eyes were wide and frightful. He stood that way a long moment. Then he made a little chittering noise in the back of his throat and pitched forward onto the stone top of a laboratory table. He clutched convulsively; flasks and burners went sliding and crashing to the floor. His thick hands seized the rim of a small tank and pulled it over, spilling a dozen sleek little synthetic coelenterates. They flapped and quivered at our feet. Lloyd sagged slowly, losing his grip on the table and toppling in several stages, landing flat on his back. His eyes were still open. He uttered one sentence, with marvelously distinct diction: Lloyd Kolff's valedictory to the world. It was in some ancient language, perhaps. None of us could identify it afterward or repeat even a syllable. Then he died.

"Life support!" Aster yelled. "Hurry!"

Two laboratory assistants came scuttling up almost at once with a life-support rig. Kralick, meanwhile, had dropped beside Kolff and was trying mouth-to-mouth resuscitation. Aster got him away, and crouching efficiently beside Kolff's bulky, motionless form, ripped open his clothing to reveal the deep chest matted with gray hair. She gestured and one of her assistants handed her a pair of electrodes. She put them in place and gave Kolff's heart a jolt. The other assistant was already uncapping a hypodermic and pushing it against Kolff's arm. We heard the whirr of the ultrasonic snout while it rose through the frequencies to the functional level. Kolff's big body shivered as the hormones and the electricity hit it simultaneously; his right hand rose a few inches, fist clenched, and dropped back again. "Galvanic response," Aster muttered. "Nothing more."

But she didn't give up. The life-support rig had a full complement of emergency devices, and she put them all into use. A chest compressor carried on artificial respiration; she injected refrigerants into his bloodstream to prevent brain decay; the electrodes rhythmically assaulted the valves of his heart. Kolff was nearly concealed by the assortment of first-aid-equipment covering him.

Vornan knelt and peered intently into Kolff's staring eyes. He observed the slackness of the features. He put a tentative hand forth to touch Kolff's mottled cheek. He noted the mechanisms that pumped and squeezed and throbbed on top of the fallen man. Then he rose and said quietly to me, "What are they trying to do to him, please?"

"Bring him back to life."

"This is death, then?"

"Death, yes."

"What happened to him?"

"His heart stopped working, Vornan. Do you know what the heart is?"

"Yes, yes."

"Kolff's heart was tired. It stopped. Aster's trying to start it again. She won't succeed."

"Does this happen often, this thing of death?"

"Once at least in everybody's lifetime," I said bitterly. A doctor had been summoned now. He pulled more apparatus from the life-support rig and began making an incision in Kolff's chest. I said to Vornan, "How does death come in your time?"

"Never suddenly. Never like this. I know very little about it."

He seemed more fascinated with the presence of death

even than he had been with the creation of life in this same room. The doctor toiled; but Kolff did not respond, and the rest of us stood in a ring like statues. Only Aster moved, picking up the creatures that Kolff in his last convulsion had spilled. Some of them too were dead, a few from exposure to air, the others from being crushed by heedless feet. But some survived. She put them back in a tank.

At length the doctor rose, shaking his head.

I looked at Kralick. He was weeping.

## * FIFTEEN *

KOLFF WAS BURIED in New York with high academic honors. Out of respect we halted our tour for a few days. Vornan attended the funeral; he was vastly curious about our customs of interment. His presence at the ceremony nearly caused a crisis, for the gowned academics pressed close to get a glimpse of him, and at one point I thought the coffin itself would be overturned in the confusion. Three books went into Kolff's grave with him. Two were works of his own; the third was the Hebrew translation of *The New Revelation*. I was enraged by that, but Kralick told me it had been Kolff's own idea. Three or four days before the end he had given Helen McIlwain a sealed tape that turned out to contain burial instructions.

After the period of mourning we headed west again to continue Vornan's tour. It was surprising how fast the death of Kolff ceased to matter to us; we were five now instead of six, but the shock of his collapse dwindled and shortly we were back to routine. As the season warmed, though, certain quiet changes in mood became apparent. Distribution of *The New Revelation* seemed complete, since virtually everyone in the country had a copy, and the crowds that attended Vornan's movements were larger every day. Subsidiary prophets were springing up, interpreters of Vornan's message to humanity. The focus for much of this activity was in California, as usual, and Kralick took good care to keep Vornan out of that state. He was perturbed by this gathering cult, as was I, as were all of us. Vornan alone seemed to enjoy the presence of his flock. Even he sometimes seemed a bit apprehensive, as when he landed at an airport to find a sea of red-covered volumes gleaming in the sunlight. At least it was my impression that the really huge mobs made him ill at ease; but most of the time he seemed to revel in the attention he gained. One California newspaper had suggested quite seriously that Vornan be nominated to run for the Senate in the next election. I found Kralick gagging over the facsim of that one when it came in. "If Vornan ever sees this," he said, "we could be in a mess."

There was to be no Senator Vornan, luckily. In a calmer moment we persuaded ourselves that he could not meet the residence requirements; and, too, we doubted that the courts would accept a member of the Centrality as a citizen of the United States, unless Vornan had some way of demonstrating the Centrality to be the legally constituted successor-in-fact to the sovereignty of the United States.

The schedule called for Vornan to be taken to the Moon at the end of May to see the recently developed resort there. I begged off from this; I had no real wish to visit the pleasure palaces of Copernicus, and it seemed to me that I could use the extra time to get my personal affairs in order at Irvine as the semester ended. Kralick wanted me to go, especially since I had already had one leave of absence; but he had no practical way of compelling me, and in the end he let me have another leave. A committee of four could manage Vornan as well as a committee of five, he decided.

But it was a committee of three by the time they actually did depart for the lunar base.

Fields resigned on the eve of the departure. Kralick should have seen it coming, since Fields had been grumbling and muttering for weeks, and was in obvious rebellion against the entire assignment. As a psychologist, Fields had been studying Vornan's responses to the environment as we moved about, and had come up with two or three contradictory and mutually exclusive evaluations. Depending on his own emotional weather, Fields concluded that Vornan was or was not an impostor, and filed reports covering almost every possibility. My private evaluation of Fields' evaluations was that they were worthless. His cosmic interpretations of Vornan's actions were in themselves empty and vapid, but I could have forgiven that if only Fields had managed to sustain the same opinion for more than two consecutive weeks.

His resignation from the committee, though, did not come on ideological grounds. It was provoked by nothing more profound than petty jealousy. And I must admit, little as I liked Fields, that I sympathized with him in this instance.

The trouble arose over Aster. Fields was still pursuing her in a kind of hopeless romantic quest which was as repugnant to the rest of us as it was depressing for him. She did not want him; that was quite clear, even to Fields. But proximity does strange things to a man's ego, and Fields kept trying. He bribed hotel clerks to put his room next to Aster's and searched for ways to slip into her bedroom at night. Aster was annoyed, though not as much as if she'd been a real flesh-and-blood woman; in many ways she was as artificial as her own coelenterates, and she minimized the Byronic heavings and pantings of her too-ardent swain.

As Helen McIlwain told me, Fields grew more and more visibly worked up over this treatment. Finally one night when everyone was gathered together, he asked

Aster point-blank to spend the night with him. She said no. Fields then delivered himself of some blistering commentary on the defects in Aster's libido. Loudly and angrily he accused her of frigidity, perversity, malevolence, and several other varieties of bitchiness. In a way, everything he said about Aster was probably true, with one limiting factor: she was an *unintentional* bitch. I don't think she had been trying to tease or provoke him at all. She had simply failed to understand what sort of response was expected of her.

This time, though, she remembered that she was a woman, and disemboweled Fields in a notably feminine way. In front of Fields, in front of everyone, she invited Vornan to share her bed with her that night. She made it quite clear that she was offering herself to Vornan without reservations. I wish I had seen that. As Helen put it, Aster looked female for the first time: eyes aglow, lips drawn back, face flushed, claws unsheathed. Naturally Vornan obliged her. Away they went together, Aster as radiant as a bride on her wedding night. For all I know, she thought of it that way.

Fields could take no more. I hardly blame him. Aster had cut him up in a fairly ultimate way, and it was too much to expect him to stick around for more of the same. He told Kralick he was quitting. Kralick naturally appealed to Fields to stay on, calling it his patriotic duty, his obligation to science, and so forth—a set of abstractions which I know are as hollow to Kralick as to the rest of us. It was a ritualized speech, and Fields ignored it. That night he packed up and cleared out, thus sparing himself, according to Helen, the sight of Aster and Vornan coming forth from the nuptial chambers the next morning in a fine full gleam of recollected delights.

I was back in Irvine while all this went on. Like any ordinary citizen I followed Vornan's career by screen, when I remembered to tune in. My few months with him now seemed even less real than when they were happening; I had to make an effort to convince myself that I had not dreamed the whole thing. But it was no dream. Vornan was up there on the Moon, being shepherded about by Kralick, Helen, Heyman, and Aster. Kolff was dead. Fields had gone back to Chicago. He called me from there in the middle of June; he was writing a book on his experiences with Vornan, he said, and wanted to check a few details with me. He said nothing about his motives for resigning.

I forgot about Fields and his book within the hour. I tried to forget about Vornan-19, too. I returned to my much-neglected work, but I found it flat, weary, stale, and unprofitable. Wandering aimlessly around the laboratory, shuffling through the tapes of old experiments, occasionally tapping out something new on the computer, yawning my way through conferences with the graduate students, I suppose I cut a pathetic figure: King Lear among the elementary particles, too old, too dull-witted, too frazzled to grasp my own questions. I sensed the younger men patronizing me that month. I felt eighty years old. Yet none of them had any suggestions for breaking through the barrier that contained our research. They were stymied too; the difference was that they were confident something would turn up if we only kept on searching, while I seemed to have lost interest not only in the search but in the goal.

Naturally they were very curious about my views on the authenticity of Vornan-19. Had I learned anything about his method of moving through time? Did I think he really *had* moved in time? What theoretical implications could be found in the fact of his visit?

I had no answers. The questions themselves became tedious. And so I wandered through a month of idleness, stalling, faking. Possibly I should have left the University again and visited Shirley and Jack. But my last visit there had been a disturbing one, revealing unexpected gulfs and craters in their marriage, and I was afraid to go back for

fear I would discover that my one· remaining place of
refuge was lost to me. Nor could I keep running away
from my work, depressing and moribund though it was. I
stayed in California. I visited my laboratory every day or
two. I checked through the papers of my students. I
avoided the cascades of media people who wanted to
question me about·Vornan-19. I slept a good deal, sometimes twelve and thirteen hours at a stretch, hoping to
sleep my way through this period of doldrums entirely. I
read novels and plays and poetry in an obsessive way,
going on binges. You can guess my mood from the statement that I worked myself through the Prophetic Books
of Blake in five consecutive nights, without skipping a
word. Those inspired ravings clog my mind even now,
half a year later. I read all of Proust, too, and much of
Dostoyevsky, and a dozen anthologies of the nightmares
that passed for plays in the Jacobean era. It was all
apocalyptic art for an apocalyptic era, but much of it
faded as fast as it moved across my glazed retina, leaving
only a residue: Charlus, Svidrigailov, the Duchess of
Malfi, Vindice, Swann's Odette. The foggy dreams of
Blake remain: Enitharmon and Urizen, Los, Orc, majestic
Golgonooza:

> But blood & wounds & dismal cries &
> clarions of war,
> And hearts laid open to the light by the
> broad grizly sword,
> And bowels hidden in hammered steel
> ripp'd forth upon the ground.
> Call forth thy smiles of soft deceit, call
> forth thy cloudy tears!
> We hear thy sighs in trumpets shrill
> when Morn shall blood renew.

During this fevered time of solitude and inner confusion
I paid little attention to the pair of conflicting mass move-

ments that troubled the world, the one coming in, the other going out. The Apocalyptists were not extinct by any means, and their marches and riots and orgies still continued, although in a kind of dogged stubbornness not too different from the galvanic twitches of Lloyd Kolff's dead arm. Their time was over. Not too many of the world's uncommitted people now cared to believe that Armageddon was due to arrive on January 1, 2000—not with Vornan roaming about as living evidence to the contrary. Those who took part in the Apocalyptist uprisings now, I gathered, were those for whom orgy and destruction had become a way of life; there was nothing theological in their posturings and cavortings any longer. Within this group of rowdies there was a hard core of the devout, looking forward hungrily to imminent Doomsday, but these fanatics were losing ground daily. In July, with less than six months left before the designated day of holocaust, it appeared to impartial observers that the Apocalyptist creed would succumb to inertia long before mankind's supposed final weeks arrived. Now we know that that is not so, for as I speak these words, only eight days remain before the hour of truth appears; and the Apocalyptists are still very much with us. It is Christmas eve, 1999, tonight—the anniversary of Vornan's manifestation in Rome, I now realize.

If in July the Apocalyptists seemed to be fading, that other cult, the nameless one of Vornan-worship, was certainly gathering momentum. It had no thesis and no purpose; the aim of its adherents seemed only to be to get close to the figure of Vornan and scream their excited approbation of him. *The New Revelation* was its only scripture: a disjointed, incoherent patchwork of interviews and press conferences, studded here and there with tantalizing nuggets Vornan had dropped. I could construct just two tenets of Vornanism: that life on earth is an accident caused by the carelessness of interstellar visitors, and that the world will not be destroyed next January 1. I suppose religions have been founded on slimmer bases than these, but I can think of no examples. Yet the Vornanites continued to gather around the charismatic, enigmatic figure of their prophet. Surprisingly, many followed him to the Moon, creating crowds there that had not been seen since the opening of the commercial resort in Copernicus some years back. The rest assembled around giant screens erected in open plazas by canny corporations, and watched en masse the relays from Luna. And I in turn occasionally tuned in on pickups from those mass meetings.

What troubled me most about this movement was its formlessness. It was awaiting the shaper's hand. If Vornan chose to, he could give direction and impetus to his cult, merely by delivering a few ex cathedra pronouncements. He could call for holy wars, for political upheavals, for dancing in the streets, for abstinence from stimulants, for overindulgence in stimulants—and millions would obey. He had not cared to make use of this power thus far. Perhaps it was only gradually dawning on him that the power was available to him. I had seen Vornan turn a private party into a shambles with a few casual movements of his hand; what could he not do once he grasped the levers that control the world?

The strength of his cult was appalling, and so was the speed at which it grew. His absence on the Moon seemed not to matter at all. Even from a distance he exerted a pull, as powerful and as mindless as the tug of the Moon itself on our seas. He was, more accurately than the cliché can convey, all things to all men; there were those who loved him for his gaudy nihilism, and others who saw him as a symbol of stability in a tottering world. I don't doubt that his basic appeal was as a deity: not Jehovah, not Wotan, not a remote and bearded father-figure, but as a handsome, dynamic, buoyant Young God, the incarnation of springtime and light, the creative and the destructive forces bound into a single synthesis. He was Apollo. He was Baldur. He was Osiris. But also he was Loki, and the old mythmakers had not contemplated that particular combination.

His visit to Luna was extended several times. I believe it was the intention of Kralick—on behalf of the Government—to keep Vornan away from Earth as long as possible, so that the dangerous emotions engendered by his arrival in the last year of the old millennium might have a chance to subside. He had been scheduled to stay only to the end of June, but late in July he was still there. On the screens we caught glimpses of him in the gravity baths, or gravely examining the hydroponics tanks, or jet-skiing, or mingling with a select group of international celebrities at the gambling tables. And I noticed Aster beside him quite often, looking oddly regal, her slim body bedecked in startlingly revealing, astonishingly un-Aster-like costumes. Hovering in the background occasionally were Helen and Heyman, an ill-assorted pair linked by mutual detestation, and I sometimes picked out the looming figure of Sandy Kralick, dour-faced, grim, lost in contemplation of his unlikely assignment.

At the end of July I was notified that Vornan was returning and that my services would again be needed. I was instructed to go to the San Francisco spaceport to await Vornan's landing a week hence. A day later I received a copy of an unpleasant little pamphlet which I'm sure did not improve the flavor of Sandy Kralick's mood. It was a glossy-covered thing bound in red to imitate *The New Revelation*; its title was *The Newest Revelation* and its author was Morton Fields. A signed copy came to me compliments of the author. Before long, millions were in circulation, not because the booklet had any inherent interest but because it was mistaken by some for its original, and because it was coveted by others who collected any scrap of printed matter dealing with the advent of Vornan-19.

*The Newest Revelation* was Fields' ugly memoir of his experiences on tour with Vornan. It was his way of vent-ing his spleen against Aster, mainly. It did not name her—for fear of the libel laws, I suppose—but no one could fail to identify her, since there were only two women on the committee and Helen McIlwain was mentioned by name. The portrait of Aster that emerged was not one that corresponded to the Aster Mikkelsen I had known; Fields showed her as a treacherous, sly, deceitful, and above all else amoral minx who had prostituted herself to the members of the committee, who had driven Lloyd Kolff into his grave with her insatiable sexual appetite, and who had committed every abomination known to man with Vornan-19. Among her lesser crimes was her deliberate sadistic torment of the one virtuous and sane member of our group, who was of course Morton Fields. Fields had written:

"This vicious and wanton woman took a strange delight in sharpening her claws on me. I was her easiest victim. Because I made it clear from the start that I disliked her, she set out to snare me into her bed—and when I rebuffed her, she grew more determined to add me to her collection of scalps. Her provocations grew flagrant and shameful, until in a weak moment I found myself about to yield to them. Then, of course, with great glee she denounced me as a Don Juan, callously humiliating me before the others, and . . ."

And so on. The whining tone was maintained consistently throughout. Fields ticked each of us off unsparingly. Helen McIlwain was a giddy post-adolescent, somewhat overripe; Lloyd Kolff was a superannuated dodderer making his way through gluttony, lechery, and the shrewd use of a mind that contained nothing but erotic verse; F. Richard Heyman was an arrogant stuffed shirt. (I did not find Fields' characterization of Heyman unjust.) Kralick was dismissed as a Government flunkey, trying hard to save everyone's face at once, and willing to make any compromise at all to avoid trouble. Fields was quite blunt about the Government's role in the Vornan affair. He said openly that the President had ordered complete acceptance of Vornan's claims in order to deflate the Apocalyptists; this of course was true, but no one had admitted it publicly before, certainly not anyone so highly placed in the circles around Vornan as was Fields. Luckily he buried his complaint in a long, clotted passage devoted to a paranoid flaying of the national psyche, and I suspect the point was overlooked by most readers.

I came off fairly well in Fields' assessments. He described me as aloof, superficial, falsely profound, a mock-philosopher who invariably recoiled in terror from any hard issue. I am not pleased with those indictments, but I suspect that I must plead guilty to the charges. Fields touched on my excessive venery, on my lack of real commitment to any cause, and on my easy tolerance of the defects of those about me. Yet there was no venom in his paragraph on me; to him, I seemed neither fool nor villain, but rather a neutral figure of little interest. So be it.

Fields' nasty gossip about his fellow committeemen alone would not have won his book much of a following outside academic circles, nor would I be speaking of it at such great length. The core of his essay was his "newest revelation"—his analysis of Vornan-19. Muddled, mazy, stilted, and dreary though it was, this section managed to carry enough of Vornan's charisma to gain it readership. And thus Fields' foolish little book achieved an influence out of all proportion to its real content.

He devoted only a few paragraphs to the question of Vornan's authenticity. Over the course of the past six months Fields had held a variety of contradictory views on that subject, and he managed to pile all the contradictions into a short space here. In effect he said that probably Vornan was not an impostor, but that it would serve us all right if he were, and in any case it did not matter. What counted was not the absolute truth concerning Vornan, but only his impact on 1999. In this I think Fields was correct. Fraud or not, Vornan's effect on us was undeniable, and the power of his passage through our world was genuine even if Vornan-as-time-traveler may not have been.

So Fields dispensed with that problem in a cluster of blurred ambiguities and moved on to an interpretation of Vornan's culture-role among us. It was very simple, said Fields. Vornan was a god. He was deity and prophet rolled into one, an omnipotent self-advertiser, offering himself as the personification of all the vague, unfocused yearnings of a planet whose people had had too much comfort, too much tension, too much fear. He was a god for our times, giving off electricity that may or may not have been produced by surgically implanted power-packs; a god who Zeus-like took mortals to his bed; a trouble-maker of a god; a slippery, elusive, evasive, self-indulgent god, offering nothing and accepting much. You must realize that in summarizing Fields' thoughts I am greatly compressing them and also untangling them, cutting away the brambles and thorns of excessive dogmatism and leaving only the inner theory with which I myself wholly agree. Surely Fields had caught the essence of our response to Vornan.

Nowhere in *The Newest Revelation* did Fields claim that Vornan-19 was *literally* divine, any more than he offered a final opinion on the genuineness of his claim to have come from the future. Fields did not care whether or not Vornan was genuine, and he certainly did not think that he was in any way a supernatural being. What he was really saying—and I believe it wholeheartedly—was that *we ourselves had made Vornan into a god*. We had needed a deity to preside over us as we entered our new millennium, for the old gods had abdicated; and Vornan had come along to fill our need. Fields was analyzing humanity, not assessing Vornan.

But of course humanity in the mass is not capable of absorbing such subtle distinctions. Here was a book bound in red which said that Vornan was a god! Never mind the hedgings and fudgings, never mind the scholarly obfuscations. Vornan's divine status was officially proclaimed! And from "he is a god" to "He is God" is a very short journey. *The Newest Revelation* became a sacred scripture. Did it not say in words, in printed words, that Vornan was divine? Could one ignore such words?

The magical process followed expectations. The little red pamphlet was translated into every language of mankind, serving as it did as the holy justification of the madness of Vornan-worship. The faithful had an additional talisman to carry about. And Morton Fields became the St. Paul of the new creed, the press agent of the prophet. Although he never saw Vornan again, never took an active part in the movement he unwittingly helped to encourage, Fields through his foul little book has already become an invisible presence of great significance in the movement that now sweeps the world. I suspect that he is due to be elevated to a lofty place in the canon of saints, once the new hagiologies have been written.

Reading my advance copy of Fields' book at the beginning of August, I failed to guess the impact it would have. I read it quickly and with the sort of cold fascination one feels upon lifting a boulder at the seashore to disclose squirming white things beneath; and then I tossed it aside, amused and repelled, and forgot all about it until its importance became manifest. Duly I reported to San Francisco to greet Vornan when he landed from space. The usual subterfuges and precautions were in effect at the spaceport. While a roaring crowd waved *The New Revelation* aloft under a gray fogbound sky, Vornan moved through a subterranean channel to a staging area at the edge of the spaceport. ·

He took my hand warmly. "Leo, you should have come," he said. "It was pure delight. The triumph of your age, I'd say, that resort on the Moon. What have you been doing?"

"Reading, Vornan. Resting. Working."

"To good effect?"

"To no effect whatever."

He looked sleek, relaxed, as confident as always. Some of his radiance had transferred itself to Aster, who stood beside him in a frankly possessive way, no longer the blank, absent, crystalline Aster I remembered, but a warmly passionate woman fully awakened to her own soul at last. However he had worked this miracle, it was undoubtedly his most impressive achievement. Her transformation was remarkable. My eyes met hers and in their liquid depths I saw a secret smile. On the other hand, Helen McIlwain looked old and drained, her features slack, her hair coarse, her posture slumped. For the first time she seemed to be a woman in middle age. Later I discovered what had harrowed her: she felt defeated by Aster, for she had assumed all along that Vornan regarded her as a kind of consort, and quite clearly that role had passed to Aster. Heyman, too, seemed weakened. The Teutonic heaviness I so disliked was gone from him. He said little, offered no greeting, and appeared remote, distracted, dislocated. He reminded me of Lloyd Kolff in his final weeks. Prolonged exposure to Vornan obviously had its dangers. Even Kralick, tough and resilient, looked badly overextended. His hand was shaking as he held it toward mine, and the fingers splayed apart from one another, requiring of him a conscious effort to unite them.

On the surface, though, the reunion was a pleasant one. Nothing was said about any strains that might have developed, nor about the apostasy of the odious Fields. I rode with Vornan in a motorcade to downtown San Francisco, and cheering multitudes lined the route, occasionally blocking it, just as though someone of the highest importance had arrived.

We resumed the interrupted tour.

Vornan had by now seen about as much of the United States as was deemed a representative sample, and the itinerary called for him to go abroad. Theoretically the responsibility of our Government should have ended at that point. We had not shepherded Vornan about in the earliest days of his visit to the twentieth century, when he had been exploring (and demoralizing) the capitals of Europe; we should have handed him on to others now that he was moving westward. But responsibilities have a way of institutionalizing themselves. Sandy Kralick was stuck with the job of conveying Vornan from place to place, for he was the world's leading authority on that chore; and Aster, Helen, Heyman and myself were swept along in Vornan's orbit. I did not object. I was blatantly eager to escape from the need to confront my own work.

So we traveled. We headed into Mexico, toured the dead cities of Chichén Itzá and Uxmal, prowled Mayan pyramids at midnight, and cut over to Mexico City for a view of the hemisphere's most vibrant metropolis. Vornan took it all in quietly. His chastened mood, first in evidence in the spring, had remained with him here at the end of summer. No longer did he commit verbal outrages, no longer did he utter unpredictably scabrous comments, no longer could he be depended on to upset any plan or program in which he was involved. His actions seemed perfunctory and spasmodic now. He did not bother to infuriate us. I wondered why. Was he sick? His smile was as dazzling as ever, but there was no vitality behind it; he was all façade, now. He was going through the idle motions of a global tour and responding in a purely mechanical way to all he saw. Kralick seemed concerned. He, too, preferred Vornan the demon to Vornan the automaton, and wondered why the animation had gone out of him.

I spent a good deal of time with Vornan as we whirled westward from Mexico City to Hawaii, and on from there to Tokyo, Peking, Angkor, Melbourne, Tahiti, and Antarctica. I had not entirely given up my hope of getting hard information from him on the scientific points that were of concern to me; but although I failed in that, I learned a bit more about Vornan himself. I discovered why he was so flaccid these days.

He had lost interest in us.

We bored him. Our passions, our monuments, our foolishnesses, our cities, our foods, our conflicts, our neuroses —he had sampled everything, and the taste had palled. He was, he confessed to me, deathly weary of being hauled to and fro on the face of our world.

"Why don't you go back to your own time, then?" I asked.

"Not yet, Leo."

"But if we're so tiresome to you—"

"I think I'll stay, anyhow. I can endure the boredom a while longer. I want to see how things turn out."

"What things?"

"Things," he said.

I repeated this to Kralick, who merely shrugged. "Let's hope he sees how things turn out fast," Kralick said. "He's not the only one who's tired of traveling around."

The pace of our journey was stepped up, as though Kralick wished to sicken Vornan thoroughly of the twentieth century. Sights and textures blurred and swirled; we zigzagged out of the white wastes of the Antarctic into the tropic swelter of Ceylon, and darted through India and the Near East, went by felucca up the Nile, trekked into the heart of Africa, sped from one shining capital to the next. Wherever we went, even in the most backward countries, the reception was a frenzied one. Thousands turned out to hail the visiting deity. By now—it was nearly October— the message of *The Newest Revelation* had had time to sink in. Fields' analogies were transformed into assertions; there was no Vornanite Church in any formal sense, but quite plainly the unfocused mass hysteria was coalescing into a religious movement.

My fears that Vornan would try to take hold of this

movement proved unfounded. The crowds bored him as much as laboratories and power plants now did. From enclosed balconies he hailed the roaring throngs like a Caesar, with upraised palm; but I did not fail to notice the flicker of the nostrils, the barely suppressed yawn. "What do they want from me?" he asked, almost petulantly.

"They want to love you," Helen said.

"But why? Are they so empty?"

"Terribly empty," Helen murmured.

Heyman said distantly, "If you went among them, you'd feel their love."

Vornan seemed to shiver. "It would be unwise. They would destroy me with their love."

I remembered Vornan in Los Angeles six months before, gleefully plunging into a mad mob of Apocalyptists. He had shown no dread of their desperate energies then. True, he had been masked, but the risks had still been great. The image of Vornan with a pile of stunned cultists forming a living barricade came to me. What joy he had felt in the midst of that chaos! Now he feared the love of the mobs that yearned for him. This was a new Vornan, then, a cautious one. Perhaps at last he was aware of the forces he had helped to unleash, and had grown more serious in his appraisal of danger. That freewheeling Vornan of the early days was gone.

In mid-October we were in Johannesburg, scheduled to hop the Atlantic for a tour of South America. South America was primed and ready for him. The first signs of organized Vornanism were appearing there: in Brazil and Argentina there had been prayer meetings attended by thousands; and we heard that churches were being founded, though the details were fragmentary and uninformative. Vornan showed no curiosity about this development. Instead he turned to me suddenly late one afternoon and said, "I wish to rest for a while, Leo."

"To take a nap?"

"No, to rest from traveling. The crowds, the noise, the

223

excitement—I have had enough. I want quietness now."

"You'd better talk to Kralick."

"First I must talk to you. Some weeks ago, Leo, you spoke to me of friends of yours in a quiet place. A man and a woman, a former pupil of yours, do you know the ones I mean?"

I knew. I went rigid. In an idle moment I had told Vornan about Jack and Shirley, about the pleasure it gave me to flee to them at times of internal crisis or fatigue. In telling him, I had hoped to draw from him some parallel declaration, some detail of his own habits and relationships in that world of the future that seemed yet so unreal to me. But I had not anticipated *this*.

"Yes," I said tensely. "I know who you mean."

"Perhaps we could go there together, Leo. You and I, and these two people, without the others, without the guards, the noise, the crowds. We could quietly disappear. I must renew my energies. This trip has been a strain for me, you know. And I want to see people of this era in day-to-day life. What I have seen so far has been a show, a pageant. But just to sit quietly and talk—I would like it very much. Could you arrange it for me, Leo?"

I was taken off balance. The sudden warmth of Vornan's appeal disarmed me; and automatically I found myself calculating that we might learn much about Vornan this way, yes, that Jack, Shirley, and I, sipping cocktails in the Arizona sunlight, might pry from the visitor facts that had remained concealed during his highly public progress around the world. I was aware of what we might try to get from Vornan; and deluded by the undemanding Vornan of recent months, I failed to take into account what Vornan might try to get from us. "I'll talk to my friends," I promised. "And to Kralick. I'll see what I can do about it, Vornan."

# * SIXTEEN *

KRALICK WAS BOTHERED at first by the disruption of the carefully balanced itinerary; South America, he said, would be very disappointed to learn that Vornan's arrival would be postponed. But the positive aspects of the scheme were apparent to him as well. He thought it might be useful to get Vornan-19 off into a different kind of environment, away from the crowds and the cameras. I think he welcomed the chance to escape from Vornan for a while himself. In the end he approved the proposal.

Then I called Jack and Shirley.

I felt hesitant about dropping Vornan on them, even though they had both begged me to arrange something like this. Jack was desperately eager to talk to Vornan about total conversion of energy, though I knew he'd learn nothing. And Shirley . . . Shirley had confessed to me that she was physically drawn to the man from 2999. It was for her sake that I hesitated. Then I told myself that whatever Shirley might feel toward Vornan was something for Shirley herself to resolve, and that if anything happened between Shirley and Vornan, it would be only with Jack's consent and blessing. In which case I did not have to feel responsible.

When I told them what had been proposed, they both thought I was joking. I had to work hard to persuade them that I really could bring Vornan to them. At length they decided to believe me, and I saw them exchange offscreen glances; then Jack said, "How soon is this going to come about?"

"Tomorrow, if you're ready for it."

"Why not?" Shirley said.

I searched her face for a betrayal of her desire. But I saw nothing except simple excitement.

"Why not?" Jack agreed. "But tell me this: is the place going to be overrun by reporters and policemen? I won't put up with that."

"No," I said. "Vornan's whereabouts are going to be kept secret from the press. There won't be a media man in sight. And I suppose the access roads to your place will be guarded, just in case, but you won't be bothered with security people. I'll make sure they stay far away."

"All right," Jack said. "Bring him, then."

Kralick had the South American trip postponed, and announced that Vornan was going to an undisclosed place for a private holiday of indeterminate length. We let it leak out that he would be vacationing at a villa somewhere in the Indian Ocean. Amid great show of significance, a private plane left Johannesburg the next morning bound for the island of Mauritius. It sufficed to keep the press baffled and misled. A little later that morning Vornan and I boarded a small jet and headed across the Atlantic. We changed planes in Tampa and were in Tucson by early afternoon. A car was waiting there. I told the Government chauffeur to get lost, and drove down to Jack and Shirley's place myself. Kralick, I knew, had spread a surveillance net in a fifty-mile radius around the house, but he had agreed not to let any of his men come closer unless I requested help. We would be undisturbed. It was a flawless late-autumn afternoon, the sky sharp and flat, free of clouds, the taut blueness practically vibrating. The mountains seemed unusually distinct. As I drove, I noticed the occasional golden gleam of a Government copter high overhead. They were watching us ... from a distance.

Shirley and Jack were in front of the house when we drove up. Jack wore a ragged shirt and faded jeans; Shirley was dressed in a skimpy halter and shorts. I had not seen them since the spring, and I had spoken to them only a few times. It struck me that the tensions I had observed in them in the spring had continued to erode them over the succeeding months. They both looked edgy, coiled, compressed, in a way that could not altogether be credited to the arrival of their celebrated guest.

"This is Vornan-19," I said. "Jack Bryant. Shirley."

"Such a pleasure," Vornan said gravely. He did not offer his hand, but bowed in an almost Japanese way, first to Jack, then to Shirley. An awkward silence followed. We stood staring at each other under the harsh sun. Shirley and Jack behaved almost ás though they had never believed in Vornan's existence until this moment; they seemed to regard him as some fictional character unexpectedly conjured into life. Jack clamped his lips together so firmly that his cheeks throbbed. Shirley, never taking her eyes from Vornan, rocked back and forth on the balls of her bare feet. Vornan, self-contained and affable, studied the house, its environment, and its occupants with cool curiosity.

"Let me show you to your room," Shirley blurted.

I fetched the luggage: a suitcase apiece for Vornan and myself. My own grip was nearly empty, holding nothing more than a few changes of clothing; but I had to struggle to lift Vornan's. Naked he had come into this world, but he had accumulated a good deal on his travels: clothing, knickknacks, a random miscellany. I hauled it into the house. Shirley had given Vornan the room I usually occupied, and a storage room near the sun deck had been hastily converted into an auxiliary guest room for me. That seemed quite proper. I set his suitcase down, and left Shirley with him to instruct him in the use of the household appliances. Jack took me to my own room.

I said, "I want you to realize, Jack, that this visit can be ended at any time. If Vornan gets to be too much for you, just say the word and we'll pull out. I don't want you going to any trouble on his account."

"That's all right. I think this is going to be interesting, Leo."

"No doubt. But it might also be strenuous."

He smiled fitfully. "Will I get a chance to talk to him?"

"Of course."

"You know about what."

"Yes. Talk all you like. There won't be much else to do. But you won't get anywhere, Jack."

"I can try, at least." In a low voice he added, "He's shorter than I thought he'd be. But impressive. Very impressive. He's got a kind of natural power to dominate, doesn't he?"

"Napoleon was a short man," I reminded him. "Also Hitler."

"Does Vornan know that?"

"He doesn't seem to be much of a student of history," I said, and we both laughed.

A little while later Shirley came out of Vornan's room and encountered me in the hall. I don't think she expected to find me there, for I caught a quick glimpse of her face, and she was wholly without the mask that we wear in front of others. Her eyes, her nostrils, her lips, all revealed raw emotion, churning conflicts. I wondered if Vornan had attempted anything in the five minutes they had been together. Certainly what I saw on Shirley's face was purely sexual, a tide of desire flooding toward the surface. An instant later she realized I was looking at her, and the mask slipped swiftly into place. She smiled nervously. "He's all settled in," she said. "I like him, Leo. You know, I expected him to be cold and forbidding, some kind of robotlike thing. But he's polite and courtly, a real gentleman in his strange way."

"He's quite the charmer, yes."

Telltale points of color lingered in her cheeks. "Do you think it was a mistake for us to say he could come here?"

"Why should it be a mistake?"

She moistened her lips. "There's no telling what might happen. He's beautiful, Leo. He's irresistible."

228

"Are you afraid of your own desires?"

"I'm afraid of hurting Jack."

"Then don't do anything without Jack's consent," I said, feeling more than ever like an uncle. "It's that simple. Don't get carried away."

"What if I do, Leo? When I was in the room with him—I saw him *looking* at me so hungrily—"

"He looks at all beautiful women that way. But surely you know how to say no, Shirley."

"I'm not sure I'd want to say no."

I shrugged. "Should I call Kralick and say that we'd like to leave?"

"No!"

"Then you'll have to be the watchdog of your own chastity, I'm afraid. You're an adult, Shirley. You ought to be able to keep from sleeping with your house guest if you think it would be unwise. That's never been much of a problem for you before."

She recoiled, startled, at my gratuitous final words. Her face crimsoned again beneath the deep tan. She peered at me as if she had never seen me in clear focus before. I felt angry at myself for my foolishness. In one breath I had cheapened a decade-long relationship. But the taut moment passed. Shirley relaxed as though going through a series of inner exercises, and said at last in a calm voice, "You're right, Leo. It won't really be a problem."

The evening was surprisingly free from tension. Shirley produced a magnificent meal, and Vornan was lavish in his praise; it was, he said, the first dinner he had eaten in anyone's home, and he was delighted by it. Afterwards we strolled together at twilight. Jack walked beside Vornan, and I with Shirley, but we stayed close to one another. Jack pointed out a kangaroo rat that had emerged from hiding a little early and went hopping madly over the desert. We saw a few jackrabbits and some lizards. It forever astonished Vornan that wild animals should be on the loose. Later, we returned to the house for drinks, and sat pleasantly like four old friends, talking of nothing in particular. Vornan seemed to accommodate himself perfectly to the personalities of his hosts. I began to think that *i* had been uneasy over nothing.

The curious tranquility continued for several days more. We slept late, explored the desert, reveled in eighty-degree heat, talked, ate, peered at the stars. Vornan was restrained and almost cautious. Yet he spoke more of his own time here than was usual for him. Pointing to the stars, he tried to describe the constellations he knew, but he failed to find any, not even the Dipper. He talked of food taboos and how daring it would be for him to sit at table with his hosts in a parallel situation in 2999. He reminisced lazily about his ten months among us, like a traveler who is close to the end of his journey and beginning to look back at remembered pleasures.

We were careful not to tune in on any news broadcasts while Vornan was around. I did not want him to know that there had been riots of disappointment in South America over the postponement of his visit, nor that a kind of Vornan-hysteria was sweeping the world, with folk everywhere looking toward the visitor for all the answers to the riddles of the universe. In his past pronouncements Vornan had smugly let it be known that he would eventually supply all the answers to everything, and this promissory note seemed to be infinitely negotiable, even though in fact Vornan had raised more questions than answers. It was good to keep him in isolation here, far from the nodes of control that he might so easily seize.

On the fourth morning we woke to brilliant sunlight. I cut out my window-opaquers and found Vornan already on the sundeck. He was nude, stretched cozily in a web-foam cradle, basking in the brightness. I tapped on the window. He looked up, saw me, smiled. I stepped outside just as he rose from the cradle. His sleek, smooth body might almost have been made of some seamless plastic

230

substance; his skin was without blemish and he had no
body hair whatever. He was neither muscular nor flabby,
and seemed simultaneously frail and powerful. I know
that sounds paradoxical. He was also formidably male.
"It's wonderfully warm out here, Leo," he said. "Take off
your clothes and join me."

I held back. I had not told Vornan of the free-and-easy
nudism of my earlier visits to this house; and thus far all
the proprieties had been carefully observed. But of course
Vornan had no nudity taboos; and now that he had made
the first move, Shirley was quick to follow. She emerged
on the deck, saw Vornan bare and myself clad in night-
clothes, and said smilingly, "Yes, that's quite all right. I
meant to suggest that yesterday. We aren't foolish about
our bodies here." And having made that declaration of
liberalism, she stripped away the flimsy wrap she had been
wearing and lay down to enjoy the sun. Vornan watched
in what struck me as remarkably aloof curiosity as Shirley
revealed her supple, magnificently endowed body. He
seemed interested, but only in a theoretical way. This was
not the ravenously wolfish Vornan I knew. Shirley,
though, betrayed profound inner discomfort. A flush
swept nearly to the base of her throat. Her movements
were exaggeratedly casual. Her eyes strayed guiltily to
Vornan's loins a moment, then quickly pulled away. Her
nipples gave her away, rising in sudden excitement. She
knew it, and hastily rolled over to lie on her belly, but not
before I had noticed the effect. When Shirley and Jack
and I had sunbathed together, it had been as innocent as
in Eden; but the stiffening of those two nubs of erectile
tissue bluntly advertised how she felt about being nude in
front of a nude Vornan.

Jack appeared a while later. He took in the situation
with an amused glance: Shirley sprawled out with upturned
buttocks, Vornan peeled and dozing, I pacing the sundeck
in distress. "A beautiful day," he said, a little too enthusi-

astically. He was wearing shorts and he kept them on. "Shall I get breakfast, Shirl?"

Neither Shirley nor Vornan bothered to get dressed at all that morning. She seemed determined to achieve the same informality that had been the hallmark of my visits here; and after her first moments of confusion, she did indeed subside into a more natural acceptance of the situation. Oddly, Vornan appeared to be totally indifferent to her body. That was apparent to me long before Shirley realized it. Her little coquettishnesses, her deftly subtle movements, flexing a shapely thigh or inflating her rib cage to send her breasts rising, were wholly lost on him. Since he evidently came from a culture where nudity among near-strangers was nothing remarkable, that was not too strange—except that Vornan's attitude toward women had always been so predatory in the past months, and it was mysterious that he so conspicuously did not respond to Shirley's loveliness.

I got down to the buff too. Why not? It was comfortable, and it was the mode. But I found I could not relax. In the past I had not been aware that sunbathing with Shirley generated any obvious tension within me. Now, though, such a torrent of yearning roared through me at times that I became dizzy and had to grip the rail of the sundeck and look away.

Jack's behavior also was odd. Nakedness was wholly natural to him here, but he kept his shorts on for a full day and a half after Vornan had precipitated the rest of us into stripping. He was almost defiant about it—working in the garden, hacking at a bush in need of pruning, sweat rolling down his broad back and staining the waistband of his shorts. Shirley asked him, finally, why he was being so modest. "I don't know," he said strangely. "I hadn't noticed it." He kept the shorts on.

Vornan looked up and said, "It is not on my account, is it?" Jack laughed. He touched the snap of his shorts and wriggled out of them, chastely turning his back to us.

Though he went without them thereafter, he appeared markedly unhappy about it.

Jack seemed captivated by Vornan. They talked long and earnestly over drinks; Vornan listened thoughtfully, saying something now and then, while Jack unreeled a strand of words. I paid little attention to these discussions. They talked of politics, time travel, energy conversion, and many other things, each conversation quickly becoming a monologue. I wondered why Vornan was so patient, but of course there was little else to do here. After a while I withdrew into myself and simply lay in the sun, resting. I realized that I was terribly tired. This year had been a formidable drain on me. I dozed. I basked. I sipped flasks of cooling drinks. And I let destruction enfold my dearest friends without remotely sensing the pattern of events.

I did see the vague discontent rising in Shirley. She felt ignored and rebuffed, and even I could understand why. She wanted Vornan. And Vornan, who had commandeered so many dozens of women, treated her with glacial respect. As if belatedly embracing bourgeois morality, Vornan declined to enter any of Shirley's gambits, backing away with just the right degree of tact. Had someone told him that it was improper to seduce the wife of one's host? Propriety had never troubled Vornan in the past. I could credit his miraculous display of continence now only to his streak of innate mischief. He would take a woman to bed out of impishness—as with Aster, say—but now it amused him to thwart Shirley simply because she was beautiful and bare and obviously available. It was, I thought, an outburst of the devilish old Vornan, the deliberate thumber of the nose.

Shirley grew almost desperate about it. Her clumsiness offended me, the involuntary witness. I saw her sidle up beside Vornan to press the firmness of a breast into his back as she pretended to reach for his discarded drink-flask; I saw her invite him brazenly with her eyes; I saw her stretch out in carefully wanton postures that she had always instinctively avoided in the past. None of it did any good. Perhaps if she had entered Vornan's bedroom in the dark hours and thrown herself upon him, she would have had what she wanted from him, but her pride would not let her go quite that far. And so she grew coarse and shoddy with frustration. Her ugly shrill giggle returned. She made remarks to Jack or to Vornan or to me that revealed scarcely hidden hostilities. She spilled things and dropped things. The effect of all this on me was a depressing one, for I too had shown tact with Shirley, not just over a few days but across a decade; I had resisted temptation, I had denied myself the forbidden pleasure of taking my friend's wife. She had never offered herself to me the way she now offered herself to Vornan. I did not enjoy the sight of her this way, nor did I find pleasure in the ironies of the situation.

Jack was totally unaware of his wife's torment. His fascination with Vornan left him no opportunity to observe what was taking place about him. In his desert isolation Jack had had no chance in years to make new friends, and little enough contact with his old ones. Now he took to Vornan precisely as a lonely boy would take to some odd newcomer on his block. I choose that simile deliberately; there was something adolescent or even subadolescent about Jack's surrender to Vornan. He talked endlessly, delineating himself against the background of his University career, describing the reasons for his desert withdrawal, even taking Vornan down into that workshop I had never entered, where he showed the guest the secret manuscript of his autobiography. No matter how intimate the subject, Jack spoke freely, like a child hauling out his most prized toys to display. He was buying Vornan's attention with a frantic effort. Jack appeared to regard Vornan as a chum. I who had always thought of Vornan as unutterably alien, who had come to accept him as genuine largely because he inspired such mysterious dread in me, found it bewildering to see Jack

234

succumbing this way. Vornan seemed pleased and amused. Occasionally they disappeared into the workshop for several hours at a time. I told myself that this was all some ploy on Jack's part to wangle from Vornan the information he desired. It was clever of Jack, was it not, to construct so intense a relationship for the sake of picking Vornan's mind?

But Jack got no information from Vornan. And in my blindness I was aware of nothing.

How could I have failed to see it? That look of bemused and dreamy confusion that Jack wore much of the time now? The moments when his eyes dropped and he turned away from Shirley or from me, cheeks glowing in unknown embarrassments? Even when I saw Vornan slip his hand possessively onto Jack's bare shoulder, I remained blind.

Shirley and I spent more time together in those days than on any previous visit, for Jack and Vornan were forever off by themselves. I did not take advantage of my opportunity. We said little, but lay side by side, baking in the sun; Shirley seemed so taut and keyed up that I scarcely knew what to say to her, and so I kept silent. Arizona was gripped by an autumn heat wave. Warmth came boiling out of Mexico toward us, making us sluggish. Shirley's bare skin gleamed like fine bronze. The fatigue washed from me. Several times Shirley seemed about to speak, and the words died in her throat. A fabric of tension took form. In a subliminal way I felt trouble in the air, the way one feels a summer storm coming on. But I had no idea what was awry; I hovered in a cocoon of heat, detecting uncertain emanations of impending cataclysm, and not until the actual moment of disaster did I grasp the truth of the situation.

It happened on the twelfth day of our visit. We were only a day short of November, now, but the unseasonal warmth was staying on; at noon the sun was like a blazing eye whose fiery stare was impossible to meet, and I could not remain outdoors. I excused myself from Shirley—Jack and Vornan were nowhere about—and went to my room. As I opaqued the window, I paused to peer out at Shirley, lying torpid on the sundeck, eyes shielded, her left knee drawn up, her breasts slowly rising and falling, her skin glistening with sweat. She was the image of total relaxation, I thought, the languid beautiful woman drowsing in the heat of noon. And then I caught sight of her left hand, fiercely clenched, so tightly fisted that it trembled at the wrist and muscles throbbed the length of her arm; and I understood that her pose was a conscious counterfeit of tranquility, maintained by sheer force of will.

I darkened the room and stretched out on my bed. The cool indoor air was refreshing. Perhaps I slept. My eyes opened when I heard the sound of someone at my door. I sat up.

Shirley rushed in. She looked wild: eyes glaring in horror, lips drawn back, breasts heaving. Her face was crimson. Bright beads of sweat, I saw with curious clarity, covered her skin, and there was a shining rivulet in the valley of her bosom. "Leo—" she said in a rusty choking voice. "Oh, God, Leo!"

"What is it? What happened?"

She stumbled across the room and sagged forward, her knees against my mattress. She seemed almost in a state of shock. Her jaws worked, but no words came forth.

*"Shirley!"*

"Yes," she muttered. "Yes. Jack—Vornan—oh, Leo, I was right about them! I didn't want to believe it, but I was right. I saw them! I saw them!"

"What are you talking about?"

"It was time for lunch," she said, gulping for calm. "I woke up on the sundeck and went looking for them. They were in Jack's workshop, as usual. They didn't answer when I knocked, and I pushed the door open, and then I saw why they hadn't answered. They were busy. With each other. With . . . each . . . other. Arms and legs all

236

over each other. I saw. I stood there maybe half a minute watching it. Oh, Leo, Leo, Leo!"

Her voice rose to a piercing shriek. She flung herself forward in despair, sobbing, shattered. I caught her as she lurched into me. The heavy globes of her breasts pressed with tips of flame against my cool skin. In the eye of my mind I could see the scene she had described for me; now the obviousness of it all struck me, and I gasped at my own stupidity, at Vornan's callousness, and at Jack's innocence. I squirmed as I pictured for myself Vornan wrapped about him like some giant predatory invertebrate, and then there was no time for further thought. Shirley was in my arms, trembling and bare and sweat-sticky and weeping. I comforted her and she clung to me, looking only for an island of stability in a suddenly quaking world; and the embrace of comfort that I offered her rapidly became something quite different. I could not control myself, and she did not resist, but rather she welcomed my invasion in relief or out of revenge, and at long last my body pierced hers and we fell joined and heaving to the pillow.

\* SEVENTEEN \*

I HAD KRALICK get Vornan and me out of there hours later. I did not explain anything to anyone. I merely said that it was necessary for us to leave. There were no farewells. We dressed and packed, and I drove with Vornan to Tucson, where Kralick's men picked us up.

Looking back, I see how panicky my flight was. Perhaps I should have stayed with them. Perhaps I should have tried to help them rebuild themselves. But in that chaotic instant I felt I had to flee. The atmosphere of guilt was too stifling; the texture of interwoven shames was too tight. What had taken place between Vornan and Jack

237

and what had taken place between Shirley and me were inextricably bound into the fabric of the catastrophe, as for that matter was what had not taken place between Shirley and Vornan. And I had brought the serpent among them. In the moment of crisis I had forfeited any moral advantage I might have had by yielding to my impulse and then by running away. I was the guilty one. I was responsible.

I may never see either of them again.

I know too much of their secret shame, and like one who has stumbled upon a file of yellowed correspondence belonging to some dear one, I feel that my unwanted knowledge falls now as a sword holding me apart from them. That may change. Already, nearly two months later, I see the episode in a different light. We all managed to look equally ugly and equally weak at once, all three of us, puppets spun about by Vornan's artfully constructed whim; and that shared knowledge of our frailty may draw us together. I don't know. I do know, though, that whatever Shirley and Jack had shared only with each other lies broken and trampled and beyond repair.

A montage of faces comes to me: Shirley flushed and dizzied in the grip of passion, eyes closed, mouth gaping. Shirley sickened and sullen afterward, slumping to the floor, crawling away from me like an injured insect. Jack coming up from the workshop, dazed and pale as if he had been the victim of a rape, walking carefully through a world made unreal. And Vornan looking complacent, cheerfully replete, quite satisfied with his work and even more pleased to discover what Shirley and I had done. I could not feel real anger toward him. He was still as much a beast of prey as ever, and had renounced nothing. He had rebuffed Shirley not out of some excess of conventionality but only because he was stalking a different quarry.

To Kralick I said nothing. He could tell that the Arizona interlude had been a disaster, but I gave him no details, and he pressed for none. We met in Phoenix; he had flown there from Washington when he got my message. The trip to South America, he said, had been hastily reinstated and we were due in Caracas the following Tuesday.

"Count me out," I said. "I've had enough of Vornan. I'm resigning from the committee, Sandy."

"Don't."

"I have to. It's a personal matter. I've given you close to a year, but now I've got to pick up the pieces of my own life."

"Give us one month more," he pleaded. "It's important. Have you been following the news, Leo?"

"Now and then."

"The world is in the grip of a Vornan mania. It gets worse each day. Those two weeks or so he was off in the desert only inflamed it. Do you know, a false Vornan showed up in Buenos Aires on Sunday and proclaimed a Latin American empire? In just fifteen minutes he collected a mob of fifty thousand. The damage ran into the millions, and it could have been worse if a sniper hadn't shot him."

"*Shot* him? What for?"

Kralick shook his head. "Who knows? It was pure hysteria. The crowd tore the assassin to pieces. It took two days to convince everyone that it had been a fake Vornan. And then we've heard rumors of false Vornans in Karachi, Istanbul, Peking, Oslo. It's that foul book Fields wrote. I could flay him."

"What does this have to do with me, Sandy?"

"I need to have you beside Vornan. You've spent more time with him than anyone else. You know him well, and I think he knows you and trusts you. It may not be possible for anyone else to control him."

"I have no way of controlling him," I said, thinking of Jack and Shirley. "Isn't that obvious by now?"

"But at least with you we have a chance. Leo, if

239

Vornan ever harnesses the power that's at his command, he'll turn this world upside down. At a word from him, fifty million people would cut their own throats. You've been out of touch. You can't comprehend how this is building. Maybe you can head him off if he starts to realize his own potential."

"The way I headed him off when he wrecked Wesley Bruton's villa, eh?"

"That was early in the game. We know better now, we don't let Vornan near dangerous equipment. And what he did to Bruton's place is just a sample of what he can do to the whole world."

I laughed harshly. "In that case, why take risks? Have him killed."

"For God's sake, Leo——"

"I mean it. There are ways of arranging it. A big, clever Government bastard like you doesn't need instructions in Machiavellianism. Get rid of Vornan while you still can, before he sets himself up as Emperor Vornan with a bodyguard of ten thousand. You take care of it and let me go back to my laboratory, Sandy."

"Be serious. How——"

"I *am* serious. If you don't want to assassinate him, try persuading him to go back where he belongs."

"We can't do that either."

"What *are* you going to do, then?"

"I told you," said Kralick patiently. "Keep him on tour until he gets sick of it. Watch him all the time. Make sure he stays happy. Feed him all the women he can handle."

"And men too," I put in.

"Little boys, if we have to. We're sitting on a megabomb, Leo, and we're trying like hell to keep it from exploding. If you want to walk out on us at this point, go ahead. But when the explosion comes, you're likely to feel it even in your ivory tower. What's the answer now?"

"I'll stick," I said bitterly.

240

So I rejoined the traveling circus, and so it was that I was on hand for the final events of Vornan's story. I had not expected Kralick to succeed in talking me into it. I had for at least a few hours believed I was quit of Vornan, whom I did not hate for what he had done to my friends, but whom I regarded as an ultimate peril. I had been· quite serious in suggesting that Kralick have him destroyed. Now I found myself committed to accompany him once more; but now I chose to keep my distance from him even when I was with him, stifling the good fellowship that had begun to develop. Vornan knew why. I'm sure of that. He did not seem troubled by my new coolness toward him.

The crowds were immense. We had seen howling mobs before, but we had never seen mobs howling like these. At Caracas they estimated one hundred thousand turned out —all that could squeeze into the big downtown plaza— and we stared in amazement as they bellowed their delight in Spanish. Vornan appeared on a balcony to greet them; it was like a Pope delivering his blessing. They screamed for him to make a speech. We had no facilities for it, though, and Vornan merely smiled and waved. The sea of red-covered books churned madly. I did not know if they waved *The New Revelation* or *The Newest Revelation*, but it scarcely mattered.

He was interviewed that night on Venezuelan television. The network rigged a simultaneous-translation channel, for Vornan knew no Spanish. What message, he was asked, did he have for the people of Venezuela? "The world is pure and wonderful and beautiful," Vornan replied solemnly. "Life is holy. You can shape a paradise while you yet live." I was astonished. These pieties were out of character for our mischievous friend, unless this was the sign of some new malice in the making.

The crowds were even greater in Bogotá. Shrill cries echoed through the thin air of the plateau. Vornan spoke again, and again it was a sermon of platitudes. Kralick was worried. "He's warming up for something," he said to me. "He's never talked like this before. He's making a real effort to reach them directly, instead of letting them come to him."

"Call off the tour, then," I suggested.

"We can't. We're committed."

"Forbid him to make speeches."

"How?" he asked, and there was no answer.

Vornan himself seemed fascinated by the size of the throngs that came out to see him. These were no mere knots of curiosity seekers; these were giant hordes who knew that a strange god walked the earth, and longed for a glimpse. Clearly he felt his power over them now, and was beginning to exert it. I noticed, though, that he no longer exposed himself physically to the mobs. He seemed to fear harm, and drew back, keeping to balconies and within sealed cars.

"They're crying for you to come down and walk among them," I told him as we faced a roaring multitude in Lima. "Can't you hear it, Vornan?"

"I wish I could do it," he said.

"There's nothing stopping you."

"Yes. Yes. There are so many of them. There would be a stampede."

"Put on a crowd shield," Helen McIlwain suggested.

Vornan swung around. "What is that, please?"

"Politicians wear them. A crowd shield is an electronic sphere of force that surrounds the wearer. It's designed specifically to protect public figures in mobs. If anyone gets too close, the shield delivers a mild shock. You'd be perfectly safe, Vornan."

To Kralick he said, "Is this so? Can you get me such a shield?"

"I think it can be arranged," Kralick said.

The next day, in Buenos Aires, the American Embassy delivered a shield to us. It had last been used by the President on his Latin American tour. An Embassy official demonstrated it, strapping on the electrodes, taping the power pack to his chest. "Try and come near me," he said, beckoning. "Cluster around."

We approached him. A gentle amber glow enveloped him. We pushed forward, and abruptly we began to strike an impenetrable barrier. There was nothing painful about the sensation, but in its subtle way it was thoroughly effective; we were thrown back, and it was impossible to come within three feet of the wearer. Vornan looked delighted. "Let me try it," he said. The Embassy man put it on him and instructed him in its use. Vornan laughed and said, "All of you, crowd around me, now. Shove and push. Harder! Harder!" There was no touching him. Pleased, Vornan said, "Good. Now I can go among my people."

Quietly, later, I said to Kralick, "Why did you let him have that thing?"

"He asked for it."

"You could have told him they didn't work well or something like that, Sandy. Isn't there a possibility that the shield will conk out at a critical moment?"

"Not normally," Kralick said. He picked up the shield, uncoiled it, and snapped back the panel to the rear of the power pack. "There's only one weak spot in the circuitry, and that's here, this integrated module. You can't see it, really. It's got a tendency to overload under certain circumstances and degenerate, causing a shield failure. But there's a redundancy circuit that automatically cuts in, Leo, and takes over within a couple of microseconds. Actually there's only one way a crowd shield can fail, and that's if it's deliberately sabotaged. Say, if someone jimmies the back-up circuit, and then the main module overloads. But I don't know anyone who'd do a thing like that."

"Except Vornan, perhaps."

"Well, yes. Vornan's capable of anything. But I hardly

think he'll want to play around with his own shield. For all intents he'll be wholly safe wearing the shield."

"Well, then," I said, "aren't you afraid of what will happen now that he can get out among the mobs and really lay the charisma on?"

"Yes," said Kralick.

Buenos Aires was the scene of the greatest excitement over Vornan we had yet experienced. This was the city where a false Vornan had arisen, and the presence of the real one was electric to the Argentines. The broad, tree-lined Avenida 9 de Julio was packed from end to end, with only the obelisk in its center puncturing the mass of flesh. Through this chaotic, surging mob moved Vornan's cavalcade. Vornan wore his crowd shield; the rest of us were not so protected, and huddled nervously within our armored vehicles. From time to time Vornan leaped out and strode into the crowd. The shield worked—no one could get close to him—but the mere fact that he was among them sent the crowd into ecstasies. They pushed up close, coming to the absolute limit of the electronic barrier and flattening themselves against it, while Vornan beamed and smiled and bowed. I said to Kralick, "We're becoming accomplices to the madness. We should never have let this happen."

Kralick gave me a crooked grin and told me to relax. But I could not relax. That night Vornan again allowed himself to be interviewed, and what he said was bluntly utopian. The world was badly in need of reform; too much power had concentrated in too few hands; an era of universal affluence was imminent, but it would take the cooperation of the enlightened masses to bring it about. "We were born from trash," he said, "but we have the capacity to become gods. I know it can be done. In my time there is no disease, there is no poverty, there is no suffering. Death itself has been abolished. But must mankind wait a thousand years to enjoy these benefits? You must act now. *Now.*"

It seemed like a call to revolution.

As yet Vornan had put forth no specific program. He was uttering only generalized calls for a transformation of our society. But even that was far beyond the sly, oblique, flippant remarks he had customarily made in the early months of his stay. It was as if his capacity for trouble-making had been greatly enlarged; he recognized now that he could stir up infinitely more mischief by addressing himself to the mobs in the street than by poking fun at selected individuals. Kralick seemed as aware of this as I was; I did not understand why he allowed the tour to continue, why he saw to it that Vornan had access to communications channels. He seemed helpless to halt the course of events, helpless to interrupt the revolution that he himself had served to manufacture.

Of Vornan's motives we knew nothing. On the second day in Buenos Aires he again went into the throng. This time the mob was far greater than on the day before, and in a kind of obstinate insistence they surrounded Vornan, trying desperately to reach and touch him. We had to get him out of there, finally, with a scoop lowered from a copter. He was pale and shaken as he rid himself of the crowd shield. I had never seen Vornan look rattled before, but this crowd had done it. He eyed the shield skeptically and said, "Possibly there are dangers in this. How trustworthy is the shield?"

Kralick assured him that it was loaded with redundancy features that made it foolproof. Vornan looked doubtful. He turned away, trying to compose himself; it was actually refreshing to see a symptom of fear in him. I could hardly fault him for fearing that crowd, even with a shield.

We flew from Buenos Aires to Rio de Janeiro in the early hours of November 19. I tried to sleep, but Kralick came to my compartment and woke me. Behind him stood Vornan. In Kralick's hand was the coiled slimness of a crowd shield.

"Put this on," he said.

"What for?"

"So you can learn how to use it. You're going to wear it in Rio."

My lingering sleepiness vanished. "Listen, Sandy, if you think I'm going to expose myself to those crowds—"

"Please," said Vornan. "I want you beside me, Leo."

Kralick said, "Vornan's been feeling uneasy about the size of the mobs for the last few days, and he doesn't want to go down there alone any more. He asked me if I could get you to accompany him. He wants only you."

"It's true, Leo," Vornan said. "I can't trust the others. With you beside me I'm not afraid."

He was damnably persuasive. One glance, one plea, and I was ready to walk through millions of screaming cultists with him. I told him I'd do as he wished, and he touched his hand to mine and murmured his thanks softly but movingly. Then he went away. The moment he was gone, I saw the lunacy of it; and as Kralick pushed the crowd shield toward me, I shook my head. "I can't," I said. "Get Vornan. Tell him I changed my mind."

"Come on, Leo. Nothing can happen to you."

"If I don't go out there, Vornan doesn't go either?"

"That's correct."

"Then we've solved our problem," I said. "I'll refuse to put the shield on. Vornan won't be able to mingle with the multitudes. We'll cut him off from the source of his power. Isn't that what we want?"

"No."

"No?"

"We want Vornan to be able to reach the people. They love him. They need him. We don't dare deny them their hero."

"Give them their hero, then. But not with me next to him."

"Don't start that again, Leo. You're the one he asked for. If Vornan doesn't make an appearance in Rio, it's

246

going to screw up international relations and God knows what else. We can't risk frustrating that mob by not producing him."

"So I'm thrown to the wolves?"

"The shields are safe, Leo! Come on. Help us out one last time."

The intensity of Kralick's concern was compelling, and in the end I agreed to honor my promise to Vornan. As we rocketed eastward over the dwindling wilderness of the Amazon basin, twenty miles high, Kralick taught me how to use the crowd shield. By the time we began our arc of descent, I was an expert. Vornan was visibly pleased that I had agreed to accompany him. He spoke freely of the excitement he felt in the midst of a throng, and of the power he felt he exerted over those who clustered about him. I listened and said little. I studied him with care, recording in my mind the look of his face, the gleam of his smile, for I had the feeling that his visit to our medieval epoch might soon be drawing to its close.

The crowd at Rio exceeded anything we had seen before. Vornan was scheduled to make a public appearance on the beach; we rolled through the streets of the magnificent city, heading for the sea, and there was no beach in sight, only a sea of heads lining the shore, a jostling, shoving, incredibly dense mob that stretched from the white towers of the oceanfront buildings to the edge of the waves, and even out into the water. We were unable to penetrate that mass, and had to take to the air. By copter we traversed the length of the beach. Vornan glowed with pride. "For me," he said softly. "They come here for me. Where is my speech machine?"

Kralick had furnished him with yet another gadget: a translator, rigged to turn Vornan's words into fluent Portuguese. As we hovered over that forest of dark upraised arms, Vornan spoke, and his words boomed out into the bright summer air. I cannot vouch for the translation, but the words he used were eloquent and moving. He spoke of the world from which he came, telling of its serenity and harmony, describing its freedom from striving and strife. Each human being, he said, was unique and valued. He contrasted that with our own bleak, harried time. A mob such as he saw beneath him, he said, was inconceivable in his day, for only a shared hunger brings a mob together, and no hunger so clawing could exist there. Why, he asked, did we choose to live this way? Why not rid ourselves of our rigidities and our prides, cast away our dogmas and our idols, hurl down the barriers that fence each human heart? Let every man love his fellow man as a brother. Let false cravings be abolished. Let the desire for power perish. Let a new age of benevolence be ushered in.

These were not new sentiments. Other prophets had offered them. But he spoke with such monstrous sincerity and fervor that he seemed to be minting each sentimental cliché anew. Was this the Vornan who had laughed in the face of the world? Was this the Vornan who had used human beings as toys and tools? This pleading, cajoling, thrilling orator? This saint? I was close to tears myself as I listened to him. And the impact on those down on the beach—those following this on a global network—who could calculate that?

Vornan's mastery was complete. His slim, deceptively boyish figure occupied the center of the world's stage. We were his. With sincerity instead of mockery now his weapon, he had conquered all.

He finished speaking. To me he said, "Now let us go down among them, Leo."

We put on our shields. I was at the edge of terror; and Vornan himself, peering over the lip of the copter's hatch into that swirling madhouse below, seemed to falter a moment and draw back from the descent. But they were waiting. They cried out for him in love-thickened voices. For once the magnetism worked the other way; Vornan was drawn forward.

"Go first," he told me. "Please."

With suicidal bravado I seized the grips and let myself be swung down a hundred feet to the beach. A clearing opened for me. I touched ground and felt shifting sand at my feet. People rushed toward me; then, seeing that I was not their prophet, they halted. Some rebounded from my shield. I felt invulnerable, and my fear ebbed as I saw how the amber glow repelled those who came too close.

Now Vornan was descending. A low roar rumbled from ten thousand throats and rushed up the scale to become an intolerable shriek. They recognized him. He stood beside me, aglow with his own power, proud of himself, swollen with joy. I knew what he was thinking: for a nobody he had done pretty well for himself. It is given to few men to become gods in their own lifetimes.

"Walk beside me," he said.

He lifted his arms and strode slowly forward, majestic, awesome. Like a lesser apostle I accompanied him. No one paid heed to me; but worshipers flung themselves at him, their faces distorted and transfigured, their eyes glassy. None could touch him. The wondrous field turned all away, so that there was not even the impact of collision. We walked ten feet, twenty, thirty. The crowd opened for us, then surged inward again, no one willing to accept the reality of the shield. Protected as I was, I felt the enormous pent-up strength of that mob. Perhaps a million Brazilians surrounded us; perhaps five million. This was Vornan's grandest moment. On, on, on he moved, nodding, smiling, reaching forth his hand, graciously accepting the homage offered.

A gigantic black man stripped to the waist loomed before him, shining with sweat, skin nearly purple. He stood for a moment outlined against the brilliant summer sky. "Vornan!" he shouted in a voice like thunder. "Vornan!" He stretched both his hands toward Vornan—

And seized his arm.

The image is engraved on my mind: that jet-black hand

249

gripping the light-green fabric of Vornan's garment. And Vornan turning, frowning, looking at the hand, suddenly realizing that his shield had ceased to protect him.

"*Leo!*" he screamed.

There was a terrible inward rush. I heard cries of ecstasy. The crowd was going wild.

Before me dangled the grips of the copter's scoop. I seized them and was pulled aloft to safety. I looked down only after climbing aboard; I saw the formless surging of the mob on the beach, and shuddered.

There were several hundred fatalities. No trace of Vornan was ever discovered.

* EIGHTEEN *

IT IS OVER, now, and yet it is just beginning. I do not know if Vornan's disappearance will steady us or destroy us. We may not know that for a while.

I have lived in Rio for six weeks, but in such isolation that I might as well have been on the Moon. When the others left, I remained. My apartment is a small one, just two rooms, not far from the beach where Vornan's final act was played. I have not left my apartment in over a month. My food is delivered through the house data-channel; I take no exercise; I have no friends in this city. I cannot even understand the language.

Since the fifth of December I have occupied myself by dictating this memoir, which shortly will be done. I do not intend to seek publication. I have set down, as accurately as recollection permits, the whole story of Vornan-19's stay among us, and of my involvement with him. I will seal the tape and have it placed in a vault, to be opened in not less than one hundred years. I have no wish to add to the flood of gospels now appearing; perhaps my testimony will be of some use a century hence, but I will not have it employed now to feed the fires that are raging in the world. I wish I could feel confident that by the time someone breaks my seal of silence, all this will have receded into oblivion. But I doubt that that will be the case.

So many ambiguities remain. Did Vornan perish in that mob or did he return to his own time? Was that black giant a courier come to fetch him? Or did Vornan transmit himself into the future at the instant his shield failed? I wonder. And why did the shield fail, anyway? Kralick had sworn that it was proof against all but deliberate sabotage. Did Kralick gimmick the shield out of fear of Vornan's growing power? And did he then use me as the cat's-paw in his conspiracy, persuading me to cooperate so that an uneasy Vornan would agree to put the flawed shield on and go into the crowd? If that is so, I am an accessory after the fact, I who pretend to abhor violence. But I am not sure that Vornan was murdered; I am not even sure that Vornan died. All I know beyond doubt is that he has gone from us.

I think he is dead. We could not risk Vornan's further presence among us. The conspirators who slew Caesar felt they were performing a public service. With Vornan gone, the question remains: can we survive his departure?

We have written the proper climax for the myth. When a young god comes among us, we slay him. Now he surely is dismembered Osiris and murdered Tammuz and lamented Baldur. Now the hour of redemption and resurrection must follow, and I fear it. Vornan alive might have undone himself in time, revealing himself to the world as foolish, vain, ignorant, and amoral, a mingling of peacock and wolf. Vornan gone is another matter. He is beyond our control now that we have martyred him. Those who needed him will wait for his successor, for someone to fill the void now created. I do not think we will lack for successors. We are coming into an age of prophets. We are coming into an era of new gods. We are coming into a century of flame. I fear that I may live to see the Time of Sweeping of which Vornan spoke.

Enough. It is nearly midnight, and tonight is the thirty-first of December. At the stroke the century will turn, for all but the purists. There is revelry in the streets. There is dancing and singing. I hear coarse shouts and the dull boom of fireworks. The sky blazes with light. If there are any Apocalyptists left, they must await the next hour in dread or in bliss, dreaming of approaching doom. It will be the year 2000 before long. The sound of that is strange to me.

It is time to leave my apartment at last. I will go out into the streets, among the crowds, and celebrate the birth of the new year. I need no shield; I am in no danger now, except only the danger in which we all must live. Now the century dies. I will go out.

# Science Fiction in Tandem editions

# Fantasy Fiction in Tandem editions

## By Lin Carter

The Chronicles of the Lost Continent of Lemuria

| | |
|---|---|
| Thongor at the End of Time .. .. .. .. .. | 25p |
| Thongor Fights the Pirates of Tarakus .. .. .. | 25p |

## By John Norman

The strange history of Tarl Cabot, once of Earth, now of Counter-Earth

| | |
|---|---|
| Tarnsman of Gor .. .. .. .. .. .. | 25p |
| Outlaw of Gor .. .. .. .. .. .. | 25p |
| Priest-Kings of Gor .. .. .. .. .. .. | 30p |

## By John Jakes

A warrior's sword against the sorcery of ancient evil

| | |
|---|---|
| Brak the Barbarian .. .. .. .. .. | 25p |
| Brak the Barbarian – The Sorceress .. .. .. | 25p |
| Brak the Barbarian – The Mark of the Demons .. .. | 25p |

## By Andre Norton

'Rich, brilliant, superbly imaginative and fully adult pure fantasy' *Lin Carter*

| | |
|---|---|
| Witch World .. .. .. .. .. .. | 25p |
| Web of the Witch World .. .. .. .. .. | 25p |
| Three Against the Witch World .. .. .. .. | 25p |
| Warlock of the Witch World .. .. .. .. .. | 25p |
| Sorceress of the Witch World .. .. .. .. | 25p |
| Year of the Unicorn .. .. .. .. .. .. | 25p |

## By Ursula Le Guin

Hugo and Nebula Award winner for 1970

| | |
|---|---|
| Planet of Exile .. .. .. .. .. .. | 25p |
| Rocannon's World .. .. .. .. .. .. | 25p |